Murder Between the Pages

by

Linda Hope Lee

The Nina Foster Mystery Series, Book 1

Murder Between the Pages

Cover Art by *Tina Lynn Stout*

The Wild Rose Press, Inc.
PO Box 708
Adams Basin, NY 14410-0708
Visit us at www.thewildrosepress.com

Publishing History
First Crimson Rose Edition, 2018
Print ISBN 978-1-5092-2367-1
Digital ISBN 978-1-5092-2368-8

The Nina Foster Mystery Series, Book 1
Published in the United States of America

The office appeared hit by a hurricane. Cupboard doors hung open, and drawers from the desk and work counter lay on the floor, their contents scattered from one end of the room to the other. A strange, metallic odor hung in the air.

Her gaze landed on a person's leg sticking out from behind the desk. A leg wearing a green stocking, and the foot a black flat.

An image of Wildeen at last night's party, wearing a yellow sweater and green stockings, popped into Nina's mind. Her throat constricted, and she pressed a hand to her chest. *Oh no, not Wildeen! Please, God, no.* She picked her way through the debris, peered around the desk, and gasped.

Wildeen lay on her stomach, one arm curled under her body, the other outstretched. Her head, turned to the left, revealed a large gash behind her ear. Her hair was blood-matted, and dried blood stained her face and the shoulder of her yellow sweater. More blood had soaked into the bare wooden floor.

Near Wildeen's outstretched left hand lay a glass horse figurine, one of her prized antique bookends. Blood covered the horse's uplifted hooves.

Blood was the strange odor. So much blood. Nausea churned Nina's stomach, while her thoughts raced. Call 911 then check for a pulse. Maybe she was still alive.

Praise for Linda Hope Lee

"A modern western, packed with secrets, intrigue, and old-fashioned romance, *FINDING SARA* is a story that won't be forgotten."

~*Joanne Hall, Writers and Readers
of Distinctive Fiction*

~*~

"*LOVING ROSE* is a sweet, heartwarming read that will tug at your heartstrings."

~*Melissa, Sizzlinghotbookreviews.net*

~*~

"Lee provides readers with emotional drama and puzzling suspense. *DARK MEMORIES* churns with guilt, passion, and intrigue."

~*Romantic Times*

~*~

"What a beautiful story! *LOVING ROSE* is full of characters who face real-life situations."

~*Nikki, Siren Book Reviews (4.5 Siren Stones)*

Dedication

To The Flexers, Joanne, Karen, and Liz,
for all your help and support.

Chapter One

"The estate looks elegant and the food tastes superb, but the book is trash," Larry Hardisty announced.

"Not so loud, Larry." Standing next to him at the buffet table, Nina Foster pressed a finger to her lips. "You might hurt Zelma's feelings. You know how sensitive some authors are about their work." She nodded across the lawn to where Zelma Duke chatted with a group of fans. The author of *My Restless Heart*, Zelma was the honored guest at tonight's party.

Larry helped himself to a cracker topped with smoked salmon. "Sorry, madam librarian, but I doubt Zelma gives a hoot what I think." He ate the appetizer and then adjusted his black-framed eyeglasses. "Now, if you'll excuse me, I'll browse the Bottses' famed art collection and catch up with you later."

"All right. We'll sit together for Zelma's reading."

Larry twisted his lips into a grimace. "A reading? Yikes. I don't know if I can survive all that purple prose." He turned and headed toward the two-story home.

Nina sighed and slowly shook her head. Larry was her assistant at the Seaview Library in Richmond, Washington, a suburb of Seattle. Although they got along well, at times like tonight, his highbrow attitude grated.

He was right about the elegant estate, though. Perched atop a cliff overlooking Puget Sound and built in the early 1900s by a timber baron, the home's stone structure, mullioned windows, and stout chimneys spoke of old money and societal position.

New money owned the property now. A few years ago, Elizabeth and Burgess Botts, who operated a chain of import shops, claimed the home and its forested environs, dubbing it "Bottswood."

Moving away from the buffet table, Nina plucked a glass of bubbling champagne from a passing waiter's tray. Tonight's June evening was perfect for Zelma's party. The temperature hovered in the low seventies, and the sun lingered in a cloudless sky like an old friend who didn't want to say good-bye.

Sipping her drink, she strolled to the table stacked with copies of *My Restless Heart*. The book cover featured a bouquet of yellow chrysanthemums tied with a scarlet ribbon. She wasn't sure what the flowers had to do with the story, but they certainly caught the eye. Zelma had proudly told her this hardcover book was her "break-out" book, designed to appeal to a larger audience than her previous romance paperbacks.

Dorothy Quinn joined Nina. In her sixties, Dorothy was a member of Literary Lights, a book discussion group that met at the library.

"I suppose you're buying multiple copies of, uh, what *is* this book's title?" Dorothy peered through her glasses at the books.

Nina nodded. "*My Restless Heart*." Our head office bought several for every branch. But you could always buy your own here and have it autographed."

Dorothy sniffed. "I think I'll pass. This book isn't

suitable for our group. We came to see Bottswood. The estate is quite grand, isn't it?" She waved a hand at the surroundings.

"Yes. I especially love the view of the sound."

Dorothy leaned to look over Nina's shoulder. "Oh, there's Myrtle Davis. I need to speak to her. Nice seeing you tonight, Nina." She fluttered her fingers and hurried off.

Continuing her stroll, Nina spotted Wildeen Bergman, owner of Bergman Books, and her employee, Hamlet Green. Wildeen's thigh-length yellow sweater and forest green tights, and Hamlet's black turtleneck and faded jeans set them apart from the more conservatively dressed guests. Wildeen's presence tonight surprised Nina. She, Wildeen, and Zelma had been friends since their days together at Pacific Northwest University, but Zelma's recent writing success had driven a wedge between her and Wildeen.

Wildeen was a writer, too, of literary short stories and poems. While Zelma sold mass-market moneymakers, Wildeen published in obscure journals, with free copies as her only payment. Moreover, Zelma now hovered on the brink of fame and fortune, everything Wildeen wanted but had been unable to achieve. Nina beckoned to the couple. "Great party, isn't it?"

Wildeen gazed around. "The view is nice."

"Awesome." Hamlet nodded, and the cross earring in his right ear danced and sparkled in the sunlight.

"I didn't expect to see you here, Wildeen." Nina studied her friend. "Did you read Zelma's book?"

Wildeen folded her arms and lifted her chin. "I did, and I found it *most* interesting. By the way, I found a book for your collection at an estate sale I attended last Saturday. A lovely copy of *The Wonderful Wizard of Oz*. The book is a first edition and in very good condition."

"Great. When can I get it?" Nina was always eager to add to her collection of children's books.

"Come by the bookstore anytime."

"How about tomorrow morning? I'll stop in on my way to work."

"Sure. I'll be there around eight-thirty, as usual…" Wildeen's eyes widened. "Oh, no, what's *he* doing here? And with *her*."

Nina turned to see a newly arrived couple strolling arm-in-arm. The "he" was Wildeen's estranged husband, Josh Loring. Nina didn't know the "her" but assumed she was the new girlfriend she'd heard about. "Maybe Josh is a friend of the Bottses," she suggested.

"Of course." Wildeen snapped her fingers. "They all belong to the Evergreen Athletic Club. Josh met Patti Hamilton there. She teaches aerobics. Are they coming this way? I hope not."

"'Fraid so." Hamlet nodded to the approaching couple. "Buck up, Wildeen. You can handle this."

Josh and Patti made an attractive couple. Tall, broad-shouldered, and with wavy brown hair, Josh could have been the hero in a Zelma Duke novel. Patti was a slender blonde who'd most likely been a cheerleader in high school. A blue tube skirt displayed her long, shapely legs to advantage. Her golden tan must have come from a salon, though. A person couldn't get a tan such as hers in the Pacific Northwest.

"Hello, Willie." Josh gestured to his companion. "You remember Patti Hamilton, don't you? From the athletic club?"

Wildeen mumbled a greeting while looking down her nose at Patti.

Patti offered a wintry smile in return.

Josh introduced Patti to Nina and Hamlet. An awkward silence followed.

Striving to keep her tone cheerful, Nina finally said, "Nice evening, isn't it?"

Josh nodded absently and focused his gaze on Wildeen.

Hugging her arms, Wildeen gazed toward the water.

Hamlet excused himself and trotted off to get another glass of wine.

Nina and Josh made small talk about the Bottses' elegant estate.

Then Patti dug her elbow into Josh's side. "Tell Wildeen."

Wildeen whirled to face Josh. "Tell me what?"

He cleared his throat. "I've asked my lawyer to set up another meeting with your lawyer. But why don't we come to an agreement on our own and save both time and expense?"

"Settle on *your* terms, I suppose."

"Of course."

Wildeen's green eyes blazed. "You can forget that. I nursed your father through his illness. I was with you at his side when he passed away. Half of the money he left is mine. He would want me to have my share. I'm entitled to the money, and I'll get it." She stuck out her chin.

Patti stepped forward. "But, Wildeen, you and Josh will have to get a divorce sometime and settle Hal's inheritance. You can't go on like this for the rest of your lives."

"Wanna bet?" Wildeen scowled. "Besides, what business is it of yours?"

Patti linked her arm through Josh's. "Anything that affects Josh affects me."

"Is that so?" Wildeen propped her hands on her hips and leaned into Patti's face. "Well, listen up, you fluffhead. I'd rather die than give in to Josh's demands. I will have what's rightfully mine, if the settlement takes forever."

Josh narrowed his eyes. "You can't talk that way to Patti."

"Oh, shut up." Wildeen snarled. "You can't tell me what to do. Not anymore."

The two faced each other, nose to nose, their gazes locked.

Tension thick enough to cut with a knife hung in the air. Nina wished she could escape.

The guests nearby looked on, open-mouthed.

Were Wildeen and Josh actually about to fight? Wanting to prevent a scene that would surely interrupt the party, Nina steeled herself to leap between them.

Patti grabbed Josh's arm and pulled him away. "Come on, Josh. We should have known better than to reason with *her*."

As the two stalked off, Josh flung over his shoulder, "See you in court, Willie!"

Wildeen stamped her foot. "That man can be so exasperating."

Nina blew out a relieved breath. "I thought you two were about to have a knock-down-drag-out. He wouldn't really hit you, would he? Has he ever?"

"Nah." Wildeen shook her head. "Oh, we've thrown things at each other, but nothing that would do any damage. I'm not afraid of him. It's just…" Her eyes glistened with tears.

Nina put her arm around Wildeen's shoulders. "You're still in love with him, aren't you?" She kept her tone soft.

"No, no, I'm not. We're over." Wildeen took a tissue from her sweater pocket and swiped her eyes. "Sorry. I have a lot on my mind tonight. Excuse me while I find the powder room." Pulling away, she marched toward the house.

Nina debated. Should she follow Wildeen? Or let her cool down on her own? She finally decided to leave her alone. From experience, she knew when Wildeen had a tantrum, she was better left to work out her emotions by herself.

Taking a deep breath, Nina gazed around. Wasn't someone here with whom she could have a nice, safe conversation? Her gaze landed on Larry, who'd finished his inspection of the Bottses' art collection and talked with a man she'd never seen before.

Larry caught her eye and waved. He spoke to his companion, and then the two men headed toward her.

She studied the stranger. In his early thirties, he was at least six feet tall and on the slender side. He strolled along in a laid-back manner, with his hands stuck in his slacks pockets.

Larry made a sweeping gesture at his companion. "Nina, meet Stephen Kraslow, new owner of *The Richmond Review*."

Nina stiffened but politely accepted his proffered hand. "Oh, yes, I've heard of you."

The Review's former owner, George Martin, became ill and had to sell the newspaper. Several local people made offers, but Stephen Kraslow, an outsider from New York, increased his until everyone else was forced to drop out.

As far as she was concerned, Kraslow was another of the annoying transplants flooding the Northwest. The steady influx of people had pushed the region's population past comfortable limits. Traffic jammed the streets at all hours, and new houses sprang up on every available piece of land like mushrooms after a rainfall. If the population infusion didn't stop, Richmond would lose its small-town character. Nina loved her hometown and didn't want the atmosphere to change. If Stephen noticed her cool greeting, he gave no indication. His handshake was firm, his smile warm.

"I've heard about you, as well," he said.

Nina carefully withdrew her hand and raised her eyebrows. "Oh? I suppose you heard something like, 'Nina Foster, that outspoken librarian'?"

Stephen tipped back his head and laughed. "As a matter of fact, I think those were the words. But I also know about you from your book review columns in the back issues of *The Review*. Good stuff."

His offhand compliment sounded sincere, and she warmed toward him. "I did enjoy writing those." In an effort to downsize the newspaper, George had eliminated her column.

"Stephen's upgrading the review page." Larry waved a hand. "With syndicated reviews of literary books."

Nina's enthusiasm faded. "Oh. Then you probably won't want to revive my column."

Stephen tilted his head. "We'll see. Right now, I'm looking for someone to review Zelma's book."

"Don't look at me." Larry raised both hands and backed away.

"I wasn't." Stephen's gaze focused on Nina. "How about it?"

She shook her head. "Zelma and I are old friends. You need someone who can be more objective."

Larry chuckled. "Nina's telling you *My Useless Heart* isn't her kind of book, either."

"The book's title is *My* Restless *Heart*, Larry." Nina pursed her lips.

Just then, a voice called out across the lawn, "Attention, everyone!" Burgess Botts, hands cupped around his mouth, stood near a lectern and several rows of metal folding chairs grouped under a large maple tree. "Come on over and take a seat," Burgess added, while his wife, Elizabeth, herded people toward the chairs.

What an odd couple. In appearances, anyway. Burgess was a short, stocky man with a fringe of black hair encircling an otherwise bald head. His thick eyebrows reminded Nina of Groucho Marx in the old movies her grandmother liked to watch. Dressed in an ankle-length gray skirt and a jacket, Elizabeth stood at least a head taller than her husband. With her long neck and long, oval face, she might have stepped from an Amedeo Modigliani painting.

Larry moaned and rubbed the back of his neck. "Oh, oh, time to hear the guest of honor read from her masterpiece. Unfortunately, I just remembered I have to be someplace. Someplace far away from here."

"Don't you dare leave." Nina frowned. "You

wanted to come tonight. You'll sit with me and listen to every word."

Larry stood tall and made a salute. "Okay, madam librarian. You're the boss." He turned to Stephen. "See what I have to put up with? Boss lady quickly turns into 'bossy lady.'"

"I do see." Stephen's eyes twinkled. "Mind if I tag along?"

"Not at all." Larry turned to Nina. "Right, Nina?"

Nina's stomach tensed, but she mustered a smile. "Of course." As Nina accompanied Stephen and Larry to the rows of chairs, she glimpsed Wildeen emerging from the house.

Wildeen strode with her shoulders straight and her head high.

The back of Nina's neck pricked. *Wildeen looks like a woman on a mission. But not about Josh. Not now. This mission is about Zelma and her book.*

Whatever Wildeen was up to, Nina feared the outcome would be unpleasant.

Chapter Two

Nina sat with Stephen and Larry on her left and Wildeen and Hamlet on her right. She introduced Wildeen and Hamlet to Stephen, leaning back in her seat while the three exchanged a few remarks.

When everyone was settled, Elizabeth Botts stepped to the lectern. "Thank you for coming this evening." Her gaze roved over the group. "Burgess and I are so excited to have as the guest of honor our very own homegrown celebrity."

"Homegrown?" Larry whispered. "What is she talking about? A tomato?"

Nina shook her head.

Stephen gave a low chuckle.

Elizabeth stepped back. "Without any more ado, let me introduce Zelma Duke."

Enthusiastic applause accompanied Zelma to the lectern.

Although a good twenty pounds overweight for her five-foot, two-inch frame, Zelma made an impressive appearance in her stylish blue dress accented with a blue print scarf. Her thick, black hair, swept back from her face, set off wide, dark brown eyes, a straight, slender nose, and full lips. Zelma confided to Nina that she'd had a makeover at a prestigious Seattle salon. She was even sporting long, scarlet fingernails. Knowing Zelma to be a compulsive nail-biter, Nina wondered how she coped without her own nails to nibble on.

"Thank you, Elizabeth." Zelma's melodious voice floated along the airwaves. "I appreciate you and Burgess opening Bottswood to all my friends and fans. And while I'm thanking people, I must not forget two who are very important. One is my literary agent, Morry Snyder. Stand up, Morry." Zelma gestured to the front row.

A heavy-set man lumbered to his feet and turned a blunt-featured, fleshy face to the audience. He grinned and then ran a hand over his high forehead and thinning black hair. "Hi, y'all." He plopped back down, and the metal seat wobbled as he settled.

"The other person," Zelma said, "is my publicist, Sondra Wagner."

Publicist? My, my. Nina knew Zelma had a literary agent, but acquiring a publicist moved her up another notch in the publishing world.

The woman sitting next to Morry Snyder stood and took a bow. A smooth cap of dark brown hair and an upturned nose gave her a pixie look.

"The past few months have been so exciting"— Zelma rolled her eyes—"from the time I learned my publisher's big plans for *My Restless Heart* to this very moment. Last week, I flew to New York and was met by a limousine. Me, Zelma Duke, from Richmond, Washington." She pointed to her chest. "I said to my editor, Joanie, 'Surely, you don't treat all your authors to a limousine,' and she said, 'Only those we plan to make into stars.'" Zelma smiled and fluttered her false eyelashes.

"Oh, gimme a break." Wildeen groaned.

Zelma gripped the lectern and swept her gaze over

the audience. "My publicist has planned a nationwide tour. But I can assure you nothing will be as special as this appearance here at Bottswood, surrounded by my friends. Why, I was telling my agent the other day, over lunch at Twenty-One." She batted her eyelashes. "You know, that famous restaurant in Manhattan?"

Nina's attention wandered to the row of madrona trees lining the cliff. Sunlight glazed their twisted trunks with an orange glow. Behind the trees, the sky was pale blue at the top and a soft peach near the horizon. She sighed. Bottswood truly was a beautiful place.

Stephen shifted and folded his arms.

She wondered idly what he, as a former New Yorker, thought of Zelma's starry-eyed account of her trip. Amusement, probably, with a dash of disdain, and perhaps boredom. Never mind. She really didn't care what he thought.

When Zelma finally finished her story, she took a copy of *My Restless Heart* from the lectern's shelf. "And now, I'd like to share a few passages from my book."

Nina expected another groan from Wildeen.

Instead, Wildeen straightened and focused on Zelma.

Zelma held up the book and pointed to the cover. "As I'm sure you all know by now, the story is about an Italian immigrant, Flavia Magnioni, who comes to our very own Northwest, where she meets Jet Houston, a prosperous banker. Here's the scene in which Flavia sees her new homeland for the first time." She opened to a page marked by a bookmark and read aloud.

As Nina listened, she thought how Zelma's writing

had improved with this new book. Apparently, the twenty books she'd already written helped to hone her craft.

Zelma finished the passage and then smiled at the audience. "I'll read one more scene."

"Read pages one hundred twenty to one hundred twenty-five," Wildeen called out.

Zelma turned the book's pages. She looked up at Wildeen and frowned. "But this section isn't one of the highlights of the story."

"Oh, but it is. Besides, I want to hear you read those pages."

Wildeen's voice dripped with sarcasm.

Nina cringed.

"Well…all right." Zelma cleared her throat and read.

The second passage was even better than the first. However, why would Wildeen want to show off Zelma's talents when she was so jealous? Nina glanced at Wildeen. A flush reddened her cheeks, and her gaze riveted on Zelma.

Zelma finished reading and closed the book. Without looking in Wildeen's direction, she stepped away from the lectern and took a bow. "Thank you all for coming tonight. And please watch my interview on the Northwest Celebrities Show tomorrow at three p.m. on channel forty."

Nina joined in the ensuing applause. Then she leaned toward Wildeen. "Why did you want Zelma to read that particular scene?"

"You'll know soon enough." Wildeen narrowed her eyes.

Nina felt her stomach clench. "Why can't I know

now?"

"Because you can't. Don't ask me any more questions about it, okay?"

"Okay." Nina gave a resigned sigh and sat back. She didn't like letting the matter go. Not one bit.

Elizabeth Botts returned to the lectern. "The evening is by no means over, folks. Burgess and I invite you to experience the nature walk we've created here at Bottswood. Thc cntrance is there." She pointed to the edge of the lawn, beyond which stood a forest dominated by towering evergreens. "You'll find plenty of interesting plants and flowers to enjoy and several lookouts."

"I'm game," Stephen said to Nina. "How about you?"

She hesitated. A walk in the forest promised to be pleasant, but did she want to spend more time in Stephen's company? Her feelings toward him were already confused. She wanted to dislike this outsider who had invaded their tight-knit community. Still, whenever he caught her eye, something inside her stirred.

Quit being such an adolescent. You can handle a walk in the woods. He's not asking for a date.

"All right," she said. "Why not?"

****

When so many others expressed interest, Burgess and Elizabeth took all of them together on a guided walk. In addition to Nina and Stephen, the group included Larry, Josh and Patti, Wildeen and Hamlet, Zelma, Sondra and Morry, and Dorothy and several other Literary Lights.

They followed Burgess and Elizabeth down a dirt

path leading into the woods. Wild rhododendron bushes, some as tall as six feet and with blossoms ranging from white to soft pink to violet, lined the way. The sweet, earthy smell made Nina's nose tingle.

"Awesome," Stephen commented as he gazed around. "One of the reasons I came to the Northwest was to enjoy places like this."

Nina pursed her lips. "The trouble is, places like this won't exist anymore if people like you keep moving here."

Stephen held up a hand. "I heard you Washingtonians do a lot of transplant-bashing. But you can save your breath on me. I'm immune."

"Is that so?" she said in a dry tone.

Ahead of them, Burgess and Elizabeth kept up a running commentary on the surroundings.

Nina couldn't hear all that was said, but phrases such as "environmentally correct" and "ecological systems" floated back to her ears.

They came to an arched wooden bridge spanning a pond full of lily pads and cattails. From there they rounded a corner and arrived at a lookout.

At the panoramic view, Nina caught her breath. Across the sound, a pale yellow sun disappeared behind the Olympic Peninsula's ridge of snow-capped mountains. Near the horizon line, caught in the sun's rays, a liner traveled north to Canada.

"This spot is the end of the line." Burgess stopped and planted his feet apart. "Feel free to watch the sunset here or on the beach." He pointed to a narrow wooden stairway leading to the rocky shore. "Or revisit anything else we've seen."

After putting their heads together in a brief

discussion, the Literary Lights remained at the lookout.

Stephen chose the stairs to the beach.

Josh and Patti wandered down one of the darker paths.

Hamlet went off to find the evergreen Burgess said had the largest girth of any in the state.

Larry wanted to check out some wildflowers he'd seen earlier.

Burgess and Elizabeth went to tend their birdfeeders.

Zelma, Sondra, and Morry started back up the trail.

Wildeen set out after them.

Nina revisited the pond. She stood at the bridge's railing, watching the lily pads drift lazily, as though nudged by an unseen hand, and listening to the chorus of frogs rising from their hiding places among the cattails. When she'd had enough communing with nature, she, too, headed back to the house. Rounding a sharp switchback, she heard Zelma say, "Wildeen, you wouldn't dare."

"Oh, wouldn't I?" Wildeen replied.

Nina ducked behind a large rhododendron bush. Pushing aside a handful of pink blossoms, she glimpsed Zelma and Wildeen only a few yards away. Never mind she was spying and eavesdropping. Since the reading, she had been worried about her two friends, and this opportunity might be ideal to discover the trouble between them.

"Can't we talk this over later?" Zelma held out both hands, palms up.

Wildeen folded her arms. "We have nothing to talk about."

"I think we do. I beg you, before you do anything,

hear me out. Meet me later tonight. Please."

"Well…" Wildeen tilted her head. "I will be stopping in the bookstore on my way home tonight. Be there around eleven, if you want to catch me."

"Okay, eleven it is." Zelma's shoulders sagged.

"But don't count on me changing my mind."

The two moved off, and the voices faded.

Nina waited several moments before abandoning her hiding place and returning to the path. Now, she was more mystified than ever. Whatever the matter was, Zelma and Wildeen planned more discussion later tonight, at Wildeen's bookstore. Surely, they would work out their differences then. Still, Nina's stomach churned with worry.

When she emerged from the forest, she saw Wildeen and Zelma standing at opposite ends of the rose garden with their backs to each other. Noticing Zelma's chalk-white face, Nina hurried to her side. "Are you okay?"

Zelma lifted her chin. "Of course, I am. The climb back up tired me out, that's all."

"I thought Morry and Sondra were with you?"

"They were, until Sondra broke a heel on her shoe. They told me to go on ahead while they searched."

That explained how Wildeen could get Zelma alone. Nina looked around, wondering when the rest of the group would return.

Just then, Morry, huffing and puffing, his suit jacket slung over his shoulder, appeared at the top of the path.

"Where's Sondra?" Zelma leaned to peek around him.

Morry took a handkerchief from his slacks pocket

and swiped at the perspiration on his forehead. "Aw, after we sent you on ahead, she insisted I take off, too, while she hunted for her heel on her own. Said she didn't want to spoil my walk." He tucked away his handkerchief and stretched his arm around Zelma's shoulders. "What's the matter, kid? You're so pale. You see a ghost on the walk, or what? Ha ha."

Zelma gave him a faint smile. "I'm just tired. These appearances are stressful."

"Hey, you're only getting started. Get a good night's sleep tonight, you hear? You gotta be fresh for your tour in a coupla days. Oh, there she is," he added, as Sondra limped into view. "You find your heel, kid?"

Sondra shook her head. "It must have gone over the cliff." She frowned at her red pumps, one with a heel and one without.

Hamlet appeared, brushing pine needles from his shoulders.

"Did you find the big tree?" Nina asked, curious to know if he had reached his destination, or if he, too, might have overheard the puzzling conversation between Zelma and Wildeen.

Hamlet's nod set his earring dancing. "The tree sits way down in a deep hollow. I had a heckuva time getting there, but the extra work was worth the trouble. That sucker is one giant tree."

Dorothy and her Literary Lights joined them, raving about the beautiful sunset.

Then came Larry, excited over the wildflowers. "I'd like to have some of them to plant at home."

Stephen loped up the path and stepped onto the lawn. "The beach was great. I would've taken a longer walk but the tide was coming in."

Josh and Patti returned. Pink lipstick smudged Josh's lower lip.

Elizabeth arrived next. "Where's Burgess?" She frowned and chewed her lower lip. "We stopped to check on our bird feeders, and when I looked for him, he was gone."

The others shrugged and shook their heads.

Tucking her slender hands into her wide jacket sleeves, Elizabeth gazed into the woods, now a patchwork of blue, green, and gray shadows.

Nina found Elizabeth's distress curious. Surely, Burgess wouldn't get lost on his own property.

At last, Burgess came trudging up the path.

"Where did you disappear to?" Elizabeth frowned at her husband.

Burgess waved a dirt-caked hand. "The sign for the Douglas Fir fell over. I had to set it up again."

"You might have told me you were going off," Elizabeth complained.

Burgess looked up at his taller wife. "But, my dear, you were busy watching the hummingbirds. I didn't want to scare them away by talking. Thought I'd slip off and take care of the sign. You know I can't get lost, don't you?"

"I suppose so." Elizabeth turned to the others, her frown morphing into a smile. "Well, I hope you enjoyed our little sojourn into Bottswood."

Everyone said they had, and soon after, the group broke up.

Nina paid her respects to Elizabeth and Burgess and then headed down the asphalt driveway to her car. As she drove away, she checked the dashboard clock. Ten fifteen. Forty-five minutes until Wildeen and

Zelma's meeting at Bergman Books. She wished she could be present, too. Maybe she could help them to resolve their conflict—whatever that conflict was.

But, as close friends as they all were, she wouldn't intrude. She'd only hope they'd settle the matter on their own.

****

Most days, even rainy ones, Nina walked the six-block distance from her Viewmont Estates' condo to the Seaview Library. The morning after the party, remembering her promise to stop at Wildeen's bookstore, she stretched the six blocks to ten, bypassing the library and continuing down Grove Street to Main. Traveling along Main, she passed the Soup and Sandwich Deli, the Yesteryear Antique Mall, and Helmer's Jewelry store. Jerry Helmer, a rosy-cheeked man in his sixties, arranged a display of diamond rings in the window. He looked up, and they exchanged a wave.

Bergman Books, New and Used, sat on the corner. Nina paused to study the array of mystery novels in the window and then approached the door. She twisted the knob, expecting the door to pop open.

The knob held fast.

How odd. Wildeen usually opened the store promptly at nine. Shading her eyes with a hand, Nina leaned against the glass and peered inside. The fluorescent nightlights cast a dim glow over the interior. Nina knocked on the wooden doorframe. She waited, expecting to see her friend emerge from the shadows and hurry to open the door.

No one appeared.

Again, she knocked, harder this time, and waited,

21

shifting from one foot to the other. Still no sign of Wildeen. Most likely, she was busy in the store's back room and failed to keep track of the time. Nina should go on to work. She didn't want to be late for this morning's ten o'clock staff meeting.

Yet, an eagerness to see the book Wildeen discovered, *The Wonderful Wizard of Oz*, made her reluctant to give up. She wanted to take the book to the library to pore over on her coffee break and at lunch. Recalling the store had a back entrance, Nina went around the corner, entered the alley, and knocked on the door. Once again, she waited.

The door remained closed. Nina grasped the knob, which turned readily. She pushed open the door. "Wildeen?" Nina stopped in the doorway and stared. The office appeared hit by a hurricane. Cupboard doors hung open, and drawers from the desk and work counter lay on the floor, their contents scattered from one end of the room to the other. A strange, metallic odor hung in the air.

Her gaze landed on a person's leg sticking out from behind the desk. A leg wearing a green stocking, and the foot a black flat.

An image of Wildeen at last night's party, wearing a yellow sweater and green stockings, popped into Nina's mind. Her throat constricted, and she pressed a hand to her chest. *Oh no, not Wildeen! Please, God, no.* She picked her way through the debris, peered around the desk, and gasped.

Wildeen lay on her stomach, one arm curled under her body, the other outstretched. Her head, turned to the left, revealed a large gash behind her ear. Her hair was blood-matted, and dried blood stained her face and the shoulder of her yellow sweater. More blood had soaked into the bare wooden floor.

Near Wildeen's outstretched left hand lay a glass horse figurine, one of her prized antique bookends. Blood covered the horse's uplifted hooves.

Blood was the strange odor. So much blood. Nausea churned Nina's stomach, while her thoughts raced. Call 911 then check for a pulse. Maybe she was still alive.

But, as she dug into her purse for her cell phone, her gaze fell on Wildeen's hand. The palm, pressed to the floor, was a mottled purple, while the back was pale white. Although she'd never actually seen lividity, the settling of blood to the bottom of a dead person's body, from reading murder mysteries, she knew instinctively that lividity was what she saw now.

No need to check for a pulse. Most certainly, Wildeen Bergman was dead.

Chapter Three

Nina huddled against the alley's brick wall, waiting for the police to arrive.

After calling 911, she ran next door to tell the Helmers what had happened. Georgia, a fiftyish woman with dyed black hair, kept murmuring about what a nice person Wildeen was. His arm around his wife's shoulders, Jerry worried the break-in was robbery motivated and their store might be targeted next.

A black-and-white police car finally pulled into the alley. Two officers, one male and one female, leaped out. The woman led the way as the two approached.

"I'm Officer Mahoney," the woman announced.

With her petite build and curly, shoulder-length blonde hair, Officer Mahoney appeared too soft to be a cop. But her authoritative tone proved otherwise.

Admonishing Nina and the Helmers to stay out, the officers entered the bookstore. "She's dead, all right," Officer Mahoney pronounced when she rejoined them in the alley.

While she and her partner took statements from Nina and the Helmers, an unmarked car, two marked squad cars, and the Medic One unit arrived. Men and women—armed with the tools of the trade—converged on the bookstore, ready to do battle at the crime scene. Richmond's resources amazed Nina.

A man dressed in navy slacks and a gray shirt

emerged from the store and joined Nina and Officer Mahoney. In his forties, he had curly, salt-and-pepper hair and a ruddy complexion.

"I'm Detective Pete Russell," he told Nina. "I understand you found the body."

She nodded and hugged her arms. "I came to pick up a book Wildeen had for me."

"I have her statement." Mahoney tapped the microphone attached to her shoulder.

"Good." Russell nodded and then turned back to Nina. "We'll still need you to come to the station, Ms. Foster, for a more complete interview. You'll have to hang around. You need to be someplace?"

"I'm the librarian at Seaview, but I've already called in and told my staff I'll be late."

Pete Russell returned to the bookstore.

Officer Mahoney put Nina in the back seat of a police car parked in the alley. Arms crossed over her chest, the officer leaned against the front fender.

A crowd gathered at the alley's entrance, held back by a ribbon of yellow crime scene tape. Among them was Stephen Kraslow. He spoke to a policeman and wrote in a small notebook. He presented quite a different picture from the casual and relaxed man she'd met last night. Today, he was an on-the-job news hound.

Oh, oh, his roving gaze landed where she sat. Nina scrunched down in the seat, wishing she could make herself invisible. *Too late*. His eyes lighted with recognition.

The officer Stephen interviewed turned to speak to someone else. Stephen ducked under the tape and headed in Nina's direction.

Just then, Officer Mahoney spotted Stephen and waved him away.

He mouthed something to Nina, but she couldn't make out the words. She shrugged, thankful for Officer Mahoney's timely intervention.

At last, Officer Mahoney drove Nina to the police station and led her to a small, windowless room furnished with only a table and straight chairs. She sat on one of the chairs, feeling more like a criminal than a witness.

Detective Russell entered, carrying a small recorder and a yellow, legal-size pad of paper. With him was a tall, lanky policewoman he introduced as Officer Valdez. He set the recorder on the table. "Okay with you to record this interview?"

Nina shrugged. "I guess so."

Officer Valdez sat at one end of the table, and Russell sat across from Nina. He propped one ankle on his knee and balanced the yellow pad on his lap.

He asked her questions about herself, questions that had nothing to do with Wildeen's death. *Why?* Then she realized he wanted her to relax. *Not possible.* Finally, she held up a hand. "Could we get on with the interview, please?"

He stopped writing and looked up with a frown.

"I, ah, really need to get back to work. My staff is waiting."

"Okay, sure." Russell nodded. "Where do you want to begin?"

She began with seeing Wildeen the night before at Bottswood and her arrangement to pick up *The Wonderful Wizard of Oz* this morning. Russell interrupted a few times to ask her to repeat or clarify a detail. When she came to finding Wildeen's lifeless body, her eyes filled with tears.

"Take your time."

Russell's tone was soft.

Officer Valdez handed Nina a tissue.

"Thanks." After wiping her eyes and blowing her nose, Nina finished her story.

Russell switched off the recorder and leaned back. "Now, Ms. Foster, I want to ask you something very important. Do you know anyone who might have a reason to kill Wildeen Bergman?"

Nina gasped. "No, I don't."

"Do you have any information other than what you have already stated that might help us? For example, do you know of anyone who was to meet Ms. Bergman last night at her bookstore?"

Nina's throat constricted. Of course, she did, and she would have to tell him. "Zelma Duke planned to meet her." She related the conversation she overheard between the two in the forest. "But Zelma wouldn't kill Wildeen. We three were friends. We all went to college together at PNU."

Pete Russell rubbed his chin. "Is that a fact? But you also said you observed tension between them earlier that evening."

"The problem concerned Zelma's new book, but I don't know the details." Feeling sick inside, she pressed a hand to her stomach. "I don't want to incriminate Zelma."

"I'm not asking you to make any conclusions about who killed Ms. Bergman. I'm just after the facts." Russell picked up his pen and notepad.

Just the facts, ma'am. He sounded like Joe Friday

on the old *Dragnet* TV series, which Nina and her grandmother watched on the Nostalgia station. Old Joe, who questioned suspects in his deadpan manner.

The time was almost noon when Russell finally ended the interview. "We may call you in again, if we need to talk further." He gathered his notepad and recorder. "I'll have someone give you a ride to the library."

"No, thank you." Nina vigorously shook her head. "One ride in a police car was enough. Now, I know how a criminal feels."

****

After a three-block, uphill walk, Nina opened the plate glass door to the Seaview Branch Library and stepped inside. An immediate sense of relief washed over her. She loved the library, and she loved her job. Shelf after shelf and row upon row of books, all arranged in precise order, offered protection from the chaotic world outside.

Behind the circulation counter, Arlette Robbins ran a metal wand over the barcodes in returned books and then placed them on a book truck. In her fifties, Arlette wore her long gray hair clipped at the nape and favored bright-colored clothing, like today's lime green blouse. She waved the wand at Nina. "Are we glad to see you. Are you okay?"

"I'm not sure." Nina offered a weak smile. "But I'm here."

Larry sat at the reference desk, narrow shoulders hunched over the computer keyboard, black-framed eyeglasses, as usual, halfway down the bridge of his nose. He looked up, pushing the glasses into place with his forefinger. "May I help you? Oh, hello, Nina." His brow wrinkled. "How are you?"

Still a bit breathless from her walk, Nina leaned against the desk. "I'm all right."

"You look stressed. What an ordeal you've been through."

"I am stressed." She straightened and gazed around, thankful to be in familiar surroundings where she could finally relax. "But I'd better get to work." She turned and headed toward the library's office.

Larry rose and followed. "We postponed the staff meeting."

"Thanks," she said over her shoulder. "We'll reschedule."

In the workroom, Myo Chung checked in a shipment of new books, while Holly Williams, the college student page, loaded a metal cart with books to shelve.

Holly's blouse had a plunging neckline and white fabric thin enough to reveal the outline of her bra. Nina sighed. Despite the many talks she and Holly had about proper work attire, the young woman persisted in dressing inappropriately. Oh, well, she'd deal with the problem later.

Myo laid one of the new books on the table and looked at Nina. "Wildeen Bergman, dead. How terrible." She shook her head and pressed her lips together.

"I've bought books at Wildeen's store." Holly added another book to her cart. "Once, when I needed a text for a lit class, Wildeen called other stores and found the book. I was impressed she went to all the trouble."

Nina smiled. "Wildeen loved to find books for

people, just like I do. Books were a bond between us."

After Holly left with her book cart, Nina tucked her purse and jacket in the closet and then stood in the center of the room, uncertain what to do.

Myo set aside a stack of books and reached for another pile. "You look tired, Nina. Maybe you should take the rest of the day off and go home."

"I'm in shock." Nina rubbed her forehead. "Even so, the library is the best place for me to be."

Arlette bustled in and stood with hands on her hips. "Can we cheer you up? Did you hear the one about the football team in the sauna?"

Larry frowned and stirred creamer into the mug of coffee he'd poured from the counter coffee maker. "Arlette, if I hear one more of your offensive jokes, I'll nail you for harassment."

As another staff problem reared its head, Nina sighed again. Despite her grandmotherly appearance, Arlette's joke repertoire came straight from the locker room. Nina had cautioned her to keep the stories out of the workplace, and she agreed to comply.

Arlette wrinkled her nose at Larry and then raised her eyebrows at Nina. "Have you eaten lunch?"

"No. I planned to stop at the deli for a take-out sandwich after I saw Wildeen, but..." Nina bit her lip and cringed inwardly at the memory.

"Not to worry."

Arlette took out her old-fashioned, round-topped metal lunch bucket and gave Nina half a tuna sandwich. Larry produced peanut butter cookies his wife made. Myo brewed Nina a cup of her favorite Earl Grey tea. Nina let them fuss over her. They were like family.

Revived by the food and the hot tea, Nina told

them about finding Wildeen's body, but not about Zelma's plans to visit Wildeen at the bookstore last night. She'd had to tell the police, but she wouldn't risk starting rumors by telling anyone else.

Holly poked her head in the door. "Larry, a lady wants to know if we have information on Morning Glory Mutual Funds. She can't find the company listed in the computer."

"The correct name is Morning*star*, Holly. And yes, we have back issues of their reports. I'll help her." Larry rolled his eyes, dumped his coffee in the sink, and hurried out.

Holly's interruption reminded Nina work needed to be done. She quickly drained her teacup. "Arlette, Myo, we'd all better get back to business. I'm fine now, thanks to all of you."

Later, Nina staffed the reference desk while Larry went to lunch. Forcing herself to keep her mind on her job, she helped a mother and her five-year-old daughter gather a stack of picture books, assisted an elderly woman in researching local retirement homes, and helped other patrons Google topics such as World Series records and the varieties of clams found on Washington's beaches.

Larry returned to take over the desk.

Needing a moment alone, Nina retreated to a quiet corner of the main reading room where large windows overlooked the city. Her gaze landed almost immediately on the domed skylight of Bergman Books. Wildeen wasn't there anymore. She would never again be in her store. Nina's heart constricted, and tears gathered behind her eyes.

"Nina…"

She turned to find Stephen Kraslow standing behind her. Her stomach tensed, but she said a polite, "hello."

"You've lost a good friend, haven't you?" Without waiting for an answer, he added, "I'm sorry."

The concern she heard in his voice brought more tears to her eyes.

Pulling a handkerchief from a back slacks pocket, Stephen held it out.

"Thanks." She took the handkerchief and dabbed her eyes. The cloth smelled faintly, pleasantly, of aftershave. "Yes, I have lost a friend."

"I understand."

"Do you?" She lifted her chin. "I'm not only sad because Wildeen is dead but horrified she died so violently."

"I had a good friend who committed suicide. He— well, I won't tell you the details, but his death was violent, and I was the one who found him." He looked away a moment and then turned back. "I met Wildeen for the first time at last night's party. She seemed like a nice person."

Nina refolded the handkerchief and held it out. "She was. She loved her bookstore and hunting down books for people. She always kept an eye out for me and my collection."

"You collect books?" He took the handkerchief and tucked it into his pocket. "How unusual."

A twinkle restored the brightness to his eyes. At his joke, she offered a wan smile. "Uh huh. Children's books."

"I was surprised to see you this morning sitting in the police car."

"I didn't expect to see you, either." Relaxed now, she allowed a smile to cross her lips. "I thought one of your staff would chase police calls."

He shook his head. "Right now, I want to answer the calls myself. The best way to become acquainted with the community is to be in it. Anyway, I learned later from my contact at the police department you were the one who found Wildeen."

She nodded, turning again toward the window. At the ferry terminal, vehicles and walk-ons streamed from a recently arrived ferry. They cleared the dock and spread out in various directions. Tragedy had upset her life, but for those unaffected, life went on as usual.

"You'd stopped by to see her this morning?"

"She had a book for me, *The Wonderful Wizard of Oz,* which she found at an estate sale. I was to pick it up on my way to work this morning."

"And?"

"When I arrived at the store, I found her on the floor of her office. Dead. Had been for some time. I could tell by the way the blood had settled to the palm of her hand. I read a lot of mysteries, you see, so I know about blood…settling." She was babbling but had no control over her tongue.

"Do you know why anyone would want to murder her? I'm assuming her death was murder. The official announcement hasn't been made yet, of course. Not until after the autopsy."

Autopsy. Nina hugged her arms, shivering at the thought of Wildeen's body being cut up and scrutinized by strangers. "No, I don't know why anyone would murder her."

"Did Wildeen have any family?"

"She has an estranged husband, Josh Loring. He was at the party last night." She wondered how Josh received the news of Wildeen's death.

"Oh, yes. The man with the blonde hanging on his arm."

"He's the one. They had no children. Wildeen's parents are both alive, but they moved to Sedona, Arizona, some years ago." The last cars were leaving the ferry now. Soon, vehicles headed for the opposite shore would board.

"What are their names?"

A clicking sound brought Nina to her senses. She whirled to see Stephen making notes in a small spiral notebook. She drew in a breath. "Are you interviewing me for your newspaper?"

Stephen wrinkled his brow. "I admit I did come here with an interview in mind."

The nerve of him, worming his way into her confidence by offering sympathy. She folded her arms and gritted her teeth. "I have nothing more to tell you. I've said too much already, and I really must get back to work." She snatched up a magazine left on a lounge chair, returned it to the rack, and then methodically straightened the stacks of back issues. She sensed Stephen behind her. Finally, she stopped short and turned. He was so close that with little effort, they could rub noses. "Please, I don't want to talk to you anymore."

"Okay." He slipped his notebook and pen into his shirt pocket. "I'll see you later, then."

Nina busied herself, straightening a set of encyclopedias in the Reference section. From the corner of her eye, she saw Stephen approach Larry at the desk.

They conversed a moment, and then Larry guided Stephen to the computers for the patrons. Was he helping Stephen locate Wildeen's parents' Arizona address and phone number? If so, she hoped Stephen would have the decency to wait awhile before calling them.

When she saw Stephen finally exit the library's glass doors, Nina breathed a sigh of relief. Why did he upset her? Was she annoyed because he was one more transplant? Or was her feeling due to something else?

Why was she thinking about him at all right now, when one of her best friends was dead and a murderer was on the loose?

Chapter Four

That evening, Nina curled up on her living room sofa, drinking Earl Grey tea and gazing out the window at the approaching twilight. Despite a lack of appetite, she finished a small tossed salad and half a sourdough roll. Even so, her stomach churned. No matter how hard she tried, she couldn't purge Wildeen's horrible death from her mind.

Her cell phone's ring broke the silence. Numbly, she picked up the phone and checked the screen. The caller was her grandmother, Jessica Bingham, who lived at Marley Manor, a local retirement home. Jessica was Nina's only living relative. The only one she knew of, anyway. Her father abandoned her and her mother when Nina was five years old, and no one knew whether or not he was still alive. Her mother passed away several years ago.

"Hi, honey."

Nina warmed to the sound of her grandmother's familiar voice. "Hello, Gran."

"I heard about Wildeen on the news," Jessica continued. "Also, Jerry Helmer's mother lives here at Marley, and he called her. He said you were the one who found the body."

"Yes, I was." Nina sketched in the details.

"How awful. Who could have done such a terrible thing?"

"I don't know. I've been asking myself that question all day."

"Well, how are *you* doing? Are you all right?"

Nina smiled at her grandmother's concern. "I think so. Finding her was quite a shock, though."

"Well, if you need me, call. You know I'm here for you."

"I know, Gran. I love you." What would she do without Grandmother Jessica?

"Love you, too, honey."

She had no more than put down the phone when it chimed again.

"Oh, Nina," Zelma wailed in Nina's ear. "I can't believe what I heard on the TV about Wildeen."

"I know." Nina glanced out the window where twilight's glow filled the sky. "I can hardly believe she's gone."

"A policeman was here today, questioning me. A grim man named Pete Russell."

Nina's chest tightened. *Of course, he was questioning you. I put him on your trail.* "I'm sure he's interviewing everyone who was at the Bottses' party."

"Nina, will you come over? I need to talk to you. Please."

Nina bit her lip. Did she want any more involvement in Wildeen's death?

"Nina?"

She heaved a sigh. What was she thinking? Zelma was her friend. If she needed to talk, Nina would listen. "Of course, Zelma. "I'll be right over."

"Thank you, Nina. Thank you sooo much."

****

Nina pulled into the driveway of Zelma's rambler

just as the sun disappeared behind the Olympic Mountains, casting shadows over the landscape. The house was in a neighborhood of modest homes located a couple miles from the harbor, on the edge of Richmond's city limits. Zelma's yard was a mess, as usual. Weeds clogged the flagstone path and the geranium beds, and at least two weeks' growth of grass waved in the light breeze.

Zelma promptly answered the door.

A sleeveless pink smock draped her ample figure. Her eyes were red-rimmed, her lipstick smudged, and wisps of dark hair had escaped the carefully swept-back wings. *So much for her makeover.*

"Oh, Nina. I'm so glad you came." Zelma gave her a hug and then waved her toward the living room. "Sit, and I'll fix us some tea."

Entering Zelma's low-ceiling living room was like crawling into a cave. A very full cave. A sofa and chairs with flat wooden arms and tweed cushions surrounded a redwood coffee table. Two worn leather chairs fought for space with a metal bookshelf overflowing with books and knick-knacks. A woven basket of logs, a stack of newspapers, and a set of fire-tending tools sat on the fireplace's brick hearth.

A huge poster depicting the cover of *My Restless Heart* occupied a narrow space between the fireplace and a Maxfield Parrish print. On an end table, a pile of Zelma's paperbacks crowded a photo of her seven-year-old twin daughters, Brittany and Angela. The odor of stale cigarette smoke hung in the air, along with the acrid smell of burned meat.

Nina wrinkled her nose and sank into one of the tweed chairs. Her gaze strayed to the archway leading to the dining room. On the round oak table sat Zelma's computer and printer. The computer screen showed a screensaver photo of Mount Rainier.

Presently, Zelma bustled in, her leather sandals slap-slapping on the carpet. She carried two mugs of steaming tea, one of which she handed to Nina.

Nina inhaled the spicy aroma. She sipped the tea and set the cup on the wide chair arm.

Zelma backed into the other tweed chair across from Nina.

On an arm rested a pack of cigarettes, a lighter, and an overflowing ashtray, the source of the room's aroma, part of it, anyway.

Zelma set down her cup, tugged out a cigarette, and lit it. As she exhaled a column of smoke, she threw Nina an apologetic look. "I quit smoking, but right now, I'm too stressed to cope. I'm in shock that Wildeen is dead." She dragged her free hand through her hair, dislodging more of the swept-back wings.

"Me, too." Nina sipped her tea.

Zelma heaved a sigh. "I keep thinking of the three of us when we were at PNU. Scenes play in my mind like reruns of old movies."

Nina nodded. She, too, had been reminiscing and feeling sad.

"Remember when we were freshmen?" Zelma took a drag on her cigarette. "Luck of the draw paired you and me as roommates. Wildeen wasn't so lucky. She drew that awful girl who smoked pot. Remember how we let Wildeen stay with us?"

At the memory, Nina smiled. "Uh huh. And she drove us crazy, washing her hair every day and using her noisy dryer while we tried to study."

"And she'd hide my cookies." Zelma wrinkled her nose.

"She was only helping you lose weight."

Zelma took another drag on her cigarette and blew the smoke at the ceiling. "I know, but she made me mad, anyway. Those days were like another lifetime, though. We were different people, and so much has happened since then." Her gaze strayed toward the photograph of her twin daughters.

"How are Brit and Angie, by the way?" Nina leaned forward to study the photo. Both girls wore their dark hair in pigtails, and their wide smiles showed a gap where a front tooth was missing.

"They're doing fine. This week is the first time they've stayed with Bob and his new wife since they moved to Tacoma. I miss the girls like crazy, but, with my tour and all, they're better off with Bob and Susie." Zelma shook her head. "Divorce is the pits. But, then, so was marriage."

Nina gave a dry laugh. "I wouldn't know about either one of those situations."

Zelma puffed on her cigarette, her nostrils flaring as she expelled the smoke. She sighed, crossed, and uncrossed her ankles.

Sensing something else was on Zelma's mind, Nina drank her tea and waited.

Finally, Zelma snuffed out her cigarette and looked at Nina, her brow wrinkled and her mouth tense. "I'm scared, Nina. I'm scared the police think I killed Wildeen."

"Why would they think that?" Nina raised her eyebrows. She knew the answer, but, on the off chance she was wrong, she wanted to hear what Zelma had to say.

Zelma twisted her fingers together. "I—I was at the bookstore last night. Someone told that awful Pete Russell I would be there at eleven. But I don't see how anyone could've had that information. Our meeting was a secret."

Nina bit her lip and looked away. She'd had to tell the police the truth, and now she must confess to Zelma. "I was the one who told Detective Russell about your meeting."

Zelma dropped her jaw. "You? But how—"

"I overheard the conversation you and Wildeen had in the woods."

"You eavesdropped?" Zelma stared.

Nina frowned and folded her arms. "By accident. On my way back to the house, I saw you two together and heard you arguing."

"You didn't have to listen, did you?"

"No. But I was worried." Nina straightened her shoulders. "When Wildeen wanted you to read those particular pages, I sensed something was wrong between you two."

Zelma tossed her head and waved a hand. "Okay, so you heard about our meeting. Did you have to tell the police?"

"Detective Russell asked me if I knew anyone who might have been at the bookstore last evening." Nina lifted her chin. "I couldn't lie. Lying would be withholding evidence."

Zelma stretched her lips into a tight line.

Nina shrugged. "He would find out eventually you were there. You must have left fingerprints or other traces. The police have all sorts of ways to determine who was at a crime scene."

"I did clutch the edge of her desk at one point. And of course, I opened the door. But I didn't kill Wildeen. She was very much alive when I left."

"I know you didn't kill her. I would never believe you did." Nina put her cup on the arm of the chair. "But why were you and Wildeen meeting at the bookstore? Can't you tell me? In the woods, I heard you beg her not to do anything before you two could talk."

Zelma gnawed her thumb's false fingernail. "Did I really grovel?"

"You sounded pretty pitiful. What were you arguing about?"

"All right." Zelma sighed. "I told Detective Russell, so I might as well tell you."

Zelma's reasoning hurt Nina. She wanted Zelma to tell her because they were friends, not because the police already had the information.

Zelma heaved herself from the chair and strode to the fireplace. "Wildeen wrote a review of *My Restless Heart* for *Pages*. You know, the prestigious magazine?"

"Uh huh." Nina subscribed to the periodical at the library. The reviews were sophisticated and insightful.

"She told me she gave my book a bad review, which would appear in next month's issue. Print and online." Zelma gazed at the poster of her book.

No wonder Zelma was upset. "Why would she tell you beforehand?"

"She wanted to see me squirm. You know how jealous she was of my success." Zelma turned from the poster and again faced Nina.

"But I believe she would write an honest review." Seeing Zelma's hurt-filled eyes, Nina cleared her throat and amended, "I mean, honest from her point of view. She wouldn't let her jealousy influence her opinion, would she?"

"I don't know. But, I thought if I could meet with her and explain my story…"

Nina pursed her lips and shook her head. "Zelma, you know a story shouldn't have to be explained."

Zelma waved a hand. "Okay, but I thought if we could at least talk, she would change her mind about trashing my book. She's gained quite a reputation as a book critic, and a bad review from her will hurt my sales."

"So, you went to the bookstore to talk about your book. Then what happened?"

Zelma shrugged. "I *tried* to reason with her, but she was in a terrible mood. I think she was pissed because Josh and Patti were at the party." Zelma narrowed her eyes. "Didn't she have a run-in with them?"

"They had some tense moments." Nina shivered at the memory of their confrontation. "Josh wanted Wildeen to settle their divorce out of court."

"I thought so. I quickly saw her mind wasn't on my book at all. So, after a few minutes, I gave up and left." She threw up her hands.

"And she stayed at the store?" Nina had the feeling Zelma wasn't telling her the whole story.

"She said she had to check on something Hamlet left undone. I don't remember what. I was too upset to listen to the details." Zelma paced in front of the fireplace.

"You didn't see anyone else around?"

"No. All the other stores nearby were closed."

Nina picked up her cup and sipped her tea. "I

thought the trouble between you two had to do with the pages she wanted you to read. She was so insistent."

Zelma stopped pacing and dropped her gaze. "I don't know why she requested those particular pages. Just a passage she particularly didn't like, I guess."

Nina didn't like to think Wildeen would be so spiteful, but she also knew Wildeen's jealousy of Zelma ran deep. "Maybe robbery was the motive. Her office was a mess."

"But why would anyone rob a bookstore? Surely, she didn't keep much money around."

"Maybe someone knew she kept rare and valuable books in her safe. The copy of *Wizard* is probably worth a few thousand."

Zelma raised her eyebrows. "Was the safe open?"

"I don't know." Nina shrugged. "The safe's in a cupboard, and I didn't think to look. My attention was on Wildeen."

Zelma returned to her chair. She picked up her cigarette pack, tapped out, and lit a cigarette. After taking a drag and exhaling the smoke, she sat back and regarded Nina. "Finding her dead must have been awful."

Nina nodded and twisted her fingers together. "The whole experience was a nightmare."

They both were quiet for a few moments while Zelma smoked and Nina drank her tea.

"I'm sorry Wildeen is gone." Zelma finally broke the silence. "But her death has certainly ruined my plans."

What was Zelma talking about? Nina frowned. "Why?"

"Because I'm the prime suspect." Zelma aimed a

thumb at her chest. "And here I am, ready to go on my tour. Plus, being a suspect will be expensive. I'll have to spend thousands of dollars defending myself and proving my innocence."

"Aren't you jumping to conclusions?" Nina frowned. "I hardly think writing a bad review of your book can be considered a motive for murder. After all, a bad review is not the end of the world."

"But if the police can't find any other suspects, they'll pin her murder on me. And I've worked hard to become a successful writer. I planned to use the money from *My Restless Heart* to buy a new house. One with a swimming pool and a sauna. I'm so tired of this dump." Zelma glanced around and wrinkled her nose.

"Your house isn't a dump. The place just needs a little attention."

Zelma waved a hand. "Whatever. Anyway, I intended to take a cruise to the Caribbean or Europe, somewhere glamorous. Until now, my writing has occupied all my time. My writing was the main reason my marriage failed. And, most of all, what will my publisher say if I'm a suspect in a murder? Will he still promote me?" Zelma twisted her lips into a grimace. "I talked to my publicist, Sondra Wagner, today. The police questioned her, too. She's really upset. We were to leave on our tour in two days."

"Can't you still go?" Zelma's cancelling her plans seemed a bit extreme.

"I suppose we could. The police haven't restricted me from leaving town. But I want to be here while they conduct their investigation."

"What does your agent think?"

A soft smile crossed Zelma's lips. "Morry's such a

dear. He told me not to worry. But I know he's counting on my success to boost his. He's never represented a really big, moneymaking writer before. Not until I came along." Shaking her head, she looked at the ceiling. "Oh, what will I do?"

"Quit worrying. Everything will be all right."

"No, everything won't." Zelma lowered her gaze and glared. "And my dilemma is all your fault, Nina Foster."

Nina felt her stomach tighten. "My fault? What are you talking about?"

Zelma shook her finger. "You were the one who told the police I planned to meet Wildeen."

Nina set her teacup aside and spread her hands in a gesture that begged Zelma's understanding. "I explained why I had to tell them. Besides, when they questioned you, you would've told them you were there…wouldn't you?" She studied Zelma from under furrowed brows.

Zelma tossed her head. "I don't know. Since I didn't kill her, why should I implicate myself? Especially when I need to promote my new book."

Shock rippled through Nina. "I can't believe what I'm hearing. Wildeen was our friend."

"Yours, maybe. Mine, once upon a time. In the last couple of years, her jealousy drove us apart."

"Maybe so, but blaming me is really unfair. I did what I had to do. Maybe I'd better leave." Nina pushed to the edge of the chair.

Zelma's eyes shot wide, and she put out a hand. "Please don't go yet. Aren't you at least a little sorry I'm in all this trouble?"

"Of course, I am. But I don't know what I can do

about it."

Zelma took a deep drag on her cigarette and then snuffed it out in the ashtray, sending bits of ash swirling into the air.

Nina picked up her cup and sipped her tea. The brew was cold and bitter, but she needed something to ease her tension.

Her eyes bright, Zelma leaned forward. "You can help me by discovering who did kill Wildeen. You're a big fan of mystery novels. Surely, you've picked up some detecting techniques from all your reading."

Nina choked out a laugh. That proposal was crazy, even for Zelma. "Sure, I like to read mysteries and, okay, sometimes pretend I'm the sleuth. But Wildeen's murder is real life, not fiction. Finding the killer is up to Detective Russell."

"I don't trust him." Zelma sat back and folded her arms. "He wants to find someone he can reasonably pin the murder on. Do you think he really cares whether or not he arrests the right person?"

"I'd like to believe he cares. But, since I've never had much to do with the police, you may be right." Nina shrugged. "Still, I don't know what I could do."

"Well, if I didn't kill Wildeen, then let's think who might have. A burglar, as you mentioned before. A stranger."

Nina gave a cynical laugh. "In which case my chances of coming across him or her are slim to none."

"But what if the killer is someone who knew her?" Zelma put a finger to her cheek and tilted her head. "How about Josh?"

"Her husband?" Nina shook her head. "Oh, Zelma, no. Not Josh."

"They had some serious fights when they were together. Wildeen had a temper and so does he. And he's strong. Don't tell me you've never noticed those muscular shoulders." Zelma rolled her eyes.

"Okay, so I have. But murder?"

"He has a motive, doesn't he?" Zelma stood and paced the floor again. "Wildeen stalled their divorce for quite a while. For that matter, maybe Patti's the murderer. With Wildeen out of the way, Josh would gain all his inheritance and be free to marry her."

"True. But I can't accept that anyone I know, personally, would resort to murder." Nina shuddered.

Zelma stopped pacing and turned to give Nina a solemn nod. "Believe it, Nina. A sneaky little murderer lurks inside all of us. Fortunately, most of us keep the little devil under control by finding acceptable outlets for our anger."

Nina widened her eyes. "Zelma, I never knew you were such a cynic. But when will I have time to track down a murderer? I have a job, you know."

"I know." Zelma sighed and paced another few steps. "Just an idea. A bad one, I guess." She stopped and slanted Nina a glance.

"Okay." Nina closed her eyes and heaved a resigned sigh. "I admit the idea is appealing. Her murder is a puzzle, and I like puzzles."

Zelma smiled and nodded. "And you have such a logical, well-organized mind. Not like me, whose brain runs in all directions. I'd really appreciate your help. You're the only one at the party I can really trust and the only one I can turn to."

Nina chewed her lower lip. Perhaps she could turn up something helpful. "All right, Zelma. But I can't promise I'll be successful."

Zelma whooshed out a breath. "Just knowing you're tackling the problem makes me feel better. Lots better. Thank you, Nina, for being my good friend."

Later, on the way home, Nina wondered if she might not regret her decision to help Zelma. What was she getting herself into?

Chapter Five

"Let's see," Nina mused, "is that everybody?" She reviewed the list of names she'd written on her pad of yellow lined paper. She could have used her electronic tablet, but sometimes, like now, she preferred pencil and paper.

Sunlight drifted through her kitchen window, reflecting off the hanging copper pots and warming the surface of the oak table where she sat. Today was Wednesday, her day off, and two days after her visit to Zelma. Two days during which she'd done considerable thinking.

Zelma was good at persuasion. At first, she decided she was a fool to let Zelma talk her into looking for Wildeen's killer. Zelma coerced her in a weak moment. Then Nina had straightened her shoulders and vowed to help her friend.

The main reason for her decision was Wildeen. Whenever she thought of Wildeen's battered body lying on the floor of the bookstore, outrage filled her. No one had the right to take another person's life.

She called upon all she'd learned from reading mystery novels and approached the problem as a detective would, which was why she made the list of names. They were her suspects. Since she overheard Wildeen and Zelma plan to meet at Bergman Books after the party, someone else might have, too. Someone who then used the occasion to kill Wildeen and frame Zelma.

She studied the list. Elizabeth Botts and Burgess Botts, the party hosts. Josh Loring, Wildeen's estranged husband. Patti Hamilton, Josh's girlfriend. Sondra Wagner, Zelma's publicist. Morry Snyder, Zelma's agent. And, finally, Hamlet Green, Wildeen's employee.

Josh and Patti were the only persons who had an obvious motive. Nina had no idea how the others could be involved, but, wanting more than two suspects, she'd added their names to her list. However, she would begin her investigation with Josh and Patti. She tapped the pencil against her chin, wondering how to determine if either—or both—was guilty. No outright accusations. She'd have to be subtle.

Perhaps she could visit Josh at work. He was a financial advisor and continually attempting to add her to his client list. Despite her polite refusal, she regularly received invitations to his investment seminars. Now was the time to accept. She went to the kitchen drawer containing miscellaneous advertising brochures and coupons and found the invitation to the latest Loring Investments Seminar. The meeting was this coming Thursday at seven p.m. and an evening she had free. She phoned Josh's office and told his secretary she would attend.

Now, how about Patti? Another item in her junk mail drawer could provide an excuse to interview her. Searching, Nina found an advertising insert from an issue of *The Richmond Review.* The included coupon was for a month's trial membership to the Evergreen Athletic Club, where Patti was an aerobics instructor.

Nina's idea of exercise was to walk to work or to dig in her patio garden. But, as was her habit, she had saved the advertisement. Now, she was glad she had.

A prospective member could visit the club any day, the ad said, without an appointment. Why not take advantage of the offer today? Upstairs in her bedroom, she packed a canvas bag with a tan T-shirt, a pair of dark brown shorts, brown socks, and white tennis shoes. Those items should do for whatever awaited her at the Evergreen Athletic Club.

She was on her way to the front door when her cell phone rang. The caller was Detective Pete Russell.

"Do you have time today to visit Bottswood with me? I want to see the spot where you overheard the conversation between Zelma and Wildeen."

"I have time later this afternoon," Nina replied, surprised and yet pleased he wanted her help.

"How about three o'clock?"

"All right... By the way, did you get the autopsy results?" She might as well use this opportunity to probe for more information.

"Yup. She died from head trauma."

Trauma to the head. An image of the bloodied, glass horse bookend popped into her mind, and she shivered. "I'm not surprised. But I'm sure Zelma Duke is not responsible."

"I'm not asking you to make a judgment. I'm only asking you to cooperate with our investigation."

Nina stiffened. "Of course."

And, maybe she could learn something from Pete Russell that would aid her own investigation.

****

At the Evergreen Athletic Club, a two-story,

yellow cement building near the waterfront, Nina presented her coupon to the young woman behind the reception desk. She wore a green body stocking, a pink tank top, and her nametag said "Helen."

"Welcome." Helen smiled and handed Nina a clipboard with a form to fill out.

Nina took a nearby seat, dutifully filled in the required information, and returned the form to Helen.

Helen perused the information and then looked up. "We'll have someone give you a tour. Then you can try out an activity. Let's see who's available." She turned to her computer screen.

"Could Patti Hamilton give me the tour?" Nina clasped her hands and rested her arms on the counter. "She's a friend of mine."

"Patti?" Helen scrolled down the screen. "She could. She's between aerobics classes right now." She picked up a microphone and announced over the intercom, "Patti to the front desk."

While Nina waited, she studied the passing parade of club members. Most of the men and women had near-perfect bodies, which they showed off in tank tops and Spandex. Where were all the overweight, out-of-shape people she expected to find in a health club? Apparently, not at the Evergreen.

A side door opened, and Patti appeared. Like the receptionist, she wore a green body stocking and a pink tank top. A pink headband corralled her long blonde hair. She bounced along as though her athletic shoes were filled with helium. She certainly fit the role of an aerobics instructor. In appearance, anyway.

"What's up, Helen?" Patti smiled at her co-worker.

"This lady registered for a trial membership and

needs a tour." Helen gestured to Nina.

Patti turned to Nina, and her smile shriveled. "Oh. You're Nina, right? Wildeen's friend."

"Yes, Nina Foster."

Patti frowned and pointed to the computer screen. "Isn't Susan available?"

Helen squinted at the screen. "Yes, but she—"

"I asked for you, specifically," Nina interrupted. "I thought talking about the club membership with someone I know would be an advantage." Would Patti see through her lame excuse and guess the real reason for her visit?

Patti narrowed her eyes, but then she shrugged. "Oh, all right. I'm here and I'm available, so I'll give you the tour." She led Nina down a hallway. "I was shocked to hear about Wildeen. So was Josh. I understand you found her."

"Yes, I went to the bookstore to get a book she'd bought for me."

"I hope they find the person who killed her."

Patti certainly sounded sincere, and Nina wanted to pursue questioning her, but just then they reached the racquetball courts. The air rang with the sounds of racquets hitting balls and balls hitting the walls.

"Do you play racquetball?" Patti gestured to the courts.

"No, I don't." Nina watched two grim-faced men battle to control the ball. "But the game looks like...fun." Actually, beating a carpet would be easier—if she wanted to exercise her arms. But, then, she had never been much for competitive sports.

Catching Patti's skeptical look, Nina vowed to sound more enthusiastic. When they visited the exercise room, with the various machines, and which in truth looked like a torture chamber, she commented on how a workout here would truly make her feel "renewed."

Next came aerobics, Pilates, and then spinning. Spinning appeared to be just another name for riding a bicycle, but Nina kept her observation to herself. At the swimming pool, a water polo game was in progress. Sensing they were nearing the end of the tour, Nina decided she'd better get down to business. "I heard about the club from Wildeen," she said as they left the noisy game behind and entered the hallway. "If I remember correctly, she and Josh joined a couple years ago."

"They did, but Wildeen rarely used her membership."

Which provided an opportunity for you and Josh to get acquainted. "I can't imagine who would kill her."

Patti stopped and pointed to double doors. "Here's the gym." She opened one of the doors and motioned Nina inside. "We have a ladies' basketball team, if you're interested."

"I'll certainly give the game some thought." Nina gazed around the court and pictured herself chasing a ball and aiming it at the basket. Okay, basketball might be fun. Maybe.

"This is the end of the tour," Patti said. "What would you like to do for your free activity?"

Nina looked at her wristwatch. "I suppose I have time for an activity. I have an appointment with Detective Pete Russell this afternoon. He's investigating Wildeen's murder, and since I discovered her, he interviewed me. Which made me a bit nervous, because I don't really have an alibi. I went home alone after the Bottses' party." She pressed a forefinger to her cheek. "I wonder if he talked to everyone who was there."

Patti propped her hands on her hips and glared. "Oh, I get it. You're fishing to see if I had anything to do with her death. Well, for your information—although my alibi is none of your business—Josh and I were together after the party. We were together all night."

Patti's defensive tone put Nina on alert. Was she only intent on proving her innocence? Or was she hiding something? "Okay…but…"

"Wildeen was not a friend of mine, but I wouldn't kill her. Neither would Josh. He wouldn't hurt a fly. He's the most kind and wonderful man I've ever known." Patti's pink cheeks matched her tank top. "Whenever I think of how she treated him, I get really mad." She made a fist and swung at the air. "But I wouldn't kill her. You think I'm stupid?"

Nina took a step back to make sure she avoided Patti's moving fist. "She refused to give Josh a divorce. And she wanted half of her father-in-law's estate. Her defiance angered Josh. I saw how furious he was at the Bottses'."

"She would have eventually granted him a divorce. And he would inherit *all* the money."

Nina frowned. "How do you know?"

"Josh's lawyer says so." Patti tilted her chin.

Nina couldn't argue with a lawyer's opinion, so she tried another tack. "Wildeen was a good friend, and I want to see her killer caught and punished."

"So, fine. You've no right to come here and harass me."

"I'm not harassing you, Patti." Nina kept her tone patient. "I want to find out what happened that night."

"Seems to me investigating a murder is a job for the police. If you weren't a prospective club member—and I wonder about that—I'd tell you to leave. Now, are you gonna use your free activity, or not?" She crossed her arms over her chest.

Better back off. She'd pushed Patti far enough. "I'll do the free activity."

"What do you choose, then?"

Nina tapped her chin with her forefinger, considering. Racquetball? Too exerting. Besides, she had no partner. A sauna? Too hot. Swimming? She hadn't brought a suit. Gazing above, she saw a railing surrounding the gymnasium at the second-story level. "What's up there?" She pointed.

"A walkway. Once around is a quarter of a mile."

"Perfect. I'll walk."

Patti snorted. "You could walk outside. But suit yourself. You brought your change of clothes, I see." She nodded at Nina's canvas bag.

"Yes, a pair of shorts and a T-shirt."

"Okay, you know where the locker room is. Oh, and don't forget your trial membership includes a free drink and snack in the lounge. If you have time before your meeting with Pete Russell."

Nina ignored Patti's smirk. "I hope I do. And, Patti, thanks for the tour."

"Yeah, sure." Patti gave a brief nod and stomped off.

Nina returned to the locker room and changed into her shorts and T-shirt. After securing her street clothes in a locker marked "Guest," she headed upstairs. She encountered no one else on the walkway. Good. The peace and quiet would allow her to think.

So, Patti and Josh were each other's alibis. How convenient. Patti denied being involved in Wildeen's murder, but her anger during the party erupted readily enough. Although slender, Patti was strong. Nina had no doubt she could have smashed the rearing horse bookend into Wildeen's skull hard enough to kill her.

Nina circled the track four times for an even mile. She might have walked another lap or two, but due to her scheduled meeting with Pete Russell, time today was short.

Dressed once again in her street clothes, she crossed the lobby, full of overstuffed furniture and potted plants, and entered the lounge. Dark wood-paneled walls and high-backed, green upholstered booths gave the place a cozy, intimate atmosphere. Behind the bar, a neon sign spelled out "Evergreen," spreading a greenish glow over liquor bottles and glasses.

She slid into a booth and consulted the drink menu. A green-vested waiter appeared, and Nina ordered an "Orange Wonder," a concoction of soda, non-fat cream substitute, and orange flavoring. An assortment of cheeses and crackers accompanied the drink. Nina munched the snack, thinking how pleased she was with her first interview. True, she hadn't found out much, but she succeeded in maneuvering Patti at least to talk about Wildeen's death. Now, on to her meeting with Pete Russell.

"Well, look who's here."

Jolted from her thoughts, she looked up to find Stephen Kraslow leaning against the back of her booth.

He wore a light blue, short-sleeved shirt, and navy slacks. A small notebook and pen peeked from the shirt's breast pocket, reminding her he was a newsman and probably on the prowl for news. Nevertheless, her stomach did a little flip-flop.

"Do you belong to the club?"

His friendly tone indicated he held no grudge for her cool dismissal the last time they'd met.

She shook her head. "I'm here on a trial membership. I used the coupon from your newspaper. I just finished the tour."

"What do you think of the club so far?"

"The facility has a lot to offer. What about you? Are you a member?"

"I am. I belonged to an athletic club in New York. Besides, like I told you the other day, I want to get to know this community."

The waiter approached. "Can I bring you something?" he asked Stephen.

Stephen hesitated, looking at Nina.

"Do join me," she felt obliged to say and gestured to the opposite bench.

"Thanks. I will." Stephen sat and turned to the waiter. "I'll have coffee. Black."

After the waiter left, Nina nudged the plate of cheese and crackers in Stephen's direction. "Help yourself. Part of my tour perks."

Stephen picked up a cracker and a piece of cheese and ate. "This hits the spot."

The waiter soon returned with Stephen's coffee.

Stephen and Nina chatted idly, mostly about the club. More people arrived, and soon talk and laughter filled the room. Classical music from speakers on the ceiling provided a soothing backdrop. For the first time that day, Nina felt relaxed.

During a lull in their conversation, Stephen put down his cup and leaned forward. "So, how are you coping with the loss of your friend?"

Nina fingered her cocktail napkin. "I miss her so much. We talked or texted nearly every day. And sometimes, I'd go to estate and garage sales with her to look for books."

He nodded. "A tough adjustment for you."

"Her memorial service is on Friday. Seeing her family will be difficult." Reminded of his visit to the library, she added in an accusing tone, "Did you call her parents? I saw Larry help you find their address from the computer directory when you were at the library the other day."

He straightened and raised his eyebrows. "You certainly jump to conclusions. Larry did not help me locate Wildeen's parents. I didn't ask him, and besides, I could do that on my own. He showed me a glitch he found in our online edition of *The Review*. He has a sharp eye, and I appreciated his pointing out our error."

Nina pressed fingers to her lips. "Oh. I thought... I'm, uh, glad Larry was helpful."

"See? I'm not as callous as you think. Did you read the article I wrote about Wildeen?"

"I did." The article appeared in the latest edition of *The Review*. The piece was well written, too, she had to admit, with crisp prose and an objective and unbiased viewpoint.

"Did you find anything there to indicate I talked to her parents?"

"No..." His apologetic tone brought heat to her

cheeks, and she suddenly wished she hadn't invited him to join her.

Stephen sat back and held up a hand. "I'm sorry. I shouldn't give you a bad time, especially when you're hurting. I'd really like to be friends."

She met his gaze. The concern reflected in his eyes calmed her, and she mustered a smile. "Apology accepted."

"Good. And now, I have something else I'd like to discuss."

"What's that?" On guard again, she narrowed her eyes.

"Your column for the newspaper."

Nina sat forward. "Really? What about my column?"

"I'd like you to write for us again and expand the topics. You could discuss library news, review books or write about whatever topic you want."

"A longer article *would* be nice. Plus, seeing my name in print does carry a certain cachet."

He grinned. "So, the lady likes to have her ego massaged, as the saying goes."

"To a point. But don't push me."

They both laughed, and another flush warmed her cheeks. This time, one of pleasure.

"I understand the thrill of seeing your name in print." Stephen helped himself to more cheese and crackers. "When I lived in New York, I was a journalist for *Newsworld* magazine."

Nina sipped her Orange Wonder, enjoying the tangy flavor. "That must have been an interesting job."

"It was. I framed my first article and saved the rest. Whenever I feel low or discouraged, I take out the articles and read them. They renew my self-confidence." He straightened his shoulders.

She couldn't imagine him lacking in confidence. He always seemed so self-assured, so in control. "What kinds of articles did you write?" She warmed to the subject, and to him.

"Just about anything. I especially liked investigative journalism."

"Why would you leave a job you liked to come here?"

He lowered his gaze. "After my wife passed away, I didn't want to be in New York any longer."

Nina wrinkled her brow. "Oh, I'm sorry." She hadn't thought he might have a sad reason for moving to the Pacific Northwest. "How long ago did she pass away?"

"Two years ago. I hung on to the job for a while afterward, but all the reminders of our life together made staying difficult. I needed to get completely away and start over. I'm originally from a small town in northern Idaho—Parkers Landing. But I didn't want to live there again, either. I roamed around for a while. Then I heard about George selling *The Review*, and here I am." He shrugged.

His life was so different from hers. She was born and raised in Richmond and hadn't done much traveling. "Did you and your wife have children?"

Stephen shook his head. "We planned to. Carly was a nurse in a children's hospital, and she loved kids. So do I. But we weren't lucky enough to have any before she died."

"What happened?" Then, afraid she was too inquisitive, she added, "Or maybe you don't want to talk about it."

"I'm okay." He waved a hand. "She got cancer. The disease spread through her like wildfire, and she was gone in six months. She was young, too, only thirty-two."

They both were silent, sipping their coffee and picking at the remaining crackers.

Presently, Stephen leaned back and gave her a soft smile. "Hey, I didn't mean to lay my sorrows on you. You have your own to deal with."

"No need to apologize. I'm interested in people."

His smile widened into a teasing grin. "Even a lowly transplant like me?"

Nina lowered her eyelids. "Well...I'll have to think about that."

Their gazes met, and they laughed simultaneously.

Suddenly self-conscious, Nina shifted in her seat. Then she thought to check her wristwatch. "Oh, I didn't realize how late it is. I have to go. I have an appointment with Pete Russell... Oops." She clapped a hand over her mouth. She hadn't meant to divulge that bit of information.

"Pete Russell?" Stephen raised his eyebrows. "I hope he doesn't consider you a suspect."

"I don't think so. He wants me to go to Bottswood with him and, um, look around."

Stephen leaned forward. "The grapevine says Zelma Duke is the prime suspect."

She wondered where he heard that news. Perhaps he had an informant at the police station. "Maybe so, but I know she couldn't be the killer."

"How do you know?" Stephen tilted his head and studied her.

Nina sat back and folded her arms. "Zelma and I and Wildeen have been friends since we attended PNU. Even if they didn't always see eye-to-eye, Zelma wouldn't kill Wildeen. She wouldn't kill anyone."

He leaned closer. "What didn't they agree about?"

"Writing, mainly. Wildeen was a writer, too, but her work was literary essays and poetry. She wasn't shy about calling Zelma's fiction writing inferior. Did you catch her dig at the party when she asked Zelma to read certain pages in her book?"

"I wondered what that request was about."

"Zelma thinks the scene was one Wildeen particularly didn't like, and she wanted Zelma to read it aloud so she could sneer."

"I thought what she read was well-written."

"I thought so, too. But, anyway, I need to go." She scooted to the edge of the booth. "Nice chatting with you."

He put out a hand. "Wait. Before you leave, we need to make a date."

"A date? What for?" Was he asking her out socially?

"To discuss the column you're to write for *The Review*. Like I said, I want something a little different than what you wrote before."

"Oh, right…the column." Nina pushed away a niggle of disappointment. Had she hoped he was asking her out? No, of course not.

"How about discussing the subject over dinner tomorrow night?"

Oh, oh, now his suggestion sounded again like a date. "Since the column is library business, why don't you come to my office? I'll check my schedule tomorrow and give you a call."

Stephen frowned. "Why are you turning down my invitation to dinner? Are you involved with someone?"

"No one special. I like to keep my personal and professional lives separate."

"I see. In that case, we'll meet again at the library."

As she left the club, Nina reflected that exactly what she feared had happened. Stephen was no longer just an irksome transplant. By sharing personal information, he'd become an individual. Worse, she found herself, well, liking him.

However, she wasn't looking for a relationship, especially not after her last one, a disaster in which the man abruptly left. Anyway, she wasn't good at relationships, which probably had to do with her father abandoning her and her mother when Nina was only five years old. Whatever, for now, she needed to keep her association with Stephen Kraslow strictly business.

Chapter Six

"This is the spot." Nina pointed to a rhododendron bush with pink blossoms.

Pete Russell pinned her with a narrowed gaze. "You're sure?"

The detective had the most disconcerting habit of asking a question and then staring until she answered. She tilted her head and focused on the bush. "Well...fairly sure."

Russell snorted. "'Fairly' doesn't work, Nina. I need you to be sure."

Nina glanced around at the nearby bushes and then pursed her lips. "What difference does it make exactly which bush I hid behind when I overheard Wildeen and Zelma?"

He ran a hand through his salt-and-pepper hair, making the curls stand on end. "Where you were might matter a lot. We might find something in the vicinity to indicate another person had been there, too. Someone who also could have overheard their plans to meet."

"Oh, of course." Mollified, she studied the bush again. But wild rhododendron bushes popped up in the Bottses' forest at every turn, and they all looked similar, especially now, when she was under pressure to select a single one.

"We'll go back to the bridge again." Russell gestured toward the path.

Start over? How exasperating. "If you wish." Nina pasted on a smile.

He waved a hand. "You lead."

Nina nodded and stepped onto the dirt walkway.

As planned, she met Detective Russell at the police station. He reviewed her statement, saying he wanted to make sure every detail was accurate. He suggested she ride to the Bottses' with him, but she declined, saying she would take her own car.

He laughed. "Right. As I recall, you have an aversion to riding in police vehicles."

"Yes, but my discomfort is not today's reason. I have an errand afterward." True, more or less. Her "errand" was to linger at the Bottses' after the detective left and talk privately with Elizabeth. She was one of Nina's suspects, although Nina couldn't imagine for the life of her why a gracious and mild-mannered woman like Elizabeth Botts would kill Wildeen. Or anyone.

At the bridge, Nina expected a quick turnaround to retrace their steps and continue the rhododendron hunt.

Instead, Russell strolled to the center of the arch and stood at the rail.

Reluctantly, she followed and stood beside him, gazing at the pond. Brownish marsh grass waved in the slight breeze, and two ducks glided effortlessly over water that in the afternoon light shone a milky green.

"My wife would like this spot." Russell rested his arms on the railing.

His remark jolted. She hadn't thought of the detective having a wife. She thought of him only as a police officer. Her attitude reminded her of how she had regarded her grade school teachers. Whenever she met her teacher in, say, the grocery store, she did a double take. For her, they had no life outside the realm of the school. "Your wife likes the out-of-doors, then?" she inquired, feeling a response was necessary.

"You bet she does. We met at The Mountaineers club. The first summer we were together, she just about killed me, dragging me all over the Olympics. I mean, I like a hike now and then, but she's a fanatic." He absently rubbed the bridge of his nose.

"Do you two still hike?"

"Rarely. I'm too busy being a cop, and she's too busy taking care of three kids." He straightened and stepped away from the railing. "Okay, enough chatter. We'll get on with our search."

They inched their way along, stopping at every fork in the path. The night of the Bottses' party Nina hadn't noticed every bush and tree she passed. Today, with hand cupping her elbow and fist against her cheek, she studied the surroundings. Still, they ended up at the same giant rhododendron as before.

"You're sure, this time?" Russell probed.

Nina fingered a pink blossom. "As sure as I'll ever be."

He plucked a small, black-covered notebook and a pen from the inside pocket of his windbreaker. "Now, tell me what you heard Wildeen and Zelma say."

Nina frowned. "I put what I overheard in my statement."

"I know, but I want to hear their conversation again." Russell flipped open the notebook and held the pen poised to write.

"I'm not sure I can remember the exact words. I'm not certain what I put in my statement were the exact words."

"Just do the best you can."

He certainly tried a person's patience. Nina sighed. What if today's words were different from those in her statement? Would the discrepancy make her look suspicious?

She couldn't worry now, though, because Russell gave her his from-under-the-eyebrows stare. One eyebrow broke rank and peaked. Oh oh, eyebrow movement signaled annoyance. She wondered how his wife responded to those looks. But, maybe he reserved them for troublesome witnesses.

Nina gazed into the trees. "Let's see, Zelma asked Wildeen not to do something, I don't know what. Then Zelma asked her why she planned to do whatever. And Wildeen said, 'You know.' Then Zelma said, 'Can't we talk this over later?' and Wildeen said she would be at her bookstore later that evening, and so they agreed to meet at eleven o'clock."

Russell stopped writing and looked up. "Which one suggested the time?"

"Wildeen, I think."

Russell wrote. "Hmmm. Why eleven, I wonder?"

"I don't know, but I sensed Zelma was eager to get the matter settled. Eleven would allow enough time for the party to break up and for them both to get downtown."

"Do you know what Wildeen meant when she said, 'You know'?"

"I don't. I already told you I didn't know."

"O-kay." He flipped shut his notebook and stuffed it and the pen into his windbreaker pocket. Hands on his hips, nose aimed at the ground, he edged away. "Stay put while I have a look around."

Now the notebook was out of sight, Nina relaxed a little. "Do you want me to help?"

"No, thanks." Leaves rustled, twigs snapped, and soon, Pete Russell disappeared into the forest.

Nina stood where her feet were planted. But, since she waited on an incline, the tendons in her calves soon ached. Surely, moving to a more comfortable spot would be okay. She scooted off the path to level ground. Russell's refusal of help annoyed her. Even though she wasn't on his payroll, why couldn't she hunt for clues, too?

Time dragged. Above the canopy of trees, an airplane droned and birds twittered. She was ready to whip out her phone and check her email, just for something to do, when the brush crackled and Russell stepped into view.

He held up a plastic baggie containing a red object. "Does this mean anything to you?"

Nina studied the baggie's contents. "That looks like the heel Sondra Wagner lost on the walk. Sondra is Zelma's publicist."

Russell nodded. "I saw her name on the guest list the Bottses gave me."

"She limped out of the woods because one of her heels broke off. She told us she couldn't find the heel and that it probably fell over the cliff. Where did you find it?"

He gestured behind him. "Not far from here and in plain sight on the path."

"I wonder why the heel was close by when the cliff is quite a distance." Had Sondra been mistaken about where her shoe had broken, or had she lied?

"That's a good question."

When they emerged from the path, they found Elizabeth Botts waiting. Her hands were tucked into the sleeves of her white jacket, and her long, thin face wore a frown. "You were gone a long time."

"Yeah, well, examining the area took awhile." Russell pulled the baggie from his windbreaker pocket and showed it to Elizabeth. "Do you recognize this shoe heel?"

Elizabeth peered at the bag. "That heel looks like the one Sondra Wagner said she lost on the trail walk."

"I thought so, too." Nina nodded to Elizabeth.

"But she said the heel went over the cliff." Elizabeth frowned. "I thought her explanation odd. All our paths near the cliff have wooden railings. A person would need to duck under the railing to lose something over the side. Why would Sondra go under the railing?"

"I'm sure I don't know, Miz Botts." Russell returned the baggie to his pocket.

"Well, I hope you're finished now." Elizabeth released her hands and tucked wisps of hair into her coiled braid. "This matter is very upsetting. I feel like the murder was committed here instead of at Wildeen's bookstore."

"I need to ask you a few more questions, Miz Botts. Somewhere in private." Russell nodded toward the house.

Elizabeth widened her eyes and pressed a hand to her chest. "Question me? Why? I had nothing to do with what happened to Wildeen."

"Just routine." Russell pinned her with his stern gaze. "We'll talk now—unless you want a lawyer present."

Elizabeth's lips thinned. "A lawyer won't be

necessary. Now will do."

Russell turned to Nina. "Thank you for coming, Nina. You've been very helpful."

"But I—" Nina wrinkled her brow. She hadn't planned the meeting to end with her dismissal.

"Yes?" The lieutenant studied her.

"I, uh, wanted to ask Elizabeth a few questions about—about their paintings. We're looking for new art to display at the library."

Russell raised his eyebrows.

Maybe she'd better back off. She waved a hand in a gesture of dismissal. "I suppose I could come another time."

"Okay with me if you stick around." Russell turned to Elizabeth. "Do you have any objections, Miz Botts?"

"None whatsoever." Elizabeth sent Nina a smile. "You can wait in the library."

The Bottses' library had three walls of floor-to-ceiling bookshelves. The fourth wall featured a marble fireplace. On either side, two large, mullioned windows looked out on the back lawn and the swimming pool. Curious to know the Bottses' taste in literature, Nina perused the book titles. She soon discovered that instead of being arranged by author or even by subject, the books were shelved haphazardly. A Sidney Sheldon novel was tucked between *Great Operas of the World* and *Birds of Western Washington*. Dostoyevski's *Crime and Punishment* bunked with *The Annotated Shakespeare*. Robert Frost's poems sat beside *Country Western Songbook*. How could they find anything? Nina tightened her hands at her sides to keep from rearranging at least a few of the books.

Faint sounds of Russell's and Elizabeth's voices

floated in from the adjacent sitting room. Nina wished she could make out the words, but in no way would she risk being caught eavesdropping. She'd search the library instead.

She plucked *History of the Alphabet* from a shelf and sidled to the mahogany desk. Holding the book open in one hand and conscious of the moments ticking by, she studied the items on the desk—a blue blotter, a gold-plated pen and pencil set, a red, egg-shaped paper weight, and a three-tiered metal paper holder. The bottom rack contained a stack of manila folders. She stepped closer to see the folders more clearly. The top folder's tab was labeled "Bell."

She stopped to listen, and reassured by the steady drone of voices, she carefully lifted the folder. The next one was labeled "Saunders." The one underneath, "Emmons." Then "Harper," "Pedersen," and the last, "Quinn."

Surnames, Nina guessed. Laying aside the alphabet book, she pulled out her phone and keyed in the names. She'd barely finished and stuffed away the phone when footsteps sounded and a door slammed. She snatched up the alphabet book and ran to the window.

"He's finally gone."

Nina took a moment to draw in a deep breath before turning to see her hostess enter the library. The sight of Elizabeth's wrinkled brow set Nina's heart hammering. Had she seen her snooping?

Hugging her waist, Elizabeth crossed the room. "I hate being interrogated."

Realizing Pete Russell caused the woman's distress, Nina exhaled a relieved breath. "Being questioned is a strain." She closed the book and gave

Elizabeth her full attention.

"Especially since our party is involved. Murder. Just hearing the word makes me sick." Elizabeth's mouth twisted into a grimace. "Murder happens somewhere else, not here. Can you remember anyone ever being murdered in Richmond?"

Nina tilted her head. "I can't."

"Crime is spreading to the suburbs. Soon, we won't feel safe in our own homes."

"I certainly share your concern." Nina went to the shelves and, in case the collection had an organization of which she wasn't aware, replaced the alphabet book exactly where she found it. "Did you know Wildeen well?"

Elizabeth shook her head. "I've bought many books from her, but we never discussed anything personal." She gestured toward the door. "Would you like a cup of coffee? I feel in need of one."

"I'd go for some tea, if it isn't too much trouble."

"Not at all. Come along to the kitchen."

The night of the party, Nina hadn't seen the Bottses' kitchen. The room had ample counter space, oak cabinets, and a butcher's block in the center.

Elizabeth touched one of the cabinets, and the door sprang open. She took out two floral patterned cups and saucers, a matching cream and sugar bowl, and a straw basket of tea bags. She handed the basket to Nina. "Help yourself."

Nina sorted through the envelopes and selected Apple Spice.

Elizabeth filled a copper teakettle with water. "I wish I'd never been involved in Zelma Duke's autograph party. What a mistake."

"How did you get involved?" Glad to have her visit extended, Nina tore open the envelope, pulled out the bag, and dangled it in the closest cup.

Elizabeth set the teakettle on the stove and then turned on the burner under a pot of previously brewed coffee. "I don't even know Zelma, really. Oh, I've heard of her. Who in Richmond hasn't? Whenever she publishes a book, she places a huge ad in *The Review* and puts a flyer on every public bulletin board."

"She is good at publicity." Nina wanted to say something positive about Zelma.

"Anyway, Sondra Wagner contacted me about having the party. Her mother and my sister are good friends. Sondra explained the book is an especially important one for Zelma."

"*My Restless Heart* is her break-out book."

"Whatever." Elizabeth waved a hand. "Anyway, Burgess and I like to give parties and share Bottswood with our friends, so I agreed. And the party was fun. Didn't you think so?" Elizabeth's expression brightened.

"The party was lovely." Nina hoped her words registered her sincerity.

"But now, how distressing to learn a murder was arranged in our very own woods, and Zelma is the prime suspect." Elizabeth shivered and hugged her arms.

She's the second person who made that claim. Nina frowned. "How did you know Zelma is the prime suspect?"

"Burgess told me."

"How did he find out?"

"Josh Loring told him." Elizabeth went to the

refrigerator and retrieved a carton of half-and-half.

Nina widened her eyes, wishing she could take notes. "Oh, really? And who told Josh?"

"Zelma." Elizabeth filled the creamer with the half-and-half. "She told him she met Wildeen at the bookstore late that night, but Wildeen was alive when she left. She also told Josh she was terrified at first to be a suspect, but now she feels better because you'll discover the real murderer."

Nina bit back a groan, hardly believing what she heard. But then, why should she be surprised? Zelma often demonstrated a lack of discretion. One particular instance occurred when they were in college and Nina had a crush on a popular student leader. Zelma told him of Nina's interest and suggested he ask her out. The young man politely declined. Nina was mortified and spent the rest of the year dodging him whenever their paths crossed.

The teakettle whistled and a few minutes later, she and Elizabeth were seated with their drinks at a round table in a sunlit corner.

"I'm guessing your role as amateur sleuth is the real reason you wanted to stay and talk." Elizabeth plucked two napkins from a wire holder, handed one to Nina, and spread the other on her lap.

Nina took a moment to sip her tea. The Apple Spice had a pleasant aroma and a tangy taste. "I was hoping to discuss the case. I'm sure you've already told Detective Russell all you know, but perhaps you'll share your comments. Did you hear or see anything on the trail walk that might help the investigation?"

Elizabeth shook her head hard enough to loosen a couple locks of hair from her coil. "I did not. Burgess and I spent the time watching the hummingbirds feed."

"But Burgess left you for a while."

Elizabeth narrowed her eyes. "He didn't."

"He did, Elizabeth. I remember you came out of the woods first, and you were upset because Burgess hadn't yet returned." Why was Elizabeth intent on convincing her otherwise?

"Your recollection is different from mine." Elizabeth sat back and folded her arms.

Nina tilted her head. "I wonder if Burgess could have overheard Wildeen and Zelma."

"I just told you he was with me." She frowned and unfolded her arms. "How dare you come here and insinuate my husband was involved in a murder!" Two red spots bloomed on Elizabeth's cheeks.

Nina spread her hands. "Please, Elizabeth, I'm not insinuating anything. I thought Burgess might have seen or overheard something, too, like I did."

"I suppose you told Mr. Russell Burgess and I were separated on the walk? I mean, that you *thought* we were."

"No, when I gave my statement, I didn't think of you two. Besides, I can't prove you weren't together the entire time." Elizabeth certainly was adamant about her and Burgess being together.

"Then what's the point of this discussion? Take my advice and let the police handle the matter."

"I promised Zelma I'd help her." Nina sighed and shook her head. "I wish she hadn't told Josh, but, since she did, my involvement is in the open. So, do you know anyone who might want to harm Wildeen?"

"I certainly do not." Elizabeth lifted her chin. "I told you, I barely knew her. I wish I'd never said yes to

Sondra Wagner."

Elizabeth's emphatic tone left no doubt about her position. So much for questioning her. Perhaps this interview was a waste of time, after all.

Elizabeth drank her coffee, tilting the cup high and then setting it on the saucer with a clack. "Are you finished with your tea?"

Nina checked her cup. "I am." Too bad, because she could've used a few more minutes to question Elizabeth.

"Let's take a walk outside. Walking always calms me."

"A walk would be nice." Elizabeth's invitation surprised Nina. Perhaps she was sincere. Then again, maybe she wanted only to hurry Nina along and away from Bottswood.

Once they were outside, Elizabeth turned to Nina. "Let me show you our prize-winning rose."

She led Nina to the rose garden bordering the woods. Blossoms of various colors—yellow, red, purple, pink—filled the garden. "That rose is our prize-winner." Elizabeth pointed to bushes with amber blossoms. "Burgess created the flower and named it 'Elizabeth Rae,' after me. The rose took first prize in Richmond's Garden Club Show last summer."

Pride rang in Elizabeth's voice, and she held her head high.

"The color is lovely." Nina leaned over the blossoms and inhaled the sweet scent. "Mmmm, they smell good." As she straightened, her gaze fell on a slip of paper folded in accordion pleats, half-hidden by the roses. Brushing aside the leaves, she picked up the paper, careful to touch only the edges, in case it proved to have fingerprints of interest to Detective Russell. Unfolding it revealed one of Zelma's bookmarks for *My Restless Heart*.

Elizabeth peered over Nina's shoulder. "Ugh, that bookmark reminds me of that awful night. I don't want it." She wrinkled her nose and flapped a hand.

"I'll dispose of it for you." Nina slipped the paper into her jacket pocket.

They strolled across the lawn to the bluff. Nina gazed past the madrona trees to the water, glistening under a bright sun. "Your estate is so peaceful."

Elizabeth nodded. "I love Bottswood. Burgess and I came to Richmond because we wanted to escape everything we hate about city life—the noise, the pollution, the crime, the congestion." She hugged her arms. "But, now, I don't feel safe here anymore."

Nina nodded soberly. "I'm beginning to feel the same way."

Chapter Seven

As soon as Nina returned home, she phoned Zelma. First came the strains of "Love Makes the World Go 'Round," then Zelma's melodious "Hell-o, this is Zelma Duke. Sorry I missed your call, but you are important to me, so please leave a message. Oh, by the way, *My Restless Heart* will be on the stands in two weeks. Look for the book in the Best Sellers' section. 'Bye now." The beep sounded.

Nina gritted her teeth. "This is Nina. Call me." She disconnected and still gripping her cell phone paced to the living room window. Across the courtyard, her neighbor, Madge, stepped out the door of her unit. Her poodle pranced at her side, ready for his afternoon walk.

Madge caught Nina's eye, and the two waved.

Not more than a minute passed before Zelma phoned. "I was screening calls, but you hung up too fast."

Nina sighed and turned from the window, ready to give her full attention to Zelma. "I appreciate your calling back so quickly."

"I'm working on my new book, but I can't focus on my characters and their problems. I have too many problems of my own. I hate reality to intrude on my fantasy world."

"Yes, well, please focus on reality now." Nina's

tone was dry.

"Okay. Why did you call? Have you found out who murdered Wildeen?"

"I haven't." Nina rolled her eyes. "Not even Sherlock Holmes could work so fast. I called to say I wish you hadn't blabbed to Josh about meeting Wildeen at the bookstore or about my investigating."

"Why not? My visit to the bookstore was bound to become known, anyway. And why shouldn't I brag about my best friend's belief in my innocence?"

"Suppose Josh is the murderer? Do you think he'll want me poking around? Or what if Patti's the killer? Will he want me to expose her?" Gripping the phone, Nina paced again.

"I didn't think of all that."

Nina waved a hand. "Besides, Josh told Burgess, who told Elizabeth. I suppose by now, even Pete Russell knows." Her stomach knotted.

"No real harm was done. If people know you're working on the case, maybe they'll tell you something important."

Okay, maybe Zelma's indiscretion wasn't so disastrous, after all. Nina sank into a chair and took a deep breath.

"So, come on," Zelma coaxed. "Tell me what you've found out, so far. I'm dying to know. Oops, poor choice of words." She giggled.

"Not a lot. I interviewed Patti at the athletic club…"

"Interviewed? Oh, you sound so professional, Nina."

Nina closed her eyes then sighed. "Will you just listen, please? Patti insists she and Josh were together the night of the murder."

"Of course, Josh would be her excuse. What else do you have?"

"Today, Pete Russell and I went to Bottswood."

"You and that horrible man? What?" Zelma's voice rose. "Are you investigating for him, too?"

"Hardly. He wanted me to show him where I stood when I overheard you and Wildeen."

"And did you?"

"As best I could recall." Nina clamped shut her jaw. Maybe giving Zelma new information would only result in more gossip. On the other hand, sharing might also help Nina to put into perspective what she'd learned. "He found Sondra's heel. The one she said she lost?"

"I can't see her shoes having anything to do with Wildeen."

"Nor can I." Nina sat straight again. "I'm just telling you what happened. Anyway, I stayed afterward and talked to Elizabeth. She is upset you and Wildeen made plans on the trail walk to meet later. She doesn't want either herself, or Burgess, or anyone else at her party, to be even remotely involved in a murder."

Zelma huffed. "She's such a snob. Why else were the Literary Lights at the party? Not one of them bought my book."

Nina pursed her lips at Zelma's self-centeredness. "I don't know why they came, but since this one is your break-out book, don't you want to court readers like them?"

"You're right, of course. Hmmm, I'll work on the idea. Meanwhile, what's next on your agenda?"

"I'm not sure." Nina hedged, fearing she had

already given Zelma too much information. "If I had any sense, I'd back off and leave the investigation to the police."

"Oh, no, you can't." Zelma moaned. "Please, Nina, don't desert me."

Zelma's pleading tone touched Nina. They had been friends for a long time, and she would honor their friendship. "All right. But keep what I tell you to yourself, will you?"

"I will. I promise. I'll concentrate on my new story—another historical, set during the American Revolution. My heroine is a spy. I do love intrigue, don't you?"

"I thought I did. Now, I'm beginning to wonder."

****

After ending the call, Nina took out her list of suspects and sat at the kitchen table. At the top of a new sheet of paper, she wrote "Patti," and then recorded the main points of that interview. On another sheet, she wrote "Elizabeth Botts" at the top.

As she made notes on her talk with Elizabeth, she remembered the bookmark found among the roses. Retrieving the paper from her jacket pocket, she unfolded the accordion pleats with a pair of tweezers and laid it front side up on the table. Nothing indicated to whom the bookmark belonged. She flipped it over. The back listed Zelma's previous titles. Only the most recent, though, because enumerating all twenty on a small piece of paper would be impossible. In the margin, someone had written "310 Main Street," which was the address of Bergman Books. Had the writer planned to visit the store later that night? Nina's pulse quickened.

Don't jump to conclusions. The person might want to remember Bergman's location for other reasons. Perhaps Wildeen gave the address to a prospective customer, someone whose purpose was to buy books, not to murder the store's owner.

Still, the bookmark was related to the crime, and she must give it to Pete Russell. No way would she withhold possible evidence. She hoped he hadn't heard about her amateur sleuthing. Or, if he had, he'd refrain from embarrassing her by mentioning it.

At the police station the next day, the officer on duty informed her the detective was out. Nina left the bookmark, enclosed in a plastic bag, and a note explaining where she found it and why it might be important.

Later, before closing time at the library, Nina made her clean-up rounds. Picking up a copy of *The Richmond Review* and placing it on the newspaper rack reminded her of Stephen Kraslow. She promised to call him and make an appointment to discuss her column. Should she phone him today? No, why not wait a day or so? She didn't want to appear too eager.

****

That evening, Nina headed toward Josh Loring's investment seminar. At exactly ten to seven, she drove her car into the parking lot at Merton Park, Josh's office complex. Lingering sunlight glittered on the five-story building's silver walls and windows. A wide semicircle of steps led her to the entrance, and revolving doors swept her inside. A sign in the lobby indicated the Loring Investment Seminar met in Conference Room 101.

Watercolors of Northwest scenery brightened the

conference room's beige walls, and tables arranged in a large rectangle stretched from end to end. A few people were already seated, while others milled around a refreshment cart, pouring cups of coffee or making tea.

Josh—handsome in a brown suit, crisp tan shirt, and striped tie—set up his laptop to beam on a pull-down screen.

Nina considered approaching him to say hello but decided not to interrupt his concentration. She headed for the refreshment cart and fixed herself a cup of tea instead. Cup in hand, she strolled to the tables and took a seat. Each place had a blue folder with "Loring Investments" printed on the cover. Inside were papers and brochures full of numbers, charts, and graphs. Just glancing at them fogged her mind. Even simple terms such as "yield" and "rate of return" went over her head. Why couldn't she have inherited even a little of her mother's talent with finances?

Nina's mother had been a successful real estate agent who invested shrewdly. When she passed away, she left enough money for Nina to buy her condo and for Grandmother Jessica to settle into Marley Manor, plus a plentiful reserve for each.

Nina maintained her assets by staying on her mother's investment track. At income tax time, her accountant, Belden Mannering, made sense of the statements she collected and dutifully transferred the proper numbers to the correct tax forms. Nina trusted Belden implicitly. Her mother had, and so did she.

At last, Josh finished his preparations and stood before the group. "Ladies and gentlemen, we're ready to begin."

Looking around the table, Nina recognized a

member of the Literary Lights who attended the Bottses' party but whose name she could not recall. In her sixties, she had salon-coifed, white hair and wore a stylish, powder blue suit.

Catching each other's eye, the two smiled and nodded. A few minutes later, when the participants introduced themselves, Nina learned her name was Amanda Harper. Something else about the woman tugged at her memory, but before she could bring the information to mind, Josh moved on to the next person.

Josh gave each participant his undivided attention. He asked questions designed to make them feel at ease. The man simply oozed charm and charisma, not to mention those football-player shoulders Zelma drooled over.

When Nina's turn came, Josh's eyes lighted. "Nina Foster, welcome."

Josh's voice rang with surprise, as though he hadn't seen her for ages, instead of just the other night at the Bottses' party. Was he being sincere? Or was his warm greeting for the benefit of the other participants?

Nina flashed him a smile. "Thank you, Josh. I'm pleased to be here."

After everyone had been introduced, he launched into a definition of terms illustrated on the screen with cartoon characters—stocks, bonds, mutual funds, and treasury notes.

He made investing sound like such fun. However, Nina's brain had gone from fog-bound to shutting down altogether. During the break, Nina refilled her teacup with hot water at the refreshment cart. Looking around, she came face-to-face with Amanda Harper. They exchanged greetings and references to the Bottses' party.

"Horrible about Wildeen Bergman." Amanda held her cup under the coffee urn's spigot.

"She was a good friend." Nina's throat constricted as she dipped an Earl Grey teabag into her cup of hot water.

"Then her death was really tragic for you." Using a pair of tongs, her pinkie finger extended, Amanda dropped a sugar cube into her coffee. "I'm so sorry."

Nina acknowledged Amanda's sympathy with a smile. "What do you think of the seminar so far?"

"I'm enjoying myself immensely. I never knew investing could be so entertaining. I already have a financial advisor, but I'm transferring to Josh. He comes highly recommended, don't you know?"

"Really? By whom, if I may ask." Nina stepped aside to allow another participant access to the hot water urn.

"Burgess Botts. He sings Josh's praises to the skies. Burgess introduced me to Josh at the party, and Josh invited me tonight."

So, Josh and Burgess were friends. "I see. Do you know anyone else who uses Josh's services?"

"My friend Lily Ciliano has been with Josh for several years. She lives at Marley Manor. Marley is a retirement home, don't you know?"

Nina nodded. "My grandmother, Jessica Bingham, lives at Marley. Perhaps your friend knows her."

"Jessica Bingham?" Amanda smiled and nodded. "Yes, I met her when I visited Lily. She's quite a livewire. I hope I have as much energy when I'm her age."

Stepping away from the refreshments, they sipped

their drinks and chatted until Josh called them to their seats.

During the second half of the evening, Josh told them that to make big money, they must take risks. Risks shouldn't be scary but looked upon as adventures. He ended by instructing them to fill out the Personal Assets sheet in their packet. "I'll use the information to design a personal program to find your pot of gold at the end of the rainbow."

After the meeting, Nina lingered. When all the others had left, she approached Josh.

"I'm surprised to see you here." He quirked an eyebrow. "I thought you had your investments all set. Or is tonight part of your sleuthing?"

Taking note his voice had lost the friendliness displayed during introductions, Nina pursed her lips. "As far as my so-called sleuthing goes, I simply told Zelma I'd be alert for anything that might help her avoid being charged with Wildeen's murder. And, yes, I'm set financially. Even so, I want to stay informed. Who knows? I might decide to take some of those risks you told us about tonight."

"Yeah, right."

His narrowed eyes and flat tone indicated what he thought of her excuse.

Nina took a deep breath. "Okay, I admit I did come tonight intending to talk about Wildeen. I hope you don't mind?"

Josh switched off his laptop and closed the cover. "Go ahead and talk. I have nothing to hide."

"I don't think Zelma killed her, do you?"

"I don't. But I certainly didn't. Neither did Patti. We were together that night. *All* night." He slapped his palm on the table.

Nina took a step back. "So she told me. But, Josh, if I may say so, you do have a motive."

A muscle in his jaw twitched. "What motive? The half of Dad's inheritance Wildeen insisted she should have? My lawyer assures me I would receive all the money in a court settlement." He slid the computer into a leather briefcase, closed the flap, and snapped the catch.

Nina gripped her purse and shifted from one foot to the other. "Do you have any theories about what did happen to Wildeen?"

Josh straightened his shoulders. "I think a burglar killed her."

"Why would anyone rob a bookstore? Surely, a thief couldn't expect to find much cash. Why not hit Helmer's Jewelry next door?"

Briefcase in hand, Josh strode to the refreshment cart and unplugged the coffee and hot water urns. "Maybe he thought he was at Helmer's. Those alley doors all look alike, and no names are on any of them. Choosing the wrong door would be easy, especially in the dark."

Josh's firm tone indicated he'd made up his mind about a burglar being responsible for Wildeen's death. "Okay, but to kill someone over a few dollars in the till?"

"Wildeen could've surprised the thief. She might have been in the front part of the store, or in the restroom, when he broke in. A person can't predict what a criminal will do when threatened. Maybe the guy was a nut case or on drugs." He gestured to the door. "Ready to go?"

"I am." Her purse slung over her arm and clutching her folder to her chest, Nina lengthened her stride to keep up. "One other thing, Josh. Wildeen always kept an eye out for children's books for my personal collection."

"I know. When we were together, we went to flea markets and estate sales to look for old books." A soft smile crossed his lips. "We had fun."

"At the Bottses' party, Wildeen told me she bought a first edition of *The Wonderful Wizard of Oz*. I was to pick it up Monday morning."

Josh led them along the hallway leading to the front door. "I wondered why you were at the store so early."

"I stopped on my way to work. I didn't get the book, of course, but I would like to have it. As community property, the bookstore is yours now, isn't it?"

Josh shrugged. "I suppose so, although I don't know what I'll do with a bookstore. For now, I'll let Hamlet run the show."

Nina was glad to hear that news. "When the police allow the store to open again, I'd like to collect the book. Do you mind?"

"Not at all. The book's probably in the safe. Hamlet must know the combination. If not, I'll find it somewhere."

"Wildeen didn't say how much she paid for the book. Maybe I can find the amount in her records. Or, I could have it appraised."

Josh waved a hand. "Consider the book a gift."

His generous gesture surprised her. "Oh, no, I couldn't—" Nina shook her head.

"Yes, you could, because I say so. No arguments." Josh set his jaw.

"Well, we'll see."

They reached the lobby. No one else was about, and only a few ceiling lights illuminated the area. They went through the double doors and down the semi-circular steps.

At the bottom, Nina paused to take a deep breath of the fresh night air. Only a few cars remained in the parking lot. She glimpsed Josh's silver car half-hidden in the shadows. A few rows away, her car waited under a laurel tree. Nina turned. "Goodnight, Josh."

"'Night, Nina. Thanks for coming, even if you did have an ulterior motive. And, good luck with your sleuthing."

The mocking edge in Josh's voice sent an unexpected shiver down Nina's spine. Perhaps confronting him with her suspicions wasn't such a good idea, after all.

Chapter Eight

Nina awoke the following morning to the patter of rain against her bedroom window. Somehow, the rain was appropriate.

Today was Wildeen's funeral.

The temperature dipped far enough to warrant turning on the electric heat and eating breakfast wrapped in a quilt. Nina sipped her tea and stared out the window at the rain. Saying a final good-bye to her good friend, who had died under such brutal circumstances, would be especially difficult. When she could delay no longer, she showered and dressed for the service. She told her staff she would be gone for only a couple hours to attend the eleven o'clock memorial, but they insisted she take off the entire day. Without argument, she agreed. She wouldn't be efficient at work today, anyway.

Nina arrived at Benson's Funeral Home in downtown Richmond twenty minutes early. The interior, smelling faintly of cedar, provided a warm and cozy retreat from the inclement weather. Furnished with blue upholstered sofa and chairs and glass-topped tables, the lobby might have been someone's living room.

A gray-haired attendant handed her a program small enough to fit in the palm of her hand. A picture of a sunset over calm water decorated the cover. "Please sign the guestbook." He pointed to an open book on a nearby table.

Nina hung her raincoat and hat on the coat rack, dutifully wrote her name in the guest book, and then turned to see Wildeen's parents, Hannah and George Bergman.

"Nina, my dear." Hannah, whose bright green eyes were the same color as Wildeen's, opened her arms.

Nina hugged her, catching a whiff of her spicy perfume, and then stepped back to shake George's outstretched hand.

Tall and thin, he towered over his petite wife. "So good of you to come."

Although George smiled, his eyes were bleak. "I'm so sorry." Nina pulled a tissue from her purse and dabbed her teary eyes.

Others arrived, including Wildeen's older sister, Sylvia, her husband, Ralph, and their two children. The family lived in Kirkwood, another Seattle suburb.

Nina offered her condolences.

Too small to understand the significance of the occasion, the boy and girl hopped and skipped about until their father finally caught and drew them to his side.

Organ strains of "Amazing Grace" signaled the beginning of the service. The attendant herded people toward the chapel door.

I don't want to go in the chapel. I don't want to go through with the service. Nina forced her feet to walk forward. Once in the chapel, she chose a pew near the back. Avoiding the closed, gladioli-draped casket, she focused on the baskets of flowers lining the front of the room and quickly picked out the petunias she sent.

Petunias were Wildeen's favorite flower. She loved their fragile, silky petals and their cheerfulness.

The attendant led Zelma Duke, Sondra Wagner, and Morry Snyder down the aisle to a pew several rows in front of Nina. She pursed her lips. How nervy of Zelma to attend, when she was a suspect in Wildeen's murder. But, then, Zelma often demonstrated a lot of nerve. Sondra and Morry definitely should not be here. They were outsiders. Other than meeting Wildeen at the Bottses' party, they didn't know her.

The minister, a young man who looked barely old enough to be out of college much less divinity school, approached the pulpit. "We are here today to celebrate the life of Wildeen Bergman," he began.

Yes, let's celebrate her life. Anything to keep our minds off her death.

At the reception, held directly after the short service, Nina sipped tea from a glass cup and munched a crustless, tuna salad sandwich, more to have something to do than because she was hungry or thirsty. She surveyed the crowd, wanting to see who was there, and who wasn't.

Josh wasn't. Neither was Patti, nor the Bottses. She spotted Hamlet Green, Wildeen's employee at the bookstore. His cross earring bobbed as he talked to Wildeen's sister. Then her roving gaze landed on Stephen Kraslow, and her stomach tightened. What was he doing here? He wasn't a friend of Wildeen's. He must have come on behalf of his newspaper. Although his presence annoyed her, she had to admit he looked handsome in his navy blue suit, white shirt, and blue-and-gray print tie. Oh oh, he saw her.

He smiled and took a step in her direction.

She gave him a quick nod and turned away, searching for someone to talk to. Her gaze landed on Zelma, Sondra, and Morry. They chatted with an older woman Nina didn't know, but she hurried to join them. Any refuge in a storm.

"*My Restless Heart* will be on the stands in a couple weeks," Zelma said to the woman. "Look for it in the best sellers' section."

Nina gritted her teeth. How brazen of Zelma to promote her book at Wildeen's funeral.

"I'm so impressed." The woman beamed at Zelma. "I've never met an author in person before."

"I'm so glad to meet you, too. What did you say your name is?" Zelma beamed at her new fan.

When the woman finally left, Nina turned to Zelma. "I didn't expect to see you here."

Zelma shrugged, and her smile vanished.

"Staying away might make me look guilty. I didn't want to come alone, though. Thank goodness, Sondra and Morry were available." Zelma gestured to her companions.

"You could have come with me," Nina pointed out.

"I suppose so, but I wasn't thinking clearly." She pressed a hand to her forehead. "I haven't been myself lately."

Zelma did look haggard. Wisps of hair escaped her makeover hairdo, gray shadows hovered around her eyes, and lines between her nose and mouth were deeper than usual. Nina softened toward Zelma. Despite their differences, Wildeen's death had taken a toll on her, too.

Morry leaned toward Nina. "Hey, kid, Zelma tells me you're gonna find out who killed Wildeen. Whatcha got, so far?"

Nina stifled a gag at the combination of tobacco and aftershave accompanying Morry's speech. "Sorry, but I can't talk about that now." Not that she'd tell him anything, under any circumstances.

Morry nodded. "Okay, keep us informed, ya hear?"

Zelma leaned toward Nina. "I told Sondra the three of us must do lunch one day next week." She laid a hand on Morry's arm. "Sorry to exclude you, but our lunch is for girls only."

"No problem." Morry stuck his hands in his slacks pockets and rocked back on his heels. "I have plenty to do. I've been settin' up appointments with potential clients. Got to get me another best-selling author."

Zelma frowned. "Now, Morry, don't worry. My tour will be underway soon." She turned again to Nina. "What day would be good for you?"

"Wednesday is my day off."

"Sondra?"

"Just a sec." Sondra pulled her phone from her white, patent leather purse, thumbed the screen, and then looked up. "I can squeeze in lunch on Wednesday."

They'd no more than settled on Sailor's Inn at noon when from the corner of her eye, Nina glimpsed Stephen heading in her direction. Her stomach clenched, and she turned toward the others. "Will you excuse me, please?" Without waiting for a reply, she hurried off. She considered finding someone else to talk to, but the room suddenly closed in, and she had to leave. On her way out, she said good-bye to Wildeen's family, adding to her parents that if she were ever in Arizona, she'd be sure to visit.

In the foyer, she shrugged into her coat and placed her hat on her head. Nodding to the attendant, she slipped out the door. The solid gray sky indicated the rain settled in for the day. The air was so cold she could see her breath. Holding onto her hat, she made a dash for her car. As she took out her key fob to open the door, she heard the gravel behind her crunch.

Then a voice called, "Nina! Wait!"

She turned to see Stephen hurrying toward her. A gray raincoat protected his suit, but he wore no hat, and raindrops glistened in his hair. She narrowed her eyes. "What do you want?"

"I wanted to speak to you inside, but I never caught up. I decided you were avoiding me." He raised his eyebrows. "Am I right? Do you still consider me an outsider, one of those annoying transplants you don't like?"

Nina planted her hands on her hips. "You are an outsider, especially today. You didn't know Wildeen or her family. I suppose you're here looking for a story."

"I came because I wanted to pay my respects, just like you."

He sounded sincere, but she wasn't ready to yield. "Well, now we have, and so we can each go our separate way."

"Where are you going?" He gestured to her car.

"Home…I guess. I have the rest of the day off." Hot tears mingled with the raindrops on her cheeks.

"You're not going home. You're coming with me." He caught her wrist and drew her away from her car.

"No, Stephen, please!"

"Let me take care of you, Nina."

The intensity in his eyes and the sincerity in his

voice melted her resolve. And so, she allowed him to lead her away and down another row of parked cars. A gust of wind swept by, and she had to secure her hat with her free hand. She glanced around to see if anyone witnessed Stephen's outrageous behavior, but no one was in sight.

He finally stopped beside a newer-model, tan SUV. He unlocked the passenger's door and motioned her inside.

With a resigned sigh, she slid onto the seat. Being sheltered from the rain did feel good.

Stephen shut her door and climbed in the driver's side. Without speaking, he started the engine and drove off.

"I could charge you with kidnapping." Only half-joking, she folded her arms and sat stiffly in the seat.

A smile hovered around his lips. "You could, but you won't."

Nina narrowed her eyes. "You're certainly sure of yourself, aren't you?"

"Sometimes. Today is one of those times."

"So, where are we going?" She shifted to gaze out the window. Through the rain-drenched glass, she recognized the town's business district.

"To my place."

His boldness jolted her. She hadn't thought of him having a "place." "Your apartment?"

He slowed to turn off Main Street onto a road leading to Puget Sound. "My house."

"A house." She raised her eyebrows. "You are settling in, aren't you?"

"When I came here, I planned the move would be permanent."

Stephen's neighborhood fronted the water and included homes from 1920s bungalows to contemporary A-frames. Judging from the style—two stories, a peaked roof, and clapboard siding—the house had been built in the 1940s.

He led Nina along a covered walkway connecting the garage to the back porch. The door they entered put them in the kitchen, which, judging from the mess, was in the midst of being remodeled. A hole gaped from underneath a counter, and several cupboards were missing their doors. An open toolbox sat on the floor nearby.

"The house was a fixer-upper." Stephen gestured toward the counter. "Right now, I'm installing a new dishwasher." He hung their coats in a small closet off the kitchen and then took her down a hallway to the living room.

The view from the picture window captured her attention. She crossed the room and looked out. A path cut through his front yard to the beach and a boat dock. Farther out, nearly obscured by the gray curtain of rain, a tug towed a load of lumber toward the Port of Seattle. The Olympic Mountains, their peaks hidden by clouds, rimmed the horizon. She turned to find him standing behind her. "You have quite a view, even on a day like today. I have a view from my condo, but nothing like this. Mostly, I watch the ferries cross the sound."

Stephen gestured to the telescope mounted on a nearby tripod. "I like to watch the ferries, too. The boat traffic is always interesting." He nodded to a brown leather sofa. "Make yourself comfortable. Would you like something to drink? How about a glass of wine?"

"Wine would be nice." Nina settled on the sofa.

Her gaze fell on the glass-top coffee table covered with stacks of books, jars of pens and pencils, and coffee mugs. Hands outstretched, she leaned forward to straighten the mess and then pulled back. Stephen's housekeeping habits were none of her business.

Stephen returned, carrying two long-stemmed glasses of white wine. He had removed his suit jacket and tie and opened the top two buttons on his shirt. He handed her one of the glasses. "Please excuse the mess. When I left this morning, I didn't know I would have company today."

"You don't have to apologize. Your place looks…" She searched for a word, ending up with, "lived in."

He laughed. "My house is definitely 'lived in.'" He tilted his head and studied her. "I have a feeling your home is as neat as the proverbial pin."

"Most of the time." She inhaled the wine's sweet bouquet then took a sip, enjoying the fruity flavor.

He shoved aside the coffee table's clutter to make room for their glasses. Then he built a fire in the arched brick fireplace, taking kindling and newspaper from a metal box on the hearth and adding alder logs from a wire basket.

Nina sat back, allowing the warmth from the fire, plus the wine, to soothe and relax her.

Stephen settled on the other end of the sofa, and for a while, they made small talk. Then he set down his glass and turned. "How about staying for dinner?"

"Oh, no, I couldn't." She didn't want to turn their business association into a personal relationship.

"Why not? Do you have another engagement?"

"Well, no." Not meeting his gaze, she brushed an imaginary piece of lint from her skirt.

"A cat or a bird or a dog that must be fed on schedule?"

She had to laugh at his persistence. "No pets."

"Then I see no reason you can't stay. The food won't be anything fancy. Just chicken soup and salad."

"All right." Nina sighed. "Once again, you've twisted my arm."

He grinned. "Not very hard, this time. I must be making progress."

"You have to let me help, though. But be forewarned. I'm not much of a cook."

"I'm sure I can find something for you to do. Come on, we'll move the party to the kitchen." He stood and held out his hand.

She grasped his fingers and allowed him to pull her to her feet. Still joined, he led her to the kitchen. She had to admit, his taking care of her was comforting.

Stephen took a kettle of chicken soup and a cutting board draped with a dishcloth from the refrigerator. After placing the kettle on the stove, he removed the cloth to reveal a pile of freshly made noodles.

Nina stared. "You made those?"

"Yep." He grinned. "With a pasta maker."

So, he could not only remodel the kitchen but also cook in it. "I received a pasta maker as a Christmas gift a few years ago. It's still in the box."

Stephen carried the noodles to the stove. "You should try using it sometime."

"Uh uh. Too intimidating." Nina turned up her hands. "What can I do? You promised to let me help."

"How about buttering slices of sourdough bread and warming them in the oven?"

She grinned. "I guess even a kitchen idiot like me

could do that."

He set out the bread and the butter and a length of foil.

Nina went to work.

Stephen scooped the noodles into the pot, stirring the soup with a wooden spoon. "Are you having any luck discovering who killed Wildeen?"

She was glad his back was turned and he couldn't see her embarrassed flush. "So, you know about my so-called investigating, too? I can't believe how fast gossip spreads, even in a small town. Who was your source?"

"Patti, on the day you and I met in the Evergreen lounge. After you left, she cornered me, needing to blow off steam about you grilling her. I provided a sympathetic ear."

Nina buttered a slice of bread and added it to the stack on the foil. "I wouldn't call my talk with her a grilling. But, anyway, Zelma asked me to see if I could find out anything about Wildeen's death, and I agreed. I felt bad about telling Detective Russell I overheard her and Wildeen plan to meet at the bookstore after the party."

He looked up from his stirring and raised an eyebrow. "You overheard them?"

She shrugged. "You might as well know that, too. Everyone else does. I'm outraged by what happened to Wildeen and want to see her killer caught. But now, I feel rather foolish. And presumptuous, to think I can do the police force's job better than they can."

"Don't you realize messing around with a murder might be dangerous?"

"I'm not worried." Nina waved a hand.

"You might change your mind if the killer comes

after you." Stephen arched an eyebrow.

"You sound as though you speak from experience." Finished with buttering the bread, Nina sealed the foil packet and put it in the oven.

"During my last year at *Newsworld*, I researched a story about illegal steroids. One night, someone took a wild shot at me outside my apartment." Stephen paused to stir the soup. "Then an anonymous phone call warned if I didn't get off their case, next time, they wouldn't miss their shot."

Nina gasped. "Did you quit your investigation?"

"No, I went deeper under cover. The bad guys were caught, but they never found out I was the one responsible for their arrest. I lost what would have been a great story, but I saved my skin."

Nina shook her head in wonder. "Pretty brave, Mr. Kraslow."

He grinned. "I thought so. So did my boss."

They ate in the dining room, which also had a view of the water. The rain still fell, but cracks in the clouds freed the hidden sun and turned the gray water to silver.

"So, how about letting me help you with your investigation?" Stephen asked after they had eaten in silence for a few minutes. "I have friends at the police station, plus connections from my former life."

Nina's stomach tensed. Accepting his help would mean spending more time together. She shook her head. "I appreciate your offer, but I can't think of anything you can do."

"Why don't you let me be the judge? What have you found out so far?" Stephen took a sip of soup.

"Nothing to speak of." Not quite true. She'd discovered a few things, such as why Zelma visited

Wildeen at the bookstore that fateful night and that Elizabeth Botts refused to admit she and husband, Burgess, were separated on the walk through their forest, but she didn't want to share her discoveries with Stephen.

Stephen frowned. "I won't use what you tell me in a newspaper article. I know when to keep information secret."

Nina stared at her plate.

He leaned forward. "You have some other reason for refusing my help."

He was right. The problem was, she wasn't sure of the reason. Personal relationships with men brought a vague uneasiness. She must not get too close. She must not trust too much.

Most likely, her reluctance had to do with her father's abandoning her and her mother when she was so young. Also, Darren Johnson, whom she was learning to trust, left her, too. "Getting to know someone takes me a while," she finally told him. "I'm more comfortable doing some things by myself."

He nodded and sat back. "I understand. I'm a bit of an introvert sometimes, too. Still, if I discover anything I think will help, I'll be sure to share the information."

Later, on the way back to the church to retrieve her car, she thought of something. "We didn't discuss the column you want me to write for your newspaper."

"The thought occurred, but I decided not to mention the subject tonight."

She turned to study his profile. "Why?"

He grinned. "Because now we have a reason to get together again."

Although surprised she could do so on such a sad

day, she had to laugh. "Pretty sneaky. I can see I'll have to be on my toes around you."

Chapter Nine

"Four in the side pocket," Jessica Bingham announced.

Holding her breath, Nina watched her grandmother lean over the pool table, her strawberry-blonde hair gleaming under the fluorescent lights.

Jessica took aim and gently tapped the white cue ball. With a click, the ball glided into the number four ball. Number four rolled to the side pocket, hovered on the edge, and then fell in. As Jessica straightened, she caught Nina's eye and winked.

Sitting on the sidelines, Nina exhaled and made an "okay" sign with thumb and forefinger.

Today was Sunday, and although Nina visited her grandmother at other times, Sunday was their special day together. On this occasion, Jessica was a finalist in a pool tournament held in the retirement home's basement recreation room.

Her opponent, Reagan, frowned and ran a hand through his thick, white hair. The game was almost over, and Jessica was ahead.

Jessica called and then made her next shot. The ball grazed another ball, which threw it off course. "Oh, drat!" She scowled and gripped her cue.

Reagan took his turn, announcing his shot and pocketing number seven. Only two balls left. He aimed again, and shot. The ball rolled along but stopped inches short of the intended pocket.

Jessica dispensed with the final two balls and then pocketed the eight ball. "Yay! I win!" She waved her cue and did a little dance.

The onlookers, including Nina, cheered and applauded.

Reagan grumbled under his breath and stomped off.

"Reagan's a poor loser." Jessica folded her cue into its black carrying case. "Especially when the winner is a woman. But he'll get over himself and be ready to challenge me again next week." She grasped Nina's elbow. "Come upstairs, my dear, and we'll have a cup of tea." In Jessica's third floor apartment, she bustled into the kitchen.

Nina stood at the window, looking out. Rain had fallen since Friday. In the garden below, rose blossoms glistened with the pelting drops. Two people, their genders hidden by voluminous, yellow-hooded ponchos, plodded along the asphalt walkway bordering Marley Lake. On the other side of the lake, in a public park, several teens tossed a Frisbee.

Moments later, Jessica appeared with a tray holding a teapot, cups, and a plate of chocolate-frosted cookies. She placed the tray on a mahogany coffee table then sat on the beige sofa.

Nina took a chair across from her and leaned forward to select a cookie. "These look good."

"I made them yesterday." Jessica poured their tea and set the pot on the tray. "After I had my hair done. How do you like my color?" She patted her curls.

"Nice," Nina said between bites. The true color of her grandmother's hair was a mystery, because she had dyed her hair for as long as Nina could remember. When Jessica was younger, she favored a bold, Lucille Ball red. As she aged, she gradually toned down the color to today's lighter shade.

Jessica frowned and sipped her tea. "How was the funeral? I've been worried about you."

"The funeral was…sad." Nina's shoulders sagged.

"You're depressed. Well, let yourself grieve. When Tyler died, I took years to recover." Jessica looked away. "Death is a shock, and adjusting takes time."

"The police suspect Zelma. She talked me into snooping to discover the true murderer.

"I know about your involvement."

Nina rolled her eyes and pursed her lips. "Of course, you do. Which branch of the grapevine whispered in your ear?"

Jessica chuckled. "Martha Mundy heard about you from Zelma's neighbor, Helga Thorgrimsen. Are you having success with your investigation?"

Nina told her about questioning Patti, Elizabeth, and Josh, and about Sondra Wagner's heel and finding the bookmark.

"I'm impressed. Sounds like you've uncovered some possibilities."

Nina finished a bite of cookie. "I do feel a sense of accomplishment. Someone told me I should be careful, though, because messing around with murder is dangerous."

Jessica widened her eyes and leaned forward. "Who told you that? Why are you being so mysterious?"

"The person was Stephen Kraslow, the new editor of *The Richmond Review.*"

"Oh, him." Jessica sat back again. "I haven't met him personally, but Rex Crawford interviewed him on KCCZ cable. He's charming and handsome. So, you two know each other already. Are you, um, dating?"

Nina waved a hand. "No, Gran, we're not dating. We've been in touch because he wants me to resume writing my column for the newspaper. I met him at the Bottses' party. He also met Wildeen there, and he came to the funeral." She wrinkled her nose. "But he's a transplant, and you know what I think of them."

"Uh huh. Vile creatures." Jessica's eyes twinkled, and then she sobered. "Seriously, Nina, he could be right about the danger involved in a murder investigation."

"Then you think I should stop? I'd feel as though I were letting down Wildeen."

"I know better than to tell you what to do. So I won't. But be careful."

"I will." Nina picked up her cup and sipped. "By the way, do you know a Lily Ciliano who lives here? I heard about Lily from Amanda Harper at Josh's seminar."

Jessica nodded. "Sure, I know Lily. Lives on the sixth floor. Had a stroke a while back. Widowed six years ago. One son, but he rarely visits. If you want to talk to Lily, I'll phone her."

"I would like to ask her opinion of Josh." Making the connection might yield useful information.

Jessica picked up her cell phone from the coffee table and made the call. "Lily's not answering," she said a few moments later. "She's probably in the building, though. Since her stroke, she doesn't get out much. I'll try again later."

When the time came for Nina to leave, Jessica accompanied her on the elevator. "I need to check with the dining room." She punched the button for the first floor. "I've arranged for a harpist to provide dinner music tonight, and I want to help her set up."

The lobby was a busy place, with residents and their guests seated in comfortable chairs or at small tables enjoying refreshments from the nearby snack bar.

"I see Lily Ciliano. Lily!" Jessica waved.

A woman wearing thick eyeglasses and pushing a walker with a bright pink basket stopped and looked around.

"Lily! Here!" Jessica waved both arms.

Lily's mauve-shaded lips curved into a smile. "Hi, Jessica."

Jessica introduced Nina, adding, "Nina wants to ask you something, if you don't mind?"

"Ask me what?" Lily looked at Nina with magnified eyes.

"I heard from a friend of yours, Amanda Harper, that Josh Loring handles your investments. I'd like to know how you like him. I attended one of Josh's seminars but can't decide if I want to hire him." Nina hoped no harm would come from her slight distortion of the truth.

Lily gripped her walker and shrugged. "I guess he's doing a good job. He's always buying and selling. But the statements he sends might as well be written in Greek. Gave up trying to understand 'em or even read 'em. Josh came highly recommended, though, and I trust him. But what else can I do?" She flattened her lips and shook her head. "My son don't give a damn. He's busy with his rock band. Can you imagine pushing fifty and still wanting to be a rock star? I wish he would've hit the big time when he was younger and got stardom out of his system."

Nina tilted her head. "Josh came highly recommended, you say? By whom?"

"Burgess Botts."

So, Burgess had recommended Josh to both Amanda Harper and Lily. "Did he say why he recommended Josh?"

"Just that Josh was their advisor, and look how rich he and Elizabeth are." She let go of her walker with one hand and waved the air. "Their big home, and all. I hope Josh will do the same for me, although sometimes I wonder why. Only person to leave my money to is my bum son." She looked at her wristwatch. "Oh, oh, got to go now. I have a date to play checkers with Wally Stern. You know him, Jessica? Lives on six."

"A date." Jessica winked at Nina. "Sure, I know Wally. Used to be manager of Associated Grocers and lived in Emerald Hills. Wife died of a heart attack. Nice guy, Wally."

Lily stuck out her chin. "He is. So, don't you horn in."

Jessica stepped back and raised both hands. "I wouldn't think of interfering. Have fun, and I'll catch up with you at dinner."

"Nice to meet you." Nina nodded to Lily. She'd truly enjoyed the lively woman. "And thanks for your information."

"You're welcome, hon." Lily pushed off.

"Poor soul," Jessica whispered behind her hand. "Her bum son drives her crazy. But she didn't give you much help, did she?"

"She gave me something to think about. Burgess Botts also recommended Josh to Amanda Harper."

Jessica raised her eyebrows. "Is that so? Well, maybe Burgess wants to help spread the wealth. Good for him."

"Maybe." Was Gran right? Or did Burgess have some other motive?

Jessica accompanied Nina to the front door. "Good-bye, dear. Don't give Stephen Kraslow too bad a time now, will you? If he wants to be friends, be friends, for heaven's sake."

Nina frowned. "I'm not sure what he wants."

Jessica heaved a sigh. "I wish Ivy hadn't bad-mouthed your father. Sure, he was a rat for leaving you two the way he did and never contacting you again. But, not all men desert their families."

"Darren Johnson left me, too."

"He was a wimp." Jessica placed her hands on her hips. "Tied to his mama, and when she moved to Palm Springs, he had to go along. You're better off without him."

"I'm better off without anyone just now." But was she, really? Wouldn't sharing her life with someone be preferable to being alone? If only she could learn to trust… Nina lifted her chin.

Jessica gave Nina a hug. "Don't give up, honey. You'll find the right person. Tyler and I had a wonderful marriage. I wouldn't have missed our relationship for the world."

"I love you, Gran," Nina said against her soft, warm shoulder.

"I love you, too. Don't know what I'd do without you."

"Nor I, without you."

****

Monday morning, before the library opened to the public, Nina and her staff assembled in the employee's lounge for their weekly meeting. She looked around the oval table at her group.

Larry sat tall with eyes alert behind his round glasses. Larry loved meetings. He was always the first to arrive and the last to leave.

Arlette sat beside him. She bent over her cup of coffee, gripping it with both hands.

On the other side of the table, Myo, never one to waste a moment, sorted order cards.

Next to Myo, Holly scrolled her cell phone. She wore a thin, ruffled blouse with her jeans, but the blouse had a camisole underneath. Perhaps Nina had made progress on the issue of proper work attire, after all.

The upcoming book drive took precedence on the agenda. Each August, Seaview Library held a book sale. Some of the books offered were discarded from their inventory, some came from area bookstores, and some from the general public. For the latter purpose, a large barrel stood near the library's front door. Nina picked up her pen. "Let's get started. Who has suggestions for the book sale money?"

Larry raised his hand. "I'd like to update the encyclopedias in the reference section. Since the head office cut our budget, we haven't bought the latest volumes for some of our sets."

Nina nodded. "Part of the reason is because the publishing companies want such exorbitant prices. One hundred dollars and up per volume."

"A lot of work goes into a reference book." Larry folded his arms. "Of course, people research online now, but we still have patrons who prefer the hard copy."

"All right, I'll put reference books on the list." Nina wrote on her yellow pad then focused on Arlette. "What do you think, Arlette?"

Arlette finished a sip of her coffee. "DVDs."

Larry frowned. "What subjects?"

Arlette tilted her head. "Oh, movies, cartoons, and how-tos."

"I thought so." He pursed his lips. "Let people buy that kind of junk. Or subscribe to online networks."

"A lot of people can't afford to buy or subscribe." Myo continued to sort cards while she spoke.

Larry removed his glasses, polished the lenses with a handkerchief, and set them back on his nose. "But my clients—"

Arlette snorted. "You mean the professors at PNU? Phooey on them. The library is for everyone."

Hoping to stop the two from arguing, Nina held out a hand. "I'm putting DVDs on the list." She wrote then turned to the other side of the table. "Holly, what do you think?"

"Huh?" Holly looked up.

Nina pursed her lips. "Could you put away your phone please, while we have our meeting?"

"Oh, sure." Holly laid the phone in her lap.

"Now, Holly, do you have any ideas about spending our sale money?"

"Uh, could we have more tables and chairs in the children's area? Lots of times, I see kids sitting on the floor to read their books."

114

"New furniture?" Larry wrinkled his nose and spread his hands. "You're talking major expenses. We don't make that much on the book sale."

"I just thought—" Holly's face flushed. "I mean, Nina asked—"

"Yes, I asked, Holly." Nina shot Larry a frown and Holly a smile. "And yours is a good suggestion. We'll add children's furniture to our list." She picked up her pencil and wrote on her notepad. "Now, Myo, anything from you?"

"I'll go along with Arlette on the DVDs." Myo shuffled her cards. "But how about a new computer, too? Sometimes our patrons have a long wait."

"Good idea." Nina added "computer" to her list then sat back and surveyed the group. "I hope we can fulfill all these requests to some extent. Larry, make a list of the reference sets you'd like to update. Arlette and Myo, choose the DVDs you want. And Holly, I have catalogs you can look through to pick out the furniture for the children's area. And all of you, please keep your minds open to more ideas."

Everyone nodded.

Pleased with their discussion, Nina turned to a new page on her yellow pad. "Now, let's talk about this week's special programs…"

****

On her lunch break, Nina visited Bergman Books. She wanted to collect the *Wonderful Wizard of Oz*, which Josh told her she could have. She hoped to talk to Hamlet, too. He was on her suspect list.

However, when she reached the store and about to enter, tears blurred her vision and her hand froze on the doorknob. Wildeen wouldn't be inside to greet her and offer a cup of tea or show her a new book. Nina blinked away the tears and straightened her shoulders. She must go in. She needed to do everything possible to help track down and expose the person who'd taken away her friend.

She crossed the threshold to the tinkle of the bell above the door. She looked around for Hamlet but didn't see him. Beyond several rows of low, freestanding shelves, customers sat in a grouping of comfortable chairs. A table held the makings of coffee and tea, and the aromas of both hung in the air.

Next to the reading area, a wrought iron spiral staircase led to the second level, where, in addition to more books, a domed skylight allowed light to beam on the lower level. Even though today's skies were gray, the window added a cheerful note. The skylight was the main reason Wildeen chose this building for her bookstore. She wanted customers to sit and enjoy the books under the dome's natural light.

"Aren't you afraid people will only read and not buy?" Nina had asked.

"Not at all," Wildeen replied. "Books are like clothes. You have to try them on to see if they fit."

Nina found Hamlet Green behind the checkout counter. His black-booted feet were propped on an old roll-top desk, and his lap held an open book. She leaned her arms on the counter. "You look relaxed."

He grinned and swung his feet to the floor. "I'm checking in a new shipment." He gestured to the volumes stacked at his elbow and then to a carton of books at his feet.

"So, you're in charge now?"

Hamlet's nod set his earring dancing. "Josh asked

me to take over until he decides what to do. Wish I had the bucks to buy the place. But right now, my college education is the priority."

"How much longer do you have?"

"One more year at the junior college, and then I hope to transfer to the U Dub."

He used the University of Washington's popular nickname. "Well, hang in there."

"You bet I will." Hamlet pointed a forefinger. "Say, I'll bet you're here to get your copy of *The Wizard*."

Nina smiled and stepped back from the counter. "I checked with Josh, and he gave me the okay to pick it up."

Hamlet laid aside his book and stood. "The book's in the office safe. Come on back." He gestured over his shoulder.

She followed Hamlet to the back room, but at the doorway, she stopped. Revisiting the place where she found Wildeen turned her stomach queasy.

"What's the matter?" Hamlet wrinkled his brow. "Oh, I get it. You don't want to come in the office because this is where Wildeen, ah—"

"I'm having flashbacks." She pressed a hand to her stomach.

"No problem. I'll get the book. You can wait in the reading area."

Nina shook her head. "I'll come in. I need to conquer my fear." She took a deep breath and stepped into the room. Her gaze strayed to the spot where on that awful morning she found Wildeen. When she saw that today a rug hid the bloodstains, she took a few more steps forward, her tension easing.

Hamlet opened a cupboard underneath a counter to reveal a small, black safe. "I memorized the combination." He knelt and turned the dial.

"The safe wasn't broken into that night?"

"No, although somebody messed with it." He pointed to gouge marks on the door.

"Was any money taken from elsewhere in the store?"

"A coupla hundred from the cash register. Wildeen usually put the money in the safe at the end of each day." He shrugged. "For some reason, that day, she didn't."

"So, Wildeen could've surprised a robber." Maybe Patti and Josh were right in their insisting a stranger was responsible for Wildeen's death.

"She could have." Hamlet twisted the safe's dial, and the door swung open. "Hey, am I smart or what?" He reached inside and pulled out a book. After glancing at the title, he handed it to Nina.

Excitement rippled down Nina's spine. She'd searched for this book for a couple years and now, thanks to Wildeen, she had found it. She ran her fingers over the title and smiled at W. W. Denslow's illustration of the Cowardly Lion. Standing on all fours, the comical creature wore round eyeglasses and a beanie.

She examined the spine, which was solid, and then opened the cover to the title page, illustrated with a picture of the Tin Woodman and the Scarecrow. Their opposite hands were clasped, ready to arm wrestle. She inspected the rest of the book. Some of the interior pages showed wear and tear, but what could she expect? Published in nineteen hundred, the book was well over a century old. Nina turned to Hamlet. "This edition is wonderful. Do you know much it cost Wildeen?"

Hamlet leaned against the counter and slowly shook his head. "I haven't a clue. She kept records of the sales she went to, but I don't know where they are."

Nina frowned. "I need to know."

"Why? Josh told me the book is a gift."

"I know, but I don't feel right accepting it. I always paid Wildeen for the books she found. I'll figure it out, Hamlet. The cost isn't your problem."

He waved a hand. "Whatever." He knelt and peered inside the safe. "Wonder what else is in here…Whoa, what's this?" He pulled out another book, a paperback. "I don't know why this book is in the safe, too, but maybe she meant for you to have it along with *The Wizard*."

Nina took the book from his outstretched hand. The title was *Love's Eternal Triumph* and the author, Eula Endicott. The cover showed a blonde woman from the late eighteen hundreds who wore a full-skirted dress with a low-cut, off-the-shoulder bodice. In the background, a dark-haired man with a square jaw and bare, muscular arms sat astride a black stallion.

The title page listed the publisher as Meredith, Ltd., London, England. The verso, the back of the title page, showed a publication date of thirty years ago. "This book appears to be an historical romance novel." Nina held up the paperback. "But I've never heard of the publisher or the author."

Hamlet studied the cover. "Me, neither. Hardly Wildeen's type of reading, huh?"

"No, it certainly isn't."

"But, like I said, maybe she was saving it for you."

Nina frowned and idly turned the book's pages. "I can't imagine why. This story is not the kind I read or collect."

"Maybe she wanted to donate it for your sale."

"Maybe. But for the sale, Wildeen usually sends us an entire box of books."

"This one might have been the beginning of her box. Let's face it, Nina, we'll probably never know. So, why don't you take the book anyway?"

"All right." Nina tapped a finger on the cover. "I'll do some research and see if it has any value."

Hamlet closed the safe and twisted the dial. "I'd better check on the customers."

Stepping aside, Nina slipped both books into her tote. "Do you mind if I look around the office? I'd like to find the record of what Wildeen paid for *The Wizard*."

He shrugged. "Okay with me. The police are all done in here."

"I suppose you had to clean up the mess?"

"Right. I wasn't sure where some stuff belonged, but I did the best I could."

After Hamlet left, Nina sat at Wildeen's desk. She opened the middle drawer and found the usual supplies—pens and pencils, paper clips, scissors, and a letter opener. A side drawer revealed half a dozen file folders. She pulled out one labeled "Garage/Estate Sales." The contents included receipts for Wildeen's purchases but none for *The Wizard*.

The other folders contained computer printouts of inventories, invoices, and miscellaneous correspondence. One thick file labeled "Reflections of a

Bibliophile" caught her eye. Several rubber bands saved the contents from being scattered when Wildeen's assailant threw the desk drawers on the floor.

"Reflections of a Bibliophile" had Wildeen's name on the title page. To Nina's knowledge, Wildeen wrote only poetry, literary essays, and book reviews, but this work appeared to be a memoir of her experiences as a bookseller and collector. Had Wildeen attempted to publish the manuscript?

Nina wanted to read the book but hesitated to remove it from the premises without permission. The next time she saw Josh, she would ask to borrow it. She replaced the file and turned her attention to the desktop. Miscellaneous invoices and bills lay in a three-tiered metal tray. The calendar pad still showed the Sunday of the Bottses' party, with Wildeen's neat handwriting of "Bottswood, Seven p.m."

She turned a few pages forward. A meeting of a booksellers group and a dental appointment were the only upcoming events. Working backward from the day of the party revealed that a week and a half before Wildeen's death, she'd had an appointment with Sondra Wagner. That surprised her, and she made a mental note to ask Sondra about the appointment when they met for lunch on Wednesday. On her way out, she found Hamlet at the checkout counter completing a sale.

"Thanks for coming in." Hamlet gave the customer her change and a paper bag of books. Then he turned to Nina. "Find what you were looking for?"

"If you mean the price of *The Wizard*, no, I didn't. When I return to the library, I'll research the value of both books." She held up her tote.

Hamlet nodded. "Sounds like a good idea. So, are we through here?" His gaze strayed to his desk still stacked with books.

"Almost. I need to ask you something." She stepped closer to the counter.

Hamlet folded his arms. "Yeah? What?"

His suddenly brusque tone made her hesitate. But perhaps he was only impatient to get back to work. She was here, so she might as well continue with her plan to question him. "I was wondering where you were at the time Wildeen was murdered."

His eyes widened, and he held up both hands. "Hey, don't pull your detective stuff on me."

Nina drew back. "I'm not. I just—"

"I heard you're nosing around, hoping to get Zelma off the hook. But you can't pin Wildeen's murder on me." He shook his head and thumbed his chest.

"Hamlet, I'm not—"

"Okay, so I was home alone after the party, with no alibi. I gave my statement to the police, and they're satisfied I'm not involved." He planted both hands on his hips. "I wouldn't murder Wildeen. Besides being my employer, she was my friend."

Embarrassed to have upset him, Nina put a finger to her lips. "Not so loud, Hamlet." She glanced over her shoulder, hoping none of the customers had overheard. Everyone within sight had his or her nose in a book. *Good.* She turned back to Hamlet. "I'm not accusing you, so calm down."

"Then what's with the alibi stuff?"

"I wanted to ask if you know who might have killed her."

"Yeah, her jerk of a husband. You want someone

with a motive, go see him. I'll bet he's the one." He clamped shut his jaw and stuck out his chin. "And now, I gotta get back to work."

Discouraged, Nina left the bookstore shaking her head. So far, everyone she'd questioned was defensive. Were they only insulted to be considered suspects, or did one of them have something to hide?

Chapter Ten

Nina took both books from the bookstore's safe to the library. She showed *The Wizard* to her staff and was pleased when they shared her enthusiasm. Then she ran an Internet check to determine the book's value and recorded her findings. She intended to do the same for *Love's Eternal Triumph*, but with the monthly circulation report due at the home office, she'd wait until another time. She put the book in her desk drawer and turned her attention to the report.

After dinner that evening, she settled into a comfortable chair and poured over *The Wizard*. But not paying for the highly collectible volume nagged her. Despite Josh's assurance the book was a gift, she felt compelled to give him some money. Why not pay him a surprise visit tonight, at his home in Sapphire Hills, for that very purpose? By dropping in, she might also learn something related to Wildeen's murder.

Pleased with her plan, she put the book in the glass case housing her other literary treasures. Then, after making sure her checkbook was in her purse, she climbed in her car and left Viewmont Estates.

In typical Northwest fashion, the rain ceased around five p.m., and now, at seven, the sun beamed. The minute the sun appeared, people shed their rain gear quicker than a lizard discards its skin. Instead of slickers, ponchos, and umbrellas, she now saw shorts,

T-shirts, and sunglasses.

Built on terraced slopes with each home having a view of Puget Sound, Sapphire Hills was one of Richmond's most exclusive neighborhoods. Nina drove through the granite pillars marking the entrance and past the marble fountain of a boy holding a dolphin. A healthy spray of water fell on the flower garden at the statue's feet.

Keeping to the right, she headed up one of the steep streets. The winding roads of Sapphire Hills were a maze in which one could easily get lost. Nina knew the way, but if she made a wrong turn, the car's dashboard GPS would set her straight. A left turn, a right, and another left led her to the top of the hill, where the view encompassed all of the town, Puget Sound, and the Olympic Mountains

The Loring home was a contemporary rambler with a cedar shake roof, red brick trim, and picture windows. A low cedar fence with LORING spelled out in large wooden letters surrounded the front yard. A walk of circular stones set in cedar bark led to the front door. To the right sat a three-stall garage. All three doors stood open, revealing Josh's silver sedan, a white sports car, and a gold-and-white motorboat.

Nina parked at the curb and followed the walk to the front door. She pressed the doorbell and heard the chimes ringing inside. No one came. Again, she rang the bell and waited. Still, the door remained closed.

Thinking Josh and Patti might be enjoying their backyard's sunshine, Nina followed more circular stones around the side of the house. Pushing her way through overgrown juniper tams and vine maples, she reached a solid wooden fence. The fence was too high to see over, but the gate might allow access. Nina flipped the latch, and the gate sprang open. She took a step forward and then stopped. Would entering the yard be trespassing? Never mind. She needed to settle the matter of paying for *The Wizard*. She walked through the open gate and around the corner of the garage.

A rectangular swimming pool dominated the landscape. No one was in the water, but towels and clothing draped over two padded lawn chairs indicated recent occupancy.

Voices and the clink of ice in glasses came from a covered patio. Nina ducked behind a bush and tilted her head to listen. Realizing she was again eavesdropping made her stifle a giggle. Was eavesdropping how the police obtained their information, too?

"Josh, how could you?" Patti's voice drifted across the lawn. "Little old ladies. Don't you have any morals?"

"Morals? Hah! Look who's talking. Besides, my l-o-ls make plenty."

"Yeah? And so do you—at their expense."

"So? My services come at a premium. How do you think I could afford this place? I don't see you complaining about enjoying my prosperity."

"Maybe I'll feel better about your livelihood after we're married."

Silence followed, giving Nina the opportunity to shift her position and ease a cramp in her left leg.

"About marriage." Josh broke the silence. "We should wait awhile before we tie the knot."

"Why?"

Nina held her breath, eager to hear Josh's reply.

"Us getting hitched too soon after my estranged

wife is murdered will look suspicious, don'tcha think?"

"Well… But I don't want to wait *too* long."

"You want to make sure you're a community property partner. Maybe we ought to have a pre-nup."

Patti and Josh's argument surprised Nina. Tonight, they sounded quite different from the loving couple they presented at the Bottses' party. Evidently, their relationship had hit a rough spot.

"Josh, honestly! You and your money. I never realized you were so obsessed."

"Money's what makes the world go 'round, babe, and I want to make sure I get my share."

"And then some." Patti grumbled.

"Don't get moody." Josh raised his voice. "One moody woman was enough to contend with. Wildeen was always pouting about something she didn't like. Got your drink mixed? Let's catch some rays before it rains again."

Nina crept from behind the bush and hurried out the gate. She leaned against the fence and took a deep breath, relieved to have escaped the yard without being caught eavesdropping. After a few moments, she straightened and knocked on the gate. "Yoo hoo! Is anyone home?" Without waiting for a response, she again stepped into the back yard. "Hello? Josh?"

She rounded the corner of the house just as Josh, in blue bathing trunks and flip-flops, drink in hand, rose from his chair. His shoulders, shiny from suntan oil, looked broader than ever, and his chest hair spiraled down to disappear under his bathing trunks.

"Nina?" He stopped and stared. "What are you— never mind, come on in." He gestured with his free hand.

Nina continued along the path. "I rang the front doorbell, but no one answered. With the cars in the garage, I knew you were home, so I checked the back yard. I hope you don't mind my showing up unannounced?"

"Of course not. Patti and I are taking advantage of the sunshine." He nodded toward Patti sitting in the adjacent chair. "Join us."

Nina followed Josh to the pool, where the breeze rippled the pale blue water and bounced a yellow inflatable raft against the tiled side. She turned her attention to Patti, who wore a pink bikini and pink, wedge-heeled shoes. Oversize, pink-framed sunglasses shaded her eyes. "Hello, Patti." Nina kept her tone cheerful.

Patti offered Nina a sour smile. "I hope you're not here to badger us with questions about Wildeen."

"I am not," Nina said firmly. Was Patti's cool reception due to their encounter at the athletic club? Or to her and Josh's current argument? Perhaps a bit of both.

"Can I offer you a drink?" Josh nodded to the bar.

Nina made a dismissive wave. "No, thanks. I can't stay. I came to—"

"I know." Josh's eyes gleamed. "You've changed your mind and want me to invest for you."

Nina shook her head. "Sorry to disappoint you, but investing is not why I'm here."

His mouth turned down. "Well, have a seat and tell us what's on your mind." Placing his drink on a wrought iron table, he pulled up another padded chair.

Nina sat, balancing her purse on her lap.

Eyeing Nina over the rim of the glass, Josh sipped

his drink.

Patti aimed her sunglasses in Nina's direction. One wedge-heeled shoe flapped as she swung her crossed leg.

"I went to the bookstore today," Nina began, "and Hamlet gave me *The Wizard* Wildeen bought for my collection. I researched its value, and I came to pay you." She fingered the clasp on her purse.

Josh knitted his brows. "I told you to consider the book a gift."

"I know you did, but I can't. I always paid Wildeen for the books she found." Nina thought of her collection at home in the glass bookcase. Wildeen had found quite a few. As a fellow booklover, she understood Nina's interest in collecting.

"I suppose arguing would be a waste of time."

"I'm glad you see it my way." Nina opened her purse and took out her checkbook. She wrote out a check, tore it off, and held it out. Curious to know Josh's reaction, she watched his face.

Josh took the check. He studied it and then looked up, his eyes wide. "That old book is worth this much? I'd no idea…"

Patti leaned to look over his shoulder. Her jaw dropped.

Josh waved the check. "I'll have to decide what to do with this money."

Patti stuck a hand on her hip. "Why don't you invest for Nina?"

Her voice dripped with sarcasm. Was she hinting he might then cheat her like he cheated his other clients?

"Hey, sweetheart, what a good idea." He smiled at

Patti and then turned back to Nina. "I'll put this money to work for your benefit."

"I told you, investing wasn't my intention." Nina slipped her checkbook into her purse and closed the clasp. "If you want to use the money for a special purpose, make a contribution to a charity. Wildeen always gave to the Literacy Fund."

"The best thing to do with money is to use it to make more money. When you earn enough, you can buy yourself a place like this." He made a sweeping gesture to include his house and yard.

Nina pursed her lips. "I can't stop you from doing whatever you want. As you said, the money's yours now. But I need to tell you I have another book from the safe. A paperback called *Love's Eternal Triumph*. Hamlet didn't know why that book was stored there, too."

Josh shrugged. "I'm sure I don't know why, either."

"Hamlet gave me the book, along with *The Wizard*. I doubt the old paperback has any value, but if it does, I'll let you know. If not, I'll add it to our library's sale."

"Sounds like a plan." Josh looked at his wristwatch.

Taking the hint, Nina stood. "I'd better be going." She turned to Patti. "I'll be at the athletic club this Wednesday, to take advantage of my trial membership."

"I look forward to seeing you."

Patti's dry tone indicated exactly the opposite. A few minutes later, Nina navigated down the road and out of Sapphire Hills in the twilight, her thoughts on the conversation she'd overheard. The "little old ladies"

Josh mentioned must be his clients. Was he cheating them? If so, and if Wildeen found out and threatened to expose him, he would have yet another motive for killing her. Nina shuddered. Could Josh really have murdered Wildeen?

When she turned onto her street, she noticed the car behind her also turned. Although she wasn't sure when the gray sedan first appeared, she had a feeling it followed her for several miles. Halfway down the block, she pulled into the Viewmont Estates' driveway. The other car drove by, and she exhaled a relieved breath.

Inside her condo, wanting to be sure the mysterious car was really gone, she went directly upstairs to her office. Leaving the room dark, she parted the blinds and peered out the window. Across the street, a gray sedan sat at the curb. The dark shadow in the front seat indicated a driver behind the wheel. The back of Nina's neck prickled. Was the car the same one that followed her?

The car's headlights blinked on, and the engine purred to life. Like a furtive cat, the vehicle slid from the curb and headed down the street. Nina kept her vigil until the taillights disappeared over the crest of the hill.

Stephen Kraslow's warning came to mind— *Messing around with murder can be dangerous.*

Downstairs in the living room, she sank into her favorite chair and switched on the TV news. She couldn't concentrate, though, and was still worrying about the mysterious car when Zelma called.

"I was at Bergman Books today—" Zelma began.

"What a coincidence. So was I." Nina picked up the TV remote and lowered the sound.

"I know. Hamlet told me. I wanted to get a book Wildeen was saving for me."

"Wildeen had a book for you?" Nina let surprise ring in her voice.

"She did. Hamlet said he gave it to you, because he didn't know the book was for me."

"Oh, you must mean *Love's Eternal Triumph*."

"That's the one."

Zelma's intense tone put Nina on alert. "Why was she saving it for you?"

"I'm collecting early romance novels. She found the book at the same estate sale where she got your *Wizard*."

"I didn't know about your collection." The TV forgotten, Nina concentrated on her conversation with Zelma.

"Never thought to mention it. Anyway, I'd like to have the book tonight. I'll come and get it."

The urgency in Zelma's voice puzzled Nina. "You need it tonight? Surely, you have other books to read—if reading it is your intention."

"Of course, I want to read the book. Why else would I want it?"

Urgency had become impatience, which wasn't unusual. Zelma often expected her requests to be immediately fulfilled. "I don't know, but it's not here at home, anyway. I left it at the library because I wanted to research the value. If it isn't worth anything, I planned to donate it to our book sale. Is that old paperback valuable?"

"Not to anyone but me. I'll pick up the book at the library tomorrow."

"Why don't I bring it Wednesday when we meet

Sondra for lunch? Then you won't need to make a special trip."

Zelma's heavy sigh echoed over the phone. "I suppose I could wait. But don't let anything happen to the book, okay?"

"I won't."

"And, Nina, don't bother to read it. *Love's Eternal Triumph* is not your cup of tea."

Nina hung up, puzzling over Zelma's concern about the book. Did she want it only for her collection, or for some other reason?

****

The following day at the library, Nina took *Love's Eternal Triumph* to the staff lounge to examine while she ate lunch. Zelma said to not read it, but Nina could not let a book pass through her hands without sampling at least some of the contents. Besides, she wanted to figure out why the book was so important to Zelma that she would have made a special trip last night to collect it.

After retrieving her brown bag lunch from the refrigerator, she sat at the oval table with Myo, while she perused back issues of *The Library Journal*.

"I'm researching computer cataloging systems for a class at the U." As Myo reached for another magazine, she glanced at Nina's book. "What are you reading?"

Nina unwrapped her turkey sandwich. "This book was in Wildeen's safe, along with *The Wizard*. Hamlet didn't know why she was saving it, and so he gave it to me."

Myo raised her eyebrows. "Doesn't sound like a book you'd enjoy."

"I'm sure it isn't, and last night, Zelma called and told me the book is for her. But I want to give it a look first. You know me and books."

"I do." Myo chuckled and took another bite of her salad.

Nina turned over the book and read the blurb on the back. The story was about Delilah Montcliff, who came to the United States to assume ownership of an estate inherited from distant relatives. Upon arrival, she met Lamont Jordan, the prosperous banker who held the mortgage to her property.

Nina frowned. The plot sounded familiar. Brushing aside the thought, she opened the book to the first page. The story began with Delilah on the ship heading for her new home. Again, the familiarity of the plot nagged Nina. She was halfway through the second chapter before she finally realized where she'd heard the story. She pressed her fingers to her lips. "Oh, no."

Myo looked up. "Something wrong?"

"I don't know. Oh, I hope not." Nina jumped up and hurried into the workroom, to a shelf of recently purchased books. She flipped through them until she found the one she was looking for. When she returned to the lounge, she saw Myo had finished her lunch and left. *Good.* If what Nina suspected were true, she didn't want anyone else to know.

She opened *Love's Eternal Triumph* to the first page and did the same with the book she took from the workroom and placed them side by side. Looking first at one and then the other, she compared them. Both stories began aboard a ship. She spotted similarities—a unique word here, a phrase there—but none that couldn't be explained as coincidence.

Scanning the lines, she turned several pages in each book. Finally, she found two paragraphs word-for-word the same. Further reading revealed more exact similarities. A sick feeling invaded the pit of her stomach. She put aside *Love's Eternal Triumph* and picked up the book from the workroom. She ran her trembling fingers over the swirl of yellow mums on the cover and then over the letters of the title, *My Restless Heart.*

Nina now knew why Zelma wanted to gain possession of *Love's Eternal Triumph.* She also knew Zelma had a very good motive for murdering Wildeen Bergman.

Chapter Eleven

All afternoon, Nina worried about her discovery. After dinner, without phoning Zelma first, she drove to her house. She wanted to give Zelma the opportunity to explain herself but without advance warning. She rang the doorbell and waited, her gaze fixed on a jagged hole in the screen.

Footsteps sounded inside the house. The steps came closer and then stopped on the other side of the door. But the door still didn't open.

Nina assumed Zelma scrutinized her through the peephole. She had the urge to press her face close to the little circle and stick out her tongue. She imagined the grotesque picture from the other side. However, she resisted and kept her expression one of polite patience.

Finally, Zelma opened the door. "Nina! What are you doing here? Have you discovered the murderer? Oh, I know, you brought the book. *Love's Eternal Triumph.*" Her lips curved into a smile. "How considerate. I could've waited until tomorrow. No hurry, really."

"Zelma, we need to talk." Nina kept her tone stern.

"Well, uh, sure. Come on in." Zelma opened the door wider and stood aside.

Dreading the conversation they were about to have, Nina stepped into the house. The odor of cooked cabbage assailed her nostrils.

"I just finished dinner." Zelma closed the door. "I've plenty left over, if you're hungry."

"I've eaten, thank you."

"Tea?"

"No, thanks."

Zelma pushed strands of hair from her forehead. "You'll have to excuse my appearance. I wasn't expecting company."

In addition to her bedraggled hair, a sleeveless smock exposed upper arms with wrinkled skin, indicating she'd lost weight. Not surprising, considering the circumstances. Despite her anger, Nina felt an apology was in order. "Sorry for the intrusion, but I needed to talk and didn't want to take the time to phone."

Zelma waved a hand. "We're friends, and friends can drop in."

Friends? Were they? Nina was beginning to wonder. In the living room, she sat in the same tweed-upholstered chair she chose on her last visit. The cave-like room appeared much the same, except messier. One corner of the *My Restless Heart* poster had come loose and curled down upon itself. The ceiling sported several spiders' threads drifting in the air currents she and Zelma created when they entered.

"You'll have to excuse the mess in here, too." Zelma picked up a magazine from the floor and tossed it onto the redwood coffee table. "I've been busy working on my new book and haven't taken time to straighten up."

Nina looked through the arched doorway leading to the dining room. Sure enough, Zelma's computer sat on the table, with rows of black letters against the white screen. Her stomach knotted. What book was she copying this time?

"So, where's the book?" Hands on her hips, Zelma stood over Nina. "In your purse? You can give it to me now." She held out a hand.

Nina met Zelma's gaze. "I read the book," she stated flatly.

Zelma flinched but then straightened and lifted her chin. "You read it? Well, you're a fast reader."

"I didn't read all of the book, but I read enough." Nina kept her gaze on Zelma.

"Enough for what? To know you didn't like it? I told you it wasn't your kind of story." Zelma snatched up a pack of cigarettes and tapped out one, spilling several more onto the carpet. Her hands shook as she scrambled to gather them.

"Come off it, Zelma." Nina waved a hand. "You know what I'm talking about. And sit down. You're making me nervous."

Zelma sank into the matching tweed chair and lit her cigarette. "No"—she exhaled a puff of smoke—"I don't know what you're talking about."

"All right, I'll tell you. I know you stole your story, *My Restless Heart*, from *Love's Eternal Triumph.*"

Zelma gave a dry laugh. "A lot of books have similar plots."

"The trouble is not only with the plot, Zelma. The words are put together similarly, too, into sentences, paragraphs, scenes, chapters. What you did is called plagiarism."

"Such an ugly word." Zelma stared at her cigarette.

Nina wrinkled her forehead. "Why, Zelma?" Dare she hope Zelma had an acceptable explanation?

Zelma took another drag. The smoke drifted upward, hovering in the air like a wispy piece of gauze. "Oh, lots of reasons."

"Why don't you tell me? I need to know. Your deception is upsetting—and perplexing."

"All right, I'll explain, and then, hopefully, you'll understand." Zelma leaned back and heaved a deep sigh. "I wanted so much to do a break-out book. Publishing is a highly competitive business, you know, and to become a best-selling writer, I needed to produce something really special."

Nina raised her eyebrows. "And you have to be a best-selling writer?"

Zelma straightened her spine. "Is anything wrong with having a goal?"

"The one you chose comes with a lot of pressure."

"Well, anyway, I thought up an idea for a longer, more complicated story than I'd previously written. I wrote sample chapters and an outline and gave them to Morry. He sent copies to several publishers. Three houses made offers, and we had an auction. He was so excited." A soft smile crossed Zelma's lips. "An auction was a new experience. Best Books Press offered the most money, and we accepted their contract."

Nina tapped her fingernails on the arm of her chair. How the book found a publisher was interesting, but she'd rather hear about the actual writing. "Then what happened?"

"I had a deadline to turn in the manuscript. But before I finished the writing, Bob and I had our trouble. Curiously, what caused our fallout was my contract with Best Books. He couldn't accept my making so much money and being on the brink of success."

"Wasn't he happy about the increase in the family income?"

"You'd think." Zelma pursed her lips. "But Bob has tried for years to have his paintings hung in a gallery, and none will accept his work. Then I write what he called 'a silly little book' and make a mint."

"Ah, he was jealous."

"Right. He couldn't handle my success. He gave me an awful time." Zelma put her chin in her hand. "I never told you or anyone. I was too embarrassed. Anyway, the deadline to turn in my manuscript loomed, and it wasn't finished. I had terrible writer's block and couldn't write a word. Whenever I sat at the computer, I ended up bawling my heart out. Even talking about that horrible time makes me cry." Zelma's eyes filled with tears.

Nina opened her purse, took out a packet of tissues, and held it out. "Go on."

Zelma accepted the packet, pulled out a tissue, and dabbed her eyes. "One day, while cleaning a closet, I found a box of old romance books I purchased years ago, when I was a reader, not a writer. To get my mind off my troubles, I read the stories again. Reading was always my escape, you know. I was such a bookworm in college."

Nina waved a hand. "Yes, yes. And then what happened?"

Zelma blew her nose into the tissue. "When I read *Love's Eternal Triumph,* I was surprised the plot was similar to mine."

Nina frowned. "Wait a minute. Didn't you realize that since you read the book in the past, you unconsciously borrowed the plot?"

Zelma widened her eyes. "My accidentally using the storyline never occurred to me. Honest. Anyway, Morry kept calling me and asking, where was the manuscript? Bob hassled me. Angie and Brit needed my attention. I couldn't concentrate. One day, I found myself sitting at the computer along with *Love's Eternal Triumph*. I looked at the book and thought, what would be the harm in using Eula what's-her-name's story to help finish mine?" She made a dismissive wave. "After all, *Love's Eternal Triumph* was published a long time ago and was surely out of print. I'd never heard of the publisher or the author. Probably no one else today had, either. I copied a sentence here and there and then an occasional paragraph. Soon, the whole process snowballed."

"So, you turned in your manuscript, and the publisher accepted and published it with no one the wiser." Could Zelma really be so dishonest?

Zelma nodded and ducked her head. "After I finished, I burned my copy of *Love's Eternal Triumph*. I didn't think my deception would ever be discovered. I doubted anyone would happen to read both books."

"But Wildeen did."

"Wildeen and her photographic memory." Zelma sighed and looked at the ceiling. "Remember how in college she used to quote verbatim from textbooks?"

Nina smiled. "Uh huh. Her memory was phenomenal."

"She found *Love's Eternal Triumph* at the estate sale and recognized the plot similarities. She compared the book to mine and discovered the identical passages then confronted me. I admitted I'd copied and begged her to keep my secret." Zelma propped a fist on her hip. "But no, she threatened to expose me as a, as a…"

"Plagiarist," Nina supplied dryly.

Zelma twisted her lips. "Such an ugly word."

Nina leaned forward. "Why did she want to destroy your career? I know she was jealous of your success, but to destroy you is extreme."

Zelma stubbed out her cigarette. "She was jealous for a lot of reasons and for a long time. Remember when we both took Professor Glazer's creative writing class? He praised me for my lively imagination and then scoffed at Wildeen's 'overblown prose.' She was mortified."

Nina wrinkled her nose. "Glazer was a literary snob."

"Wildeen didn't think so. She valued his opinion."

Wildeen must have had more reasons to turn on a friend. "So, what else caused her jealousy?"

"My relationship with Bob. She had her eye on him when we were in college, you know, but he ignored her and dated me. When we married, she was devastated, even though she ended up with one hunk of a guy." Zelma rolled her eyes. "Anyway, my publishing success was the last straw, so to speak."

Nina snapped her fingers. "So that's why you went to the bookstore that night. You hoped to talk her out of exposing your secret."

"I offered her half the advance for *My Restless Heart*—which is a considerable sum—if she'd keep quiet. She laughed and said no amount of money would stop her from telling the world about my 'crime.'"

Was she about to hear Zelma was involved in Wildeen's death, after all? "And when she wouldn't agree to keep quiet, you…"

Zelma's eyes blazed. "I did not kill her! I didn't!" She made a fist and pounded the arm of her chair. "When I left, she was still very much alive."

"I wasn't about to accuse you of her murder." Nina sat back and spread her hands. "I wanted to know what you planned to do about her exposing you."

"Oh." Zelma's shoulders sagged, and then she sat straight again. "Well, I decided to reason with her when she was in a better frame of mind. I was plenty scared, but I figured eventually I would convince her to keep my secret. You do understand, don't you?" Zelma's eyes pleaded.

Nina sighed. "I can understand how all the trouble could have happened."

Zelma scooted to the edge of her chair then stood. "Good. Now, we'll burn the copy you brought, just like I did with the first book." Taking kindling from the basket on the hearth, she tossed it onto the grate. After adding crumpled newspaper, she touched her lighter to the pile. Flames sprouted and grew. Turning to Nina, she held out her hand. "I'll take the book now."

Nina hugged her waist. "We're not burning *Love's Eternal Triumph*."

Zelma lifted her chin. "Yes, we are. I insist." She stepped close to Nina.

Nina looked up and met Zelma's gaze. Did she really think burning both copies of the book would solve her problem? "I didn't bring the book."

"You didn't bring it?" Zelma's eyes widened and then narrowed. "Are you serious?"

"I am." Nina set her jaw. "The book is evidence."

"Evidence?" Zelma screeched. "What are you

talking about?"

"Wildeen's discovery of your plagiarism gives you a motive for murdering her."

"Then I suppose you want to turn over the book to Detective Russell. Nina, you can't. You just can't. I'm begging you." Zelma clasped her hands together. "Don't you understand? My career will be ruined. Everything I've worked for."

Nina clutched her churning stomach. "I'm sorry, Zelma, but I couldn't live with myself if I didn't give the book to Russell."

Zelma paced in front of the fireplace, her sandals slapping against the carpet. Without *Love's Eternal Triumph* to fuel the fire, the flames dwindled to embers.

"I can't believe your betrayal." Zelma stopped pacing, closed her eyes, and shook her head. "I thought we were friends. I asked for your help, and instead you cause more trouble. I *must* have the book. If only Wildeen had given it to me that night." She opened her eyes and glared. "This dilemma is all your fault. You shouldn't have read the book. I told you not to."

Nina huffed. How like Zelma to blame someone else for her own mistakes. "You should know I always examine any book called to my attention. Books are my business."

"So, you think I killed Wildeen." Zelma propped a fist on her hip.

Nina sat back and folded her arms. "I already told you I don't believe you did."

"Then why are you working to have me arrested?"

"I'm obeying the law. Not my fault if the evidence I uncover points to you. If you'd written your own book, like you are fully capable of writing…"

Zelma frowned. "What do you mean, 'capable'?"

"You've become a really good writer. You're ready for a break-out book."

"But, I told you, I couldn't write because Bob and I were having trouble." Zelma stamped her foot.

Nina kept her back rigid. "Are you sure your failure wasn't because you lacked confidence in yourself and used the other book as a crutch?"

Zelma pressed her lips together and shook her head. "Of course not. The idea is ridiculous."

"I'm angry with you, Zelma, for not believing in yourself, and also for not being truthful in the first place. I feel used and betrayed." Nina set her jaw.

Zelma propped her hands on her hips. "I didn't betray or use you. I didn't want anyone to find out about the other book."

"No one else knows but me?" Nina pointed to her chest. "Sondra and Morry don't know about your deception?"

"Of course not." Zelma twisted her lips. "Do you think I'm crazy? If they knew I cheated, they'd both drop me in a minute. My publisher would, too." She turned her back on Nina and stared into the fireplace.

The embers had lost all glow and now were black. Nina folded her arms and clamped shut her jaw, waiting for Zelma to make the next move.

Finally, Zelma whirled and faced Nina. Her eyes narrowed to slits, and her mouth stretched into a tight, grim line. "If you think I murdered Wildeen, aren't you afraid I might kill you, too? After all, you're the only other person who knows about my cheating."

Goose bumps popped out along Nina's arms, and her throat went dry. Truly, she hadn't thought confronting Zelma might be risky. Determined to hide her fear, she swallowed and strove to keep her tone firm. "You'd find yourself in the same situation you're in now. You still wouldn't have the book."

"Oh, I expect I'd find it, eventually." Zelma tossed her head. "The book's either at your home or at the library. I'd track it down."

Nina held up a forefinger. "Even if you have my copy, others may surface."

Zelma frowned. "I doubt many copies are floating around. Two turning up so close together was a fluke."

"Doesn't matter." Nina lifted her chin. "I've already given the book to Detective Russell. If something happens to me, you'll be the prime suspect." Her threat wasn't true, of course. She hadn't had time to visit the police station. The book was at home, in the glass case with her children's literature collection.

"I can't believe you would ruin me." Zelma's voice trembled, and she dropped into her chair. "I thought we were friends."

"I thought we were, too." Sadness twisted Nina's stomach into a knot. "But, Zelma, even with your motive, I don't believe you killed Wildeen. I'm sure the truth will win out."

"Well, I don't have your confidence. The police want to find someone they can pin the crime on, guilty or not. Do you know how many people are convicted for crimes they didn't commit?"

Suddenly too weary to continue, Nina scooted to the edge of her chair. "I need to leave now." She gripped the wooden arms and stood. "I'll see you tomorrow, for our lunch with Sondra."

Zelma widened her eyes. "Are you kidding? Do

you expect me to have lunch with you tomorrow, as if tonight hadn't happened? You really are something else, Nina Foster. I don't care if I ever speak to you again."

Nina gasped. "Zelma…"

"You can find your own way out." Zelma folded her arms and glared.

Sick at heart, Nina drove home. The affair tore her apart, and she wished she'd never become involved. As both Zelma's and Wildeen's friend, however, she could never remain a disinterested observer.

Sleep that night was a long time coming. Even then, dreams of *Love's Eternal Triumph* and of Zelma's angry, accusing eyes kept her tossing and turning.

****

The following morning, Nina pulled herself together and vowed to continue the investigation. She was far too stubborn to give up now. After breakfast, she went into the living room, sat on the sofa, and called Sondra Wagner. "Are we still meeting today for lunch? Zelma's canceled."

"I know. She called to say she isn't feeling well. I'm not surprised, considering the strain she's under. I told her to rest up for our tour. We'd be gone now, but she insisted leaving so soon after Wildeen's murder would make her look guilty. But, sure, I'll still meet you for lunch. I have something I want to discuss."

Nina straightened. "You do? What?"

"I'll tell you when I see you. Sailor's Inn, in Ballard, right?"

"Yes, at noon." Her next call was to Detective Russell. He was in his office and would see her that morning. Nina breathed a sigh of relief. She wanted to give him *Love's Eternal Triumph* as soon as possible, to make good her lie to Zelma.

As she entered the police station, Nina encountered Stephen on his way out. He looked handsome in neatly pressed tan slacks and a plaid sports shirt. Her heart skipped a beat.

He stopped and regarded her with raised eyebrows. "Hello. What are you doing here?"

Not wanting to reveal the true reason for her visit, she thought fast. "I might ask you the same thing."

"Checking the police blotter for our Police Beat feature." He gestured to the hallway leading to inner offices. "But seeing you saves me a phone call. We need to discuss your column. You do want to write for us, don't you?"

"Yes. I just forgot about the column. So much going on right now."

He leaned against the counter. "Are you free for lunch today? Wednesday's your day off, as I recall."

"Sorry, I already have plans for lunch. This afternoon I'm visiting the Evergreen Athletic Club."

His eyes lighted. "Really? I plan to be at the club this afternoon, too. How about a game of racquetball? Afterward, we can go to my office and talk."

"Sorry, I don't play racquetball."

"I'll teach you. The game's easy to learn and good exercise."

She bit her lower lip, debating. What could be the harm? Why not consider the game a part of their business meeting? "All right, but I must warn you I'm not much of an athlete."

He chuckled. "You'll do fine. By the way, how's the investigation coming? Is that why you're here?

Because you've found something for Pete Russell?"

Nina tensed. "What time do you want to meet at the club?"

"Okay, I can take a hint." He flashed a grin. "I don't have your confidence yet. Gotta work on that. Will two o'clock give you enough time for your lunch date?"

"I'm sure it will." Nina breathed a sigh of relief.

"Good. I'll see you at the club."

A few minutes later, Pete Russell ushered Nina into his stuffy, windowless office. "Have a seat." He motioned to a straight chair in front of his desk then sank into his swivel chair and leaned back. "What do you want to see me about?"

She took the two books from her purse and laid them side-by-side on the desk, with the titles and authors' names positioned so he could read them. "I brought you these books…"

"You were brave to confront Zelma," Russell commented when she finished her story.

"I didn't feel brave at the time. I was angry she hadn't told me about her deception in the first place." Nina stared at the books, wishing she'd never seen— much less read—either of them.

"But you can understand why she didn't."

"Oh, yes." Nina shifted on the hard seat. "But I didn't bring her plagiarism to your attention because I want to see Zelma arrested for Wildeen's murder. I still believe in her innocence. I just couldn't withhold something that might be evidence."

Pete Russell made notes on his clipboard and then looked up. "I appreciate your coming in today, Nina."

His voice carried an understanding she didn't

expect. "Will Zelma be charged?"

"I can't say. Bringing charges is the prosecutor's job." He slipped his pen into his shirt pocket.

"Do you have any other suspects?" Surely, Zelma wasn't the only one on their radar.

Russell shook his head. "I'm not at liberty to discuss suspects."

Nina left the police station, wondering if exposing Zelma as a plagiarist was the right decision. She honestly didn't know. She couldn't ponder the dilemma now, though. A glance at her watch indicated if she were to meet Sondra Wagner at noon, she'd better be on her way. Sondra said she wanted to discuss something. What could that possibly be?

Chapter Twelve

The drive to Ballard, Seattle's Scandinavian suburb bordering Puget Sound, took twenty minutes. Nina traveled through the neighborhood's business district, which included a meat market featuring lutefisk and a restaurant famous for its Swedish pancakes. The road wound past the Hiram Chittenden Government Locks, where boats left the higher inland waterways and entered the lower waters of the sound. The locks were a popular tourist attraction, and today was no exception. Vehicles filled the parking lot, and sightseers streamed through the park's arched entrance.

A few miles beyond the locks, Sailor's Inn occupied the top floor of a two-story building overlooking a marina. As she climbed the steps to the restaurant, Nina glanced at her wristwatch. One minute to twelve. Her good timing brought a satisfied smile to her lips.

The hostess seated her at a window table offering a view of the hundreds of boats moored at the marina. Nina watched a yacht with colorful flags attached to the stern leave its slip and head for the open water. On the deck of an incoming sailboat, a man holding a coiled rope stood poised to dock the boat. Then Sondra's arrival captured Nina's attention.

Setting her brown leather briefcase on the floor, Sondra slid into the seat across the table. "Sorry I'm late, but I have a big event planned for this weekend and a million details to attend to."

"What's the event?" Nina shifted in her seat to face Sondra.

"A 4K charity walk from the Westlake Mall to Safeco Field, where a rally will be held. The mayor's giving us a send-off, and all the local channels will feature us on the five o'clock news."

Nina raised her eyebrows. "Sounds like you have a busy job."

Sondra beamed. "I do, and I love my work. But right now, I'm starved. Let's look at the menu." She picked up the plastic-encased menu the hostess left.

Nina opened her menu, too, and studied the selections. Not surprisingly, seafood was the house specialty. After perusing dishes such as blackened catfish and deep fried calamari, she settled on a crab salad.

Sondra chose a turkey croissant sandwich.

The waiter appeared and took their orders.

After sipping her water, Sondra sat back and studied Nina. "How is your investigation? Have you turned up anything to help Zelma prove her innocence?"

"Not really." Nina wondered what Sondra would say if she told her Zelma was a plagiarist.

Sondra waved a hand in dismissal. "I didn't think you would. Finding the killer is a job for the police, not an amateur sleuth."

At the scorn she heard in Sondra's voice, Nina bristled. The term "amateur sleuth" reminded her of the old Nancy Drew books in her collection. "I'm not establishing myself as any kind of sleuth, amateur or otherwise. I'm only helping a friend." She leaned forward. "What about you? Do you know of anything that might help Zelma?"

Sondra shrugged. "I wish. I hardly knew Wildeen."

"But her desk calendar showed you had an appointment with her a week and a half before she was killed."

"My, you have been busy, haven't you? All right, I did have an appointment with Wildeen. I wanted her to have a book signing for Zelma, but she refused. Not only refused but also laughed at the idea." She pursed her lips. "I'll admit her attitude didn't sit well, but her refusal is hardly a motive for murder. Besides, I found other bookstore owners eager to host a signing."

Nina gazed out the window a moment and then turned back to Sondra. "Do you know anyone who might have wanted to kill Wildeen?"

"Sure, I do. Her husband."

Sondra's quick answer indicated she was prepared for the question. Nina studied her. "You know about their conflict?"

"Zelma told me about the trouble over their divorce." She tilted her head. "Or maybe his girlfriend was the murderer. What are Patti's and Josh's alibis?"

"As far as I know, each other."

Sondra snorted. "Figures. I was married once. Never again. How about you?"

"I haven't tried marriage yet. But why didn't yours work out?" Nina was determined to keep the focus on Sondra, rather than on herself.

"Spending so much time with the same person became boring. I need excitement in my life." She shrugged. "Guess that's why I'm in the publicity biz."

Boredom was hardly an excuse to give up a marriage, but perhaps other reasons she chose not to mention contributed to Sondra's failed relationship.

Their meals arrived. Sondra's croissant was tucked in a basket, and Nina's crab salad came in a large plastic clamshell. For the next few minutes, they concentrated on eating. Nina enjoyed her salad, served with a generous portion of fresh crabmeat and a tangy dressing. However, despite being branded an amateur sleuth, she was eager to pursue questioning Sondra. "By the way," she began, "did you know Detective Russell found the heel you lost at the Bottses' party?" Not wanting to miss Sondra's reaction, she kept her gaze focused on her.

Sondra nodded and with thumb and forefinger picked up a potato chip. "He called me. I could've sworn the heel went over the cliff. I stood close to the edge admiring the view. I backed up"—she gestured with a free hand—"and my shoe hit a huge rock. The heel broke off." She wrinkled her nose. "The shoes weren't cheap, either."

Nina finished a bite of her salad. "Will he return the heel?"

"He said he would. But I don't want the thing. I've already tossed the shoes." She popped the chip into her mouth and munched.

"He found the heel close to where I overheard Zelma and Wildeen plan to meet at the bookstore."

"Maybe an animal dragged it there." Sondra glanced around and then leaned forward. "Oh, I see where you're headed. You think I overheard their conversation, too, and went to the bookstore after Zelma left, and then I killed Wildeen. But even if I had a motive, why would I pick a time when Zelma might be blamed? Her success is important. She's the first best-selling author I've represented. We've planned a fabulous tour. Why would I want to jeopardize her success?" She sat back and ate another chip.

"You wouldn't, I'm sure. But would you mind telling me where you were when Wildeen was murdered?"

Sondra finished chewing and touched her napkin to her lips. "I've already told Detective Russell, but, okay, I'll play your game—in the interest of helping Zelma, mind you." She took a breath. "After the Bottses' party, Morry and I went for a drink at the Harbor Bar and Grill. We were still there when the murder occurred."

Morry Snyder was on Nina's suspect list, too. She hadn't had a chance to interview him yet. "Did Morry know Wildeen? Other than meeting her at the Bottses'?"

Sondra shook her head. "I don't think so. But you'll have to ask him yourself." She wrinkled her brow. "Why aren't *you* a suspect? What's your alibi?"

"I don't have one. I went directly home after the party, but I didn't see or talk to anyone who can help me prove that."

"Okay, what's to have kept you from killing Wildeen and then discovering her body in the morning?" Sondra made air quotes around "discovering."

"Nothing, I guess." Nina shrugged. "Except I have no motive. Wildeen and I were friends."

"So were she and Zelma."

At the memory of their lost friendship, Nina experienced a pang of regret. "Not as good now as in the past. Wildeen's jealousy of Zelma cooled their friendship."

The waiter appeared and refilled their water glasses.

Sondra sipped her water, eyeing Nina. "So, are you finished with your interrogation?"

Nina let a smile hover over her lips. "For now."

"Good." Sondra straightened her shoulders. "Now we can talk about my idea."

Nina put down her fork. "I remember you said you had something to discuss."

"Right. I read a notice in *The Richmond Review* about your library's book sale. What do you do for publicity?" She pulled her cell phone from her purse and laid it on the table.

Nina thought a moment. "We advertise in the newspaper and on our website and distribute flyers around town. Oh, and we hang a banner across Main Street with the date and time of the sale."

Sondra made notes on her phone and then looked up, a wide smile on her lips. "Have you ever thought of TV coverage?"

Nina laughed. "I hardly think the television stations would be interested in a library book sale."

"I can get them interested in anything." She tapped her chin with her forefinger and looked at the ceiling. "You could have…a parade."

Nina wrinkled her brow. "A parade? What for?"

"Why, for books, of course. Give the sale a literacy theme and donate part of your proceeds to a literacy fund."

Nina shook her head. "We've already decided what we'll do with our money."

"Make some changes. But that idea's just off the top of my head. Give me time, and I'll come up with a bunch more."

"I appreciate your offer, Sondra." Nina speared the last bit of crab from her salad. "But I doubt our modest budget would allow for your services."

"My help would be well worth the price. Your sales would increase, and you'll take in more money than ever before."

Sondra's eyes sparkled. Nina finished chewing and put down her fork. "We usually sell almost all our books. During the last hour, we charge only a dollar a bag. Any leftovers are donated to thrift stores."

Sondra waved a hand. "I'll show you what I'm doing for Zelma." Pushing aside her food basket, she lifted her briefcase to the table and opened the clasp. She took out two pieces of paper and handed them to Nina. "Here are a bookmark and a flyer, for starters."

The bookmark was identical to the one Nina found in the Bottses' garden. The full-page flyer was much the same, except for the inclusion of Zelma's bio. "These bookmarks are very, ah, nice." Nina ran her fingers over the paper's glossy surface. The comment sounded lame, but she didn't know what else to say.

"I've also created a blog tour with a contest. Here's the prize." Sondra dug into the briefcase and pulled out a long-sleeved, yellow sweatshirt. The cover of Zelma's book blazed across the shirt's front.

Speechless, Nina gulped. She couldn't imagine anyone wanting to be a walking advertisement for another person's book. From the corner of her eye, she noticed two women diners craning their necks in Sondra's direction.

Glancing around, Sondra turned the shirt to face the women and jiggled it.

The two exchanged looks and then nodded and smiled.

"Excuse me a sec." Grabbing her bookmarks and flyers, Sondra jumped up and approached the women. She spoke to them for a few minutes, holding up the shirt and giving them the advertising material. When she returned, she sat and beamed a smile. "They're in."

"In?" Nina darted a glance at the women.

They smiled and waved.

"The contest." Sondra held up the flyers. "All they have to do is visit Zelma's website and fill in a form that tells where the hero and heroine share their first kiss."

"That task seems easy enough." Wouldn't readers realize they were just being suckered in to buying the book or to checking it out at the library?

"We'll get lots of correct answers, so in addition to the shirts, we'll have a drawing for a grand prize, a gift card and a basket of goodies."

"I'm sure your contest will be a big success for Zelma, but—"

Sondra snapped her fingers. "I know. We could do a similar version for your book sale. How about giving a T-shirt to everyone who donates books and a gift card and goodie basket to whoever donates the most books? The shirt could say 'Readers are Leaders.'" With thumb and forefinger, she traced a line in the air.

Nina visualized her staff sorting through the huge piles of books. "Keeping track of the donations would be a lot of work—"

Sondra widened her eyes. "But you do want

donations, don't you?"

Being able to purchase all the items on the staff's wish list would be nice. "Of course, but—"

Just then, the waiter laid their check on the table.

Nina reached for the slip at the same time Sondra put out her hand. Actually, Nina wanted only to see her share. She assumed the lunch was Dutch treat.

Sondra grabbed the slip of paper from under Nina's fingers. "Lunch is on me." She held the check to her chest.

"Oh, no, really—"

"I insist. You sat here listening so politely to my spiel."

True enough. "Well, thank you. I appreciate being your guest." But had Sondra picked up the bill so Nina would feel obligated to use her publicity services?

However, Sondra said no more about the book sale. She stuffed everything into her briefcase, snapped it shut, and looked at her wristwatch. "Gotta run. I have a meeting with reps from channel forty to discuss covering a dog show."

"Is a contest involved with the show?" Nina couldn't help asking.

Sondra shook her head. "Uh uh. But each entrant gets a free poop scoop."

As she picked up her purse, Nina hid a smile. "A poop scoop ought to be a good incentive."

They left the restaurant together. At the parking lot, Sondra turned to Nina. "I'm sorry Zelma couldn't come today, but I'm glad you did. I'll be in touch."

"All right. If you think of anything that might help catch Wildeen's murderer, I hope you'll let me and Detective Russell know."

Sondra quirked an eyebrow. "In that order?"

Nina laughed good-naturedly. "Yes, I want to make sure we're both informed."

****

"Oh, darn!" Once again, Nina missed hitting the ball with her racquet.

The ball hit the court's hardwood floor and then bounced into Stephen's outstretched hand. "Game over," he called.

"I know, and you won. Again." Breathless, Nina pressed a hand against her chest.

"Don't be discouraged." Stephen came to her side and touched her shoulder. "You have a smooth serve and good arm strength. But I sense your mind's not on the game. Am I right?"

She straightened and tucked a lock of hair behind her ear. "I admit to being preoccupied."

"Wildeen's murder."

"Uh huh." Plus the new development of Zelma's plagiarism. But, of course, she couldn't tell him that discovery.

However, as she met his gaze, a look passed between them that made her want to confide. She steeled herself against the feeling. He was an outsider. Besides, she wasn't interested in being close to a man. Intimacy was too scary. She tore away her gaze and held up her racquet. "Do you want to play another game?" *Please say no.*

"I wouldn't mind, but I think you've had enough. We'll play again some other time. Now we'll go to my office and discuss your column." He tucked his racquet under his arm and gestured toward the court's glass door.

160

Nina breathed a sigh of relief. "Good idea. I do want to start on the column."

On their way to the locker rooms, they met Josh Loring and Burgess Botts, heading for the racquetball courts. Josh wore blue Spandex shorts and a tank top that showed off his broad shoulders and muscular arms. His wavy, dark brown hair was smoothed back from his forehead in its usual neat style.

Burgess' over-large T-shirt failed to hide his potbelly, if that was the intent, and khaki shorts exposed hairy legs with knobby knees.

The four stopped to exchange greetings.

Josh and Stephen discussed an advertisement Josh placed in *The Richmond Review*.

Burgess turned to Nina. "I hear you're a detective now."

Heat flushed her cheeks. Had everyone in town heard about her investigation? She gave a dismissive wave. "Don't worry, I'm not taking over Detective Russell's job. I merely told Zelma I'd keep an eye out for anything that might help catch the murderer."

He peered from under his thick eyebrows. "Have you found something?"

"Nothing significant." Nina pulled out a tissue and dabbed at the perspiration on her forehead. "But on that subject, I'm confused about who was where on the trail walk. You probably know I overheard Zelma and Wildeen plan to meet later?"

Burgess nodded. "Elizabeth told me about your eavesdropping."

Nina bristled. "I didn't *intend* to eavesdrop. I came upon them by accident."

"Okay, but what're you confused about?"

"Detective Russell and I wondered if anyone else could have overheard their conversation." Nina hoped the addition of the detective would add authenticity to her query. "You were setting up a fallen sign, and Elizabeth remained at the bird feeder."

"I couldn't have overheard Wildeen and Zelma. The sign was at the other end of the woods from them."

Obviously, he and his wife hadn't coordinated their stories because Elizabeth insisted she and Burgess remained together on the walk. Nina tilted her head. "How do you know where Zelma and Wildeen were?"

He shrugged. "I dunno. Somebody told me. Maybe Russell."

Just then, Patti Hamilton appeared in the hallway.

Josh took a step toward her. "Hey, Patti."

Keeping her head averted, Patti brushed by him and continued down the hall.

"What's the hurry?" Josh frowned.

"I have an aerobics class," she called over her shoulder.

"Okay, see you afterward." Josh waved his racquet.

Patti made no further reply as she hurried along.

Nina watched her until she turned a corner and disappeared.

"What's with Patti?" Stephen commented when he and Nina were on their way to the locker rooms. "Is something wrong between her and Josh? They were cozy at the Bottses' party."

"They were, but she sure brushed him off today."

Maybe Patti was still upset over Josh's questionable business practices. Once again, Nina had the impulse to confide in Stephen. Still, she resisted.

Chapter Thirteen

The home of *The Richmond Review* was a one-story, white stucco building on Fir Street. Nina had been there many times when George Martin was the publisher, but today was the first time she'd had a tour.

Stephen began with the waiting area, furnished with inexpensive yet attractive chrome tables and matching chairs with black vinyl seats. Then he led Nina down a hallway, popping into offices and introducing her to staff. "Here's where I hang out," he said when they reached the last office. "Come in, and we'll talk about the column." He opened the door and motioned her to enter.

Nina stepped into the room. She quickly saw the clutter rivaled what she'd seen at his home. The desk was all but hidden under file folders, papers, and coffee mugs. Two side chairs held cardboard boxes, and the stuffed drawers of a metal file cabinet hung open. "How can you get any work done in this mess?"

Stephen laughed. "Because I know where everything is, and, besides, I can clean up at a moment's notice. Like now." He scooped up files, papers, and books from a straight chair and set them on the floor. "Here, have a seat." He made a sweeping gesture at the chair.

Nina sat, balancing her purse on her lap.

Stephen went behind his desk and sank into a

leather swivel chair. "Okay, down to business." He took a folder from a stack on the desktop. "Here are copies of all your columns, which I have read."

Nina shifted in her seat. Having her words under Stephen's scrutiny made her uncomfortable. Why was his opinion important? She wasn't like Wildeen or Zelma, who needed constant approval for their writing. She was a librarian hoping to interest people in books.

Stephen opened the file and paged through the contents. "The articles are well written, and each month has a theme, like this column on gardening books." He held up a photocopied page.

His compliment brought a smile to her lips. "Themes give the articles focus."

"I agree, and I'd like you to continue. You might ask your patrons for their recommendations."

Warming to the idea, she nodded. "No doubt they'll have suggestions."

"Good. Then we're agreed."

They talked more about the column, the newspaper, and the library. Relaxed and comfortable, Nina lost track of time. When she thought to check her wristwatch, she saw the time was almost four o'clock. She scooted to the edge of her seat. "I should be going. You probably have work to do."

He closed the file folder and returned it to the stack. "How about getting together later for dinner?"

"I hadn't given dinner a thought." Dinner usually meant foraging in the refrigerator to discover what was still edible.

He smiled. "We could go to a waterfront restaurant, one with a good view and tasty food."

"But I—our business is over." His suggestion

sounded too much like a date. "We've discussed the column. What else is there?" She ended with a shrug.

"Oh, Nina, we could have a lot more." He leaned forward. "I want to spend time with you. I think you feel the same way about me, although you're not ready to admit it."

She met his steady gaze. "You think you know me so well already?"

He nodded. "I do. What do you say?"

While she searched for an answer, Nina closed her eyes. Then an utterly outrageous idea popped into her mind. Her heartbeat raced. "All right, but why don't we eat at my place?"

He sat back and stared. "Are you serious?"

"I am. But be warned dinner will be plain and simple. I'm not the cook you are."

"I'll bet whatever you make will taste just great. I'll jump at the chance to visit you because you look like you might change your mind at any moment. What time should I be at your place?"

"When is your workday over?"

"Usually, around six."

"Come any time after that." She took a business card from her purse, added her home address and phone number, and held it out.

He took the card and tucked it into his shirt pocket. "See you then."

After leaving the newspaper office, reality hit Nina, and her shoulders tensed. What had possessed her to invite Stephen to dinner? He might think she wanted to get to know him better, too. Did she?

No, but she was attracted. Her feelings went deeper than just liking his looks. She admired his good-humored patience with her attitude toward outsiders and his understanding her distress over Wildeen's death. Plus, his relaxed and casual manner made him easy to be with.

However, now he was coming to dinner. What would she prepare?

On the way to her car, she decided to build her menu around the stuffed chicken breasts from the grocery store's deli. She stopped at the store and purchased the chicken, along with a few other items. At home, she set the dining room table with her best dishes, flatware, crystal glasses, and cloth napkins. Six o'clock came all too soon. Nina ran from dining room to kitchen to living room, straightening anything that looked the least out of place.

The buzzer rang.

She answered, heard Stephen's voice, and pressed the button to release the gate. Moments later, the doorbell chimed. *Here goes.* After checking her appearance in the hall mirror, she ran to open the door.

He held a bouquet of red and white carnations in one hand and a bottle of wine in the other.

Surprise—and pleasure—rippled through her. "Well, look at you. But you didn't have to bring anything."

"Tonight is an important occasion. Our first dinner together at your place." He handed her the bouquet.

She took the flowers and led him down the hall to the kitchen. Rummaging in a drawer, she found the corkscrew. In the cupboard under the sink, she located a crystal vase large enough for the flowers.

Stephen uncorked the wine with the practiced ease of someone used to managing corkscrews.

"Something sure smells good."

"Stuffed chicken breasts." She opened a cupboard, took out two wine glasses, and set them on the counter.

He gave her a sly grin. "And you said you couldn't cook."

She shrugged. "The chicken we're eating is from the deli. I hope you don't mind."

"Not at all." He poured the wine. "Here's to us." He handed her a glass.

She wanted to say, "There is no us," but the remark would be not only cliché but also rude. Instead, she nodded and touched her glass to his before sipping. The wine tasted refreshing. Picking up the vase of flowers, she led them into the dining room where she set the vase on the table. Then they went into the living room.

He stopped and gazed around. "You went to a lot of trouble to prepare for tonight."

"Not really." She surveyed the room.

He raised an eyebrow. "You mean your place always looks so neat and orderly?"

Nina stiffened. "What's wrong with neatness? Having everything in its place comforts me."

"Comforted is how I feel with *dis*order." He laughed and placed a hand on a nearby chair. "Anyway, your condo has a good floor plan."

"You're welcome to see the rest of the place." Oh, oh. Did she really want to take him upstairs to her bedroom and her study?

He nodded. "I'd like a tour. Maybe I'll find ideas for my remodeling."

She showed him the downstairs, including the flagstone patio furnished with wrought iron table and chairs and redwood tubs of geraniums, daisies, and marigolds. Upstairs, she allowed only a quick peek at her bedroom and then went to her study.

Stephen approached the bookcase housing her children's books. "Ah, your collection. Did you get the book Wildeen had for you?"

Feeling a surge of pride, she opened a glass door, removed *The Wizard*, and held it out. "This book is the one."

He set his wineglass on her desk before opening the book and turning the pages. "Very nice. I remember reading this story as a kid. Not a collectible edition like this one, though." Tilting his head, he scanned the other titles. "You have some of Howard Pease's books. I read *The Jinx Ship* and *The Tattooed Man*. My grandfather gave them to me."

Surprised, and pleased they shared a common interest, she warmed toward him. "I acquired mine when I began collecting as an adult."

Finished perusing her books, they went downstairs. At dinner, he told her about his hometown of Parkers Landing, Idaho. "The town is in the northern part of the state, only about thirty miles from the Canadian border. So you see, I'm really a Northwesterner at heart."

"Do you have family there?"

He added another helping of steamed rice to his plate. "My older sister, Judy, and her husband, and their three kids. Our parents passed away ten or so years ago."

Reflecting on how his family life had been different from hers, Nina sipped her wine. "Why did you go to New York?"

"I wanted to make a big splash as a journalist, and to do that I had to work for a large operation."

"So did you? Make a big splash? At the athletic club, you mentioned investigative reporting."

Smiling, he nodded. "A series of articles I wrote on organized crime received a Pulitzer nomination. Didn't win, but the recognition was a great honor."

"I'm sure it was," she agreed.

They took their after-dinner coffee into the living room. He settled into an easy chair while she sat on the sofa. Conversation eventually led to Wildeen's murder.

"Have you found out anything new?" He sipped his coffee, studying her over the rim of his cup.

Here was the perfect opportunity to take him into her confidence, but did she dare? Could she trust him? In the past, she would have chosen Wildeen or Zelma, but Wildeen was dead, and Zelma a possible suspect. Why not take a chance on Stephen? She set her cup and saucer on the coffee table. "I did learn something shocking about Zelma." She launched into her discovery of Zelma's plagiarism.

"That's why you were at the police station this morning."

Nina nodded. "I gave Pete Russell *Love's Eternal Triumph*."

"Confronting Zelma was risky." Brow furrowed, Stephen studied her.

Nina squirmed under his scrutiny. Perhaps she shouldn't have shared what she knew after all. "Russell mentioned risk, too. But, honestly, the thought never occurred." She looked up and met his gaze.

A smile touched his lips. "Understandable, given the two of you are close friends."

Nina twisted her fingers together. "Now, I wonder if I should have given the book to Russell. I believe

169

Zelma is innocent, so why did I turn in evidence that gives her a motive?"

Stephen leaned forward and patted her arm. "You did what you thought was right. I'd have done the same thing."

"You would?" The weight of guilt lifted from her shoulders. Then she sobered again. "Still, the book is on my conscience. What if the police arrest Zelma? I'm more anxious than ever to find the murderer."

Stephen sat back. "Any new ideas?"

"Well, Josh Loring might be cheating his elderly female clients." She told him about seeing Amanda Harper at Josh's seminar, about Lily Ciliano at Marley Manor, and about her visit to Josh's home and the conversation she overheard between him and Patti. "Patti's knowledge of Josh's scam might explain why she was so upset at the club today. If he knew Wildeen found out, too, he'd have a motive for her murder."

"Makes sense. How about any of the others?"

"I had lunch today with Sondra Wagner, Zelma's publicist. She admitted to being annoyed because Wildeen refused to give Zelma a book signing, but pointed out her refusal is hardly a motive for murder. I don't consider Sondra a strong suspect."

He tilted his head. "What about Burgess and Elizabeth Botts?"

"I found inconsistency in what each told me. She insists they were together during the trail walk, but at the club today, Burgess confirmed he left her to fix a sign. Elizabeth might be afraid Burgess overheard Wildeen and Zelma, too, and is involved in the murder." She wrinkled her nose. "I don't know what motive he would have, though."

Stephen picked up his coffee and sipped. "Burgess and Josh are pals. I see them together a lot at the athletic club."

"Josh is Burgess' financial advisor." Nina pressed a finger to her cheek. "Hmmm, I wonder if Josh is cheating him. I hardly think he'd cheat a friend, but you never know."

Stephen put down his cup and snapped his fingers. "The night of the party, I remember Burgess introducing Josh to Dorothy Quinn, head of…what's her book group called?"

"Literary Lights."

"Right. Anyway, Burgess said to Josh something like, 'Here's the little lady I've been telling you about.'"

Catching his excitement, Nina sat straight. "At Josh's seminar, Amanda Harper told me Burgess recommended Josh. Lily Ciliano said Burgess introduced her to Josh, too."

"I see a pattern…"

"I have some notes I think will help." She put out a hand. "Wait here." Nina went to the kitchen drawer and dug out her notes on the investigation. Returning, she handed the list to Stephen. "Here are the names on the file folders I saw in the Bottses' library. Bell, Saunders, Emmons, Harper, Pedersen, and Quinn. Harper and Quinn could be the last names of Amanda and Dorothy."

Stephen studied the list. "The files might contain information Burgess gathers on elderly women to pass along to Josh. He receives a cut in whatever Josh rips off, of course."

Excitement quickened Nina's pulse. "Then, if

Burgess knew Wildeen discovered their scam, he had a motive for killing her."

"Great theory…"

Doubt shadowed his eyes.

"But we have no actual proof." She sat back and heaved a sigh.

Stephen handed Nina the notes. "First, one of the victims needs to press charges against Josh. From what you've told me, no one has realized she is a victim. They all think he's wonderful."

Nina, too, had noticed the women's high approval of Josh. She bit her lower lip. "I wish we knew a way…"

"Let me talk to Dorothy Quinn." Stephen leaned forward and clasped his hands. "She's placed ads in our newspaper for her antiques store, and we've struck up an acquaintance. I'll ask if she can suggest someone to help with my investments. If she says her financial advisor is Josh, and on Burgess's recommendation, we'll add her to our list."

Nina felt her stomach tighten. She made a fist and pounded her palm. "If Josh is cheating his clients, he ought to be stopped."

"Yes, but we need to proceed very carefully. If we accuse him and he's innocent, we could be in big trouble. In the meantime, I'll have one of my contacts run a check on your list of suspects, to see if any has a criminal record."

"Great, Stephen. I'd appreciate the help." They'd have to keep in touch, though. Would that be a problem?

Stephen studied her. "What will you do next?"

"Talk to Morry Snyder, although I don't know

172

what possible motive he would have. I doubt he knew Wildeen, other than meeting her at the party. But he might have useful information."

"In the snooping business, one never knows where the answers will be found. Leave no stone unturned, as the saying goes. Here's another tip." He held up a forefinger. "If you aren't satisfied with an answer, look at the situation from a different point of view. A new perspective might lead to a solution."

"Thanks. I'll keep your advice in mind."

He looked at his wristwatch and stood. "Hey, I'd better get going. Don't want to outstay my welcome."

At the front door, he grasped both her hands. "Thanks for dinner and for the tour, and the talk—everything. I had a really good time tonight."

Warmth spread through her. "You're welcome. So did I."

Their gazes locked, and in the next moment, he leaned forward and kissed her.

The touch of his lips sent a tingling all the way down to her toes. Then, frightened by her response, she pulled away.

He drew back. "Moving too fast, am I?"

"Moving in a direction I can't go," she whispered.

After he left, she rushed upstairs to the hallway window and watched him drive through the gate. Wanting to hold onto the connection as long as possible, she kept her gaze on his car until the taillights disappeared over the brow of the hill.

Before turning away, she noticed a dark-colored car parked across the street. Thoughts of Stephen and their enjoyable evening fled. The car looked like the same one she thought had followed her home from

Josh's. A chill slithered down her spine, and she hugged her arms. Was someone watching her?

She yanked the cord to close the blinds, and the plastic slats came together with a resounding snap. Outside, a car's engine started. She edged up one of the slats and peered out just as the car pulled away from the curb and headed down the hill.

Nina leaned against the wall and blew out a relieved breath. Still, a creepy feeling came over her, and she had the feeling she hadn't seen the last of the mysterious car.

Or of its occupant.

Chapter Fourteen

Since she wasn't an aspiring writer, Nina had no professional reason to make an appointment with Morry Snyder. Therefore, she'd be honest. Everyone knew what she was up to anyway. She simply called his office and told him she wanted to discuss Zelma and her predicament.

"Sure, kid, come on down, and we'll knock it around." Morry's deep voice boomed over the phone. "The sooner Zelma is out of this mess, the better."

His concern for Zelma reassured her. "Are you free tomorrow around five-thirty? I know the time is rather late, but I'm not off work until five."

"No problem. I usually work late, anyway. Got a lot of manuscripts to read."

The address he gave her was in Seattle's Fremont District, a neighborhood full of old stone and brick buildings with just enough facelift to make them appear trendy rather than shabby. Parking places were scarce, but, luckily, Nina came upon a car pulling away from the curb. She slid into the space, alighted, and fed the meter for the minutes remaining until the six o'clock cut-off time.

The door to Morry's second floor office was set in a recess between an architectural firm and a furniture refinishing shop. She entered the building and climbed the narrow stairs. A single bulb in the high ceiling cast deep shadows, and the smell of stale pizza and cigarette smoke hung in the air. Why did Morry have his office in such a dismal place? Couldn't he afford anything better?

At the top of the stairs, a hallway branched to the left and to the right. The two offices on the left belonged to lawyers and the first office on the right to an accountant. The last door had "Morry Snyder Literary Agency" painted in black on the glass window.

Several chrome chairs with vinyl seats and a square, metal end table all but filled the small waiting room. Above the table, a copper-shaded ceiling lamp beamed on a scattering of magazines. In one corner, an artificial philodendron sat in a large plastic tub, its broad, flat leaves dulled by an accumulation of dust. Ugly brown paint covered the walls, and the tweed carpet, a cheap, indoor-outdoor, shone threadbare in spots. Nina wrinkled her nose. The whole place needed a good scrubbing and deodorizing.

A man in his fifties occupied one of the chairs. He looked up, nodded, and offered her a faint smile.

Nina returned his smile and sat across from him. Then she noticed he trimmed his fingernails with a metal clipper. With each snip, a nail fragment flew into the periphery of her vision, and she cringed inwardly.

Finally, he finished his grooming and tucked the clippers into his slacks pocket. He studied her. "You a writer?"

"No, I'm not."

"Me, neither. But the wife is. Or so she thinks. We'll see what he has to say." He tipped his head toward the closed door. "We come all the way from Bellingham so's she could show him some of her writin'. Couldn't find any lit-er-ary agents up our way and can't afford to go to New York. We was glad to find one so close."

"What does your wife write?" Knowing more about a potential client might help her to learn more about Morry, plus, being in the book business herself, she was interested in writers.

"Kids' stories." He chuckled. "Actually, they're kinda cute. We live on a farm, see? And she's always namin' the animals. She gets this idea that maybe all the animals can be in a story. And, by golly, she sat down and wrote it. Then her friend made some pictures. She's got this friend, see, that makes pictures out of straws."

"Straws?" Nina visualized the type of straw used on a farm.

"You know, the kind you drink from?"

"Oh, of course." Nina shifted her mental image.

He waved a hand. "Well, anyway, Mary Sue makes these pictures out of straws. Kinda clever, I must say. Now the wife has pictures for her story. But she's gotta find a literary agent. Or so she tells me. I don't see why she can't send her story straight to a publisher herself. But, no, she has to have an agent." He made a fist and pounded the table. "The gals in her what-you-call-it 'critique group' said so."

"So, how did your wife choose Morry as a potential representative?"

"You didn't see his big ad in the paper?" He took a folded piece of newsprint from the pocket of his plaid shirt and held it out. "Here."

Nina accepted the paper and unfolded it to reveal a large advertisement. *Star Search*, proclaimed the bold headline, and under that, *Literary Agent Seeks Manuscripts*. According to the ad, Morry represented dozens of best-selling authors. Moreover, he could make anyone who responded a best-selling author, too. He was open to any kind of manuscript but especially wanted commercial fiction. Impressive promises, Nina thought. But could Morry live up to them?

"Don't know what he means by 'commercial,'" the man commented.

"A commercial book will sell a lot of copies to the mass market." Nina handed back the article.

He frowned. "Mass market?"

Just then, the door to Morry's private office opened, and a woman stumbled out. Not over five feet tall, she wore an ankle-length, brown cotton skirt, a print blouse with a gold, oval pin at the neck, and a wrinkled, brown linen jacket. Gray hair fanned out around her shoulders. She had barely closed the door behind her when she stopped short, covered her face with her hands, and burst into tears.

The man leaped from his seat, strode to the woman, and put his arms around her. "What's wrong, Martha?"

"H-he d-didn't l-like my story." She let out a mournful wail.

Nina glanced at Morry's door, expecting him to emerge, curious about the noise. The door remained closed.

"What?" The man dropped his jaw. "Why not?"

"H-he c-called my story a-amateur."

"Well, he's got his nerve. I'll straighten him out on that subject." Balling a fist, he took a step toward the closed door.

"No, Jerry, don't." She shook her head. "I just want

to get out of here." Grabbing her husband's arm, she dragged him toward the outer door. Before leaving, she stopped and turned to Nina. "I hope you have better luck, honey."

"Nice talkin' to ya," Jerry added. He pulled his wife out the door, slamming it shut.

Well, that scenario was interesting. Nina glanced at her watch. Five forty-five. Where was Morry? Perhaps, he didn't know she was here. He could pop his head out the door to check, couldn't he? She waited, tapping her fingers on the chair's chrome arm.

Finally, the door opened, and Morry appeared. His eyes widened. "Nina, you're here already."

She was tempted to say she'd waited for twenty-five minutes but didn't want to begin the interview on a negative note. Instead, she offered a tight smile. "Hello, Morry."

"Come on in." Elbowing the door farther, he stood aside and waved her through.

As she passed him, a whiff of spicy aftershave mixed with tobacco drifted past her nose.

His desk filled most of the small room. The desktop displayed only a green blotter, a pen in a holder, a glass paperweight, and an empty In and Out basket. A nearby table supported a computer and a printer. In one corner, a brown jacket hung on a coat rack.

Morry waved at a straight chair across from his desk. "Sit down, kid." He lumbered around his desk and plopped into his chair with a thud. "Nice you could come see me."

Nina sat. "I appreciate your making time." The image of the unhappy Martha lingered in her mind.

"Your previous visitor was quite upset because you didn't like her story."

Morry leaned back and clasped both hands over his ample stomach. "The wannabes are so hopeful when they come here. They don't realize many are called but few are chosen." He looked at the ceiling. "Huh. Somebody else said that, but I can't remember who."

Inwardly, Nina rolled her eyes. "The saying is from the Bible, but I don't think Jesus was talking about writers."

Morry waved a hand. "Whatever."

"Was her story really so bad?" Nina hoped pursuing Martha's experience would help her become better acquainted with Morry.

"Not so much the story. The problem is Martha herself. She's not promotable."

"Promotable?" Did he mean he was more interested in appearances than in the quality of the author's work?

"Her screechy voice hurt my ears." Frowning, he covered his ears with both hands. "She's such a scrawny little thing." Morry lowered his arms and leaned forward. "You see, Nina, a publisher doesn't buy just words on a page, he buys the person who wrote them, too. Publishing a book is a package deal."

"I understand. But maybe a makeover like Zelma had would improve Martha, too."

Morry shook his head. "Nah. Zelma had raw material to work with but just let herself go. Underneath all the mess is a pret-ty classy lady."

Nina gazed around the room, noting little evidence Morry was a literary agent. Wouldn't he at least display jackets of some of the books he'd sold? "Martha's husband showed me your newspaper ad that states you represent a lot of best-selling writers. Who are some of them?"

"Why, Zelma, of course." Morry looked at the ceiling again. "As for the others, I can't say. Clients are confidential, unless they give me permission to release their names. Most want to maintain their privacy."

Nina shifted in her seat. "How did you become an agent?"

Morry pursed his lips. "I thought we were meeting to talk about Zelma."

"We are, but I'm curious about your background. However, if you'd rather not talk about yourself…"

He held up a hand. "No reason why I can't. I worked for a small publishing house in Oregon. They publish mostly regional books, like hiking and fishing guides. Small potatoes stuff."

"Were you a writer?" Somehow, she couldn't imagine Morry sitting at a computer turning out manuscripts, but she wanted to make sure.

"Me, a writer?" Shaking his head, he thumbed his chest. "No, I was on the sales end. Selling is what I'm good at. But I wasn't making enough money. I read about how much literary agents make with big commercial books. That's for me, I said. So, I came to Seattle to try my hand at agenting."

"But aren't most literary agents located in New York?"

"A lot of 'em are. I'm movin' there as soon as Zelma's tour gets underway. She's my ticket outa here." He gestured toward the door. "Once her book hits the bestseller lists, I'll pick and choose my authors. No more bothering with the likes of Martha Potts. No, siree."

What would Morry say if he knew his setup with Zelma could collapse at any moment? If her plagiarism became public knowledge, her book would be derided rather than admired. She might be sued, as well. But Morry seemed blissfully unaware, and Nina wouldn't burst his bubble.

"Reading manuscripts must take a lot of your time."

Morry snorted. "I don't read 'em all the way through. First, I read the author's bio. If that looks good, then I go to the manuscript. Even then, I only read a coupla pages then skim the synopsis. I can tell early on whether or not a book's got commercial potential. But, hey, how about we go for a drink? Today's Friday, and it's been a helluva week. You wouldn't believe how many answers I've had to my Star Search ad. Phone's been ringing all day." He pushed back his chair.

"Well..." Nina wasn't sure she wanted to move their meeting to a bar. Still, she hadn't learned anything about Wildeen, and spending more time with him might yield useful information.

"Come on," Morry urged. "We haven't talked about the murder yet. I want to hear what you know about it, but I sure as hell don't wanna sit in this hot office a minute longer."

Perfect. Morry wanted to discuss the murder, too. "All right." Nina stood. "Do you have a specific place in mind?"

Morry lurched to his feet. Shuffling to the corner coat rack, he grabbed his jacket and slung it over his shoulder. "I know a bar you'll like. Only a coupla blocks away, and we can walk. Full of singles and with lots of action."

Certain she wasn't interested in the type of action Morry referred to, Nina hid a smile.

The place Morry selected was a tavern called Billy's Leg. Furnished in medieval style, the interior had high-backed, dark wood booths, electric wall sconces, and wood-sculpted coats-of-arms. An alcove in the back housed several pool tables and dartboards. They settled into one of the booths.

A server carrying a tray approached. He was in his twenties, with blond hair pushed straight up from his high forehead. His white apron, worn over jeans and a plaid shirt, hung below his knees. "Hey, Morry."

Morry nodded. "Hi ya, Drake. I'll have a beer, whatever ya got on tap." He looked across the table at Nina. "How 'bout you?"

"I'll have a beer, too."

Morry raised his eyebrows. "Funny, I never figured you as a beer drinker. Thought you'd go for one of them fancy drinks with paper umbrellas. They got 'em here. Don'tcha, Drake?" He clasped his hands on the table and looked up at the waiter.

"We certainly do." Drake smiled at Nina.

Nina returned his smile. "Beer is fine."

"You got it." Drake turned to Morry. "By the way, you got a bum tip on the seventh at Longacres yesterday. Abba Babba? Glad I didn't bet on him."

"Don't remind me." Morry scowled and ducked his head.

"Sure, Morry. I'll get ya those beers right away." He turned and headed for the bar.

"So, you like the horses?" Nina settled back in the

booth, taking note of this interesting bit of information.

"Once in a while. What do you think of this place?" Morry waved at their surroundings.

Nina gazed around. "The décor is interesting. But what a strange name for a tavern."

"I know the story. Billy, the guy who owns the place, is behind the bar." He nodded to a dark-haired man mixing drinks. "He was a movie actor, until a freak explosion on the set cost him his leg. Lost his career, too. But a lawsuit got him big bucks. He bought this place and named it Billy's Leg. Clever, huh?"

Nina smiled and nodded. "Very."

Their drinks arrived, bubbles rising to the top of tall mugs.

Morry raised his glass. "Here's to ya."

Nina clinked her glass against his and drank, enjoying the refreshing taste.

Morry took two big swallows and then leaned back and grinned. "Ah, hits the spot." He sobered and studied her. "So, whadja find out about Wildeen's murder? I was real pleased to hear you're helping Zelma."

"Nothing conclusive yet. I was hoping you know something that will help."

He blinked, his eyes going wide. "Me? Why would I?"

"You were at the Bottses' party. You saw the tension between Wildeen and Zelma, didn't you?"

"Tension? No kidding? What about?" Morry took another swig of beer and smacked his lips.

Was he being evasive? "Wildeen was jealous of Zelma's success."

"Oh, yeah." He nodded. "Zelma mentioned

Wildeen's problem."

Nina sipped her beer. "Wildeen was a writer, too, of poetry and literary essays."

He raised his eyebrows. "Is that so?"

"Why, yes. I thought perhaps she contacted you about representing her." Nina recalled Wildeen mentioning she wanted to find an agent.

Morry pulled his napkin from under his glass and folded it into accordion pleats. "Nope. I'm not interested in literary stuff, anyway. Commercial fiction's where the big money is."

"So you indicated earlier. But, did you hear or see anything the night of the Bottsses' party that might be helpful?" She studied him, watching for a change in his expression, hoping to gain something useful from their conversation.

"Can't say I did."

Nina sat back and gave an inward sigh. So far, her questions hadn't yielded any significant information. Still, she was determined to press on. "Do you have any theories about who did kill Wildeen?"

"Yeah, I do." Morry leaned across the table and narrowed his eyes. "I think the murderer was Wildeen's husband's gal. What's her name? Muffy?"

"Patti." Nina hadn't expected her to be Morry's pick as a suspect.

"Whatever. Yeah, she's the one. Talk about jealous." He rolled his eyes. "Know what? I bet Josh and Wildeen still had something going for each other. You know." He wiggled his eyebrows.

She'd often thought the same. "Maybe they did. But Josh and Patti said they were together after the party."

Morry drained his glass and then pointed to Nina's half-full glass. "You want another?"

"I'm good." Nina shook her head.

Carrying a tray aloft, Drake passed their table.

Morry waved and pointed to his mug. "Hit me again, buddy."

Drake gave a salute. "You got it."

Morry turned back to Nina. "Yeah, sure, Josh and Patti were together. They could be lying, ya know."

"Do you mind telling me where you were that night after the party?"

"No problem. Sondra and I had a little after-the-party party at the Harbor Bar and Grill." He gave an exaggerated wink. "You can ask her. She'll back me up."

"I have spoken with her, and she told me you were together." Nina was disappointed to learn two of her suspects had alibis.

"Good ol' Sondra. She's a peach. Helluva good publicity gal, too. Between her and me, Zelma's cookin'."

Drake delivered Morry's beer.

Morry took a long swallow, set down the glass, and turned in the direction of the pool tables and dartboards. "I gotta have some action. I've been sittin' on my ass all day, talkin' to the wannabes and scannin' manuscripts." He swiveled and tilted his head. "Don't suppose you play pool."

"As a matter of fact, I do." She couldn't be Jessica Bingham's granddaughter without knowing how to play pool.

His jaw dropped. "You're kiddin'. A librarian who plays pool. Hah."

Nina straightened and lifted her chin. "What's so funny? Just what is your idea of a librarian, Morry?"

"Oh, someone who has her nose in a book all the time. Someone who says 'Shhh' a lot." Grinning, he put a finger to his lips.

Nina gritted her teeth. Encountering a person who still held the stereotypical idea of a librarian always annoyed her. "You need to change your old-fashioned view of our profession. If you want to play pool, I'll stand you to a game."

He slapped his palm on the table. "You're on, lady."

In the alcove, after they claimed a table and chose their cue sticks, Nina made the break. She hit square, and with a hearty crack the balls popped loose and scattered about the table. However, she missed pocketing her first shot.

Morry sent her a sly grin and pocketed his target ball. He then dispensed with two more balls before missing a shot.

Taking a deep breath, Nina rolled her shoulders, and with her next attempt, her accuracy improved and the ball disappeared into the pocket. Her score leaped ahead, and she eventually sent the eight ball into the corner pocket, winning the game.

Morry frowned. "We'll play another."

Nina headed for the cue stick rack. "No, Morry, I really must go."

"Hey, give me a chance to win one, can'tcha?"

"Oh, all right." Nina returned to the table.

He won the next game.

Expecting success to finally satisfy his ego, she again approached the cue rack.

Morry waved his cue stick. "Aw, come on, you can't leave now. What'sa matter? 'Fraid I'll win again?"

His arrogant tone grated, and she heard herself saying, "You're on." Nina won the third game. "I really do have to leave now." She made her tone firm. "Thanks for the beer."

"Sure, sure. I was off my game tonight. Next time, I'll show ya some real pool playing."

Nina was tempted to say she doubted "a next time" would ever occur but kept the remark to herself. She left the bar, glad to have met with Morry but wondering if anything she had learned would help her investigation.

Chapter Fifteen

"Want to go all the way around the lake?" Stephen asked Nina.

Nina studied the path ahead where morning sunshine turned the gray asphalt to silver. "Even though I'm used to walking, three miles sounds like a long hike."

"Okay, we'll go as far as you like. We can stop and rest along the way."

Stephen had phoned her the night before, after she returned from her meeting with Morry, to ask if they could get together the following day. "I want to visit someplace new," he'd said, "and hope you'll be my tour guide."

Since she knew he'd already explored Richmond's two parks, Nina suggested Green Lake, a popular retreat near downtown Seattle. Today was perfect for an outing, with the temperature in the mid-seventies and the sky clear. The blue-green water shimmered in the sunlight. Cattails waved in the breeze, and red and white wildflowers lined the shore.

As they continued their stroll, she finished telling him about her visit with Morry. "I can't see Morry as the killer. He certainly wouldn't want to see Zelma implicated. According to him, she's his 'ticket out of here to New York.'"

Stephen brushed windblown hair from his

forehead. "He sounds like a very ambitious person. How sincere is he about being an agent, do you think?"

"Quite sincere, as long as he represents best-selling manuscripts." Nina tightened the scarf she'd worn around her neck. "Nothing wrong with that approach, but I felt sorry for poor Martha. I can imagine how a writer feels when her work is ignored or passed off as unworthy."

"She could always self-publish. These days, authors don't have to rely on agents or publishers to see their work in print."

"True. Maybe she will. I hope she finds success. I'd love to see her prove Morry wrong. Oh, look at the ducks. Aren't they cute?" Nina pointed to a pair of ducks gliding along the water amid the cattails.

"Want to take a break and watch them for a while? I see a place to sit." He nodded toward a wooden bench near the shore.

"Sure." Resting sounded like a good idea.

Stephen grasped her hand and guided her off the path to the bench.

She sat and, with a sigh, leaned back.

He settled next to her, stretching his arm around her shoulder.

Talk and laughter from the path, along with an occasional honk from the ducks, drifted their way, and the sweet scent of the wildflowers filled the air. After her long work week, relaxing in the out-of-doors felt refreshing.

"The lake's a beautiful place," he said after a while. "Good choice for our outing."

"Glad you like it. When I was in high school, my friends and I came here to roller skate."

"We passed a group of skaters awhile ago. Maybe we'll skate next time, huh?"

"Maybe." But how long would their association continue? Wildeen's tragic death brought them together, but once the killer was caught... "Have you learned anything that might be helpful in Wildeen's murder?"

"I'm still checking our list of suspects." Stephen shifted to face her. "Also, I spoke with Dorothy Quinn and learned that on Burgess's recommendation, she turned her financial matters over to Josh. Her husband managed their investments, but since he passed away, she hasn't known what to do. We might be on to Josh's scam."

Nina watched the ducks swim in and out of the cattails, leaving ripples in their wakes. "We still need solid proof." She heaved a sigh. "I've questioned everyone I can think of and the only clue I've uncovered—besides the possibility of Josh's scam—is Zelma's plagiarism."

"We'll continue to keep our eyes and ears open. One thing I've learned in this business is that you can't hurry the answers."

They ended their walk at a frozen yogurt stand across the street from the lake. Perched on stools at the outdoor counter, they ate cones filled with strawberry yogurt while watching the passing parade of people.

"What are you doing tomorrow?" Stephen asked after awhile.

Nina finished a bite of the crunchy cone. "On Sundays, I usually visit my grandmother who lives at Marley Manor."

"The retirement home. I know the place. Sounds

like a nice way to spend a Sunday." He slanted her a glance.

She met his gaze with a raised eyebrow. "Are you angling for an invitation?"

"Maybe."

Stephen's eyes sparkled

Nina planted a hand on her hip. "Come on, Stephen, visiting an old folks' home can't be your idea of fun any day of the week."

"I'd like to meet your grandmother. Family is important." He placed a hand on her arm. "Although I don't see my sister often, we were close when we were growing up. As I've told you, I was always sorry my wife, Carly, and I didn't have children before she passed away."

Family. Children. Difficult subjects even to think about, much less to discuss. Still, she hadn't the heart to refuse him. "All right, you're welcome to come along. I'm sure Gran would like to meet you, too."

Nina needn't have worried about Stephen and Jessica meeting because the two immediately took to each other. They ate lunch in the dining room and then strolled the grounds, where Jessica proudly showed off the ripening blueberries in her section of the residents' garden. The afternoon ended with a game of pool in the basement recreation room.

"I'm making progress," Stephen said later when he walked Nina to her front door. "I didn't hear one complaint all weekend about my being an outsider." Then his eyes narrowed. "Oh oh, I probably shouldn't have brought up the subject."

Tipping back her head, Nina laughed. "Don't worry, I won't spoil our weekend. I had a good time."

"I enjoyed myself, too." He leaned forward and, with only their lips touching, kissed her. Then Stephen put his arms around her waist and pulled her close.

Hesitant at first, she finally placed her hands on his shoulders and then around his neck.

"Nice," he whispered when the kiss finally ended. "But are we moving too fast? I don't want to scare you away now."

"I don't know if we are or not. But I sure did want you to kiss me."

He laughed. "I am making progress. On that high note, I'd better leave."

Long after she went to bed, Nina stayed awake, worrying about her and Stephen's relationship. Including him in her visit to her grandmother had made her feel close. But were they traveling a dangerous path that would end up hurting them both?

****

For the next couple of weeks, Nina concentrated on her work at the library. However, when Stephen called and suggested they spend the Fourth of July together, she agreed. They attended the parade in downtown Richmond, followed by a barbecue at his house with his employees and other friends. The enjoyable day ended with fireworks set off from a barge in the sound.

Zelma's problem continued to nag, but Nina didn't phone or text, and neither did Zelma contact her. Nina figured she was still angry. Maybe she didn't even consider her a friend anymore.

Sondra Wagner came to the library to discuss her suggestions for the library book sale. To Nina's surprise, Sondra's ideas appealed. "I'll run these suggestions by the staff at our next meeting," she told her.

"Great. Let me know which ones you prefer." Sondra tucked her papers into her briefcase. "By the way, have you talked to Zelma lately?"

Nina put her copies of the plans in a file folder. "No, I haven't."

Sondra wrinkled her brow. "What's wrong between you two? I thought you were best friends."

Not wanting to reveal Zelma's plagiarism, Nina carefully phrased her reply. "We've both been busy. I'm planning our sale, and Zelma's writing another book."

"Are you still investigating? Or have you given up?"

Was it only her imagination, or did she see a hopeful gleam in Sondra's eye? "I'm not abandoning Zelma." Nina pressed her lips together and shook her head. "Not by any means."

Sondra seemed inordinately interested in Nina's investigation into Wildeen's murder. Was curiosity part of her nature, or did she have an ulterior motive?

****

At Monday's staff meeting, Nina presented Sondra's ideas for the book sale publicity. Predictably, Larry's response was a disdainful sniff.

"Have a parade and turn our sale into a circus?" He picked up the coffee carafe and refilled his cup. "I don't think so."

"You want those new reference books, don't you?" Arlette held out the plate of homemade cookies she'd brought. "Here, have a treat. Might put you in a better mood."

"I doubt that, but thanks, Arlette. Yes, of course, I

want the reference books." Larry took a couple cookies and passed the plate to Myo.

Myo transferred a cookie to her napkin. "We do have a lot on our wish list. If we increased our donations and our sales, maybe we all could have what we asked for."

Nina turned to Holly. "What do you think, Holly?"

"Huh?" Holly jolted and looked at Nina.

"About having a parade to publicize our book sale." Nina strove to keep her tone patient. At least, Holly hadn't brought her cell phone to the meeting.

A smile lit the young woman's face. "I love a parade. We could dress up. I have a clown suit."

Larry snorted. "See what I mean about a circus?"

"Oh. I just thought—" She ducked her head.

Nina frowned at Larry and then turned back to Holly. "Thank you for your suggestion. I'm adding it to my notes." She dutifully wrote on her yellow pad.

"Where will we get the money to pay Ms. Wagner?" Larry asked.

"We have money in the discretionary fund," Nina assured him.

A vote on the ideas resulted in the decision to award gift cards and goodie baskets for the most books donated. However, deciding exactly what should go in the baskets brought more dissention. With time running out, Nina finally told them to give the matter more thought and to bring a list of suggestions to the next staff meeting.

On Tuesday, Nina conducted the children's weekly story hour, which she always enjoyed. After seating the children in the story pit, she looked up to see Stephen standing nearby. Frowning, she joined him. "What are you doing here? If you need to do research, Larry can help you." She nodded to Larry sitting at the information desk.

He shook his head and gestured to the children. "I came for the story."

A grown man for a kids' story? She raised her eyebrows. "Are you serious?"

"I am. Will my being in the audience make you nervous?"

"Not at all. You can join the parents." She gestured to the adults sitting in chairs behind the story pit. Despite what she'd told Stephen, when she opened the picture book and began reading, she noticed her hand shook a little. However, she soon lost herself in the story and forgot about him.

"You're good," he said after story hour was over. "But, then, I knew you would be."

Stephen decided to do research after all, and when Nina's shift ended, they left together. At his suggestion, they went to the deli for sandwiches and soup. Afterward, they strolled Main Street. Finally, he drove her home. He walked her to her front door and grasped both her hands. "I had a good time tonight, Nina."

"Me, too. The evening has been fun."

"Tomorrow's your day off, right? How about racquetball at the club?"

She smiled and shook her head. "Still trying to make me an athlete?"

"Among other things." He leaned closer.

His suddenly serious tone set off an alarm. She looked away. "Um, maybe we're seeing too much of each other…"

He brushed a thumb over her cheek. "Not as far as

I'm concerned."

Debating, Nina bit her lip. Finally, she took a deep breath. "All right… I'll meet you at the club."

A few minutes later, she watched him climb into his car and drive away. Was she entering into a relationship she'd ultimately regret? Or one for which she'd be thankful?

****

The following day at the athletic club, Nina hummed a tune as she went down the hall to the ladies' locker room. She hadn't won today's racquetball game, but she was improving. Plus, she thoroughly enjoyed herself. Now, to shower and then meet Stephen in the lounge for drinks and snacks.

Stepping from the shower, Nina saw Patti Hamilton sink onto a bench and bury her head in her hands. Considering her hostile attitude on previous occasions, Nina hesitated to speak. Still, the young woman's apparent distress prompted her sympathy. She finished dressing, picked up her racquet and tote, and approached Patti. "Can I help?"

Patti looked up, and her lips twisted. "Oh, it's *you*." She pulled a tissue from her tunic pocket and wiped her eyes. "I'm sorry, I—I didn't mean to be rude. But, no, you can't help. I just haven't felt well lately."

"You do look a little pale." Nina nodded to Patti's reflection in the mirror. "Can you leave now and go home?"

"Home." Patti's shoulders slumped "No, I don't want to go there."

"How about resting somewhere here for a while?"

"The employee's lounge has a sofa, but I don't want my co-workers to see me. Bad enough they might find me here." She glanced around. "I didn't plan to stay more than a minute or two."

Nina sat on the bench beside Patti. "If you don't want to go home, you could come to my condo."

"That offer is kind, Nina, but I'll be all right." She took a deep breath and straightened her shoulders.

"If you're sure—"

Patti smiled. "You don't have to stay with me. Stephen must be waiting. I saw the two of you playing racquetball. He's such a nice man. You're lucky to have caught his interest."

"He is a good person. But Josh is, too...isn't he?"

"I thought so." She heaved a sigh.

Her attitude was quite different from the night of the Bottses' party when she hung on his arm and defended him to Wildeen. Nina waited, hoping she would continue. She didn't, and although Nina wanted to hear more, she didn't want to further upset Patti. "I'll leave now. You take care."

Patti nodded. "I will."

Nina picked up her tote and racquet and headed for the door.

"Nina, wait."

She turned to see Patti reaching out. "Can I help, after all?"

"Are you still investigating Wildeen's murder?"

Startled by the unexpected question, Nina frowned. "I am, but I'm not having much luck. Why?"

Patti looked down and twisted her fingers together. "Oh, nothing. I just wondered."

A few minutes later in the club's lounge, over glasses of wine and a plate of nachos, Nina related the incident to Stephen. "I wonder if Patti's distress has to do with Josh and his clients."

Stephen finished eating a nacho. "Patti may have the proof we need to expose Josh as a cheater and possibly as a murderer, too. If only she'd tell us what she knows. You made progress with her today. Talking again might help her to open up."

Nina nodded and sipped her wine. "I'll look for an opportunity to reach out. I just hope nothing disastrous happens first."

****

On Friday, while Nina was at work at the library, Stephen called. "I have some bad news."

Her heart skipped a beat. "What?"

"My source at the police station tells me Russell is close to arresting Zelma for Wildeen's murder."

"Oh, no." The news hit her like a punch in the stomach. "Do you think Zelma knows? Even though she's angry with me, maybe I should call her."

"Okay, but don't mention you've heard the news. Wait and see what she says."

As soon as her break rolled around, Nina went into her office, closed the door, and phoned Zelma.

"I don't want to talk to you," Zelma said. "Do you know I'm about to be arrested? When something bad happens, I usually say, 'Just use the experience as grist for the mill.' But I can't make that statement this time."

Zelma's distressed tone roused Nina's sympathy. "I'm so sorry…"

"Sorry?" Zelma screeched. "Sorry doesn't help. I'm glad for my real friends, Sondra and Morry. They'll stand by me. They offered to contribute to my bail. Even Bob said he'd chip in. Still, I'll have to use my advance money *and* mortgage my house. To say nothing of lawyer fees. Do you know how much lawyers cost?"

Nina pressed a hand to her forehead. "I wouldn't worry about the charges now—"

"You wouldn't, huh? Well, you're not in my situation, are you? I'm in this horrible mess, thanks to you. I hope you're satisfied, Nina. And don't ever call me again!"

That evening, sitting in a booth at the Hot Spot Café and eating halibut and chips, Nina related the conversation to Stephen. "I feel awful," she told him. "Why can't Zelma understand I did what I had to do? Her copying another author's work is not my fault. Nor is Wildeen's jealousy."

Stephen dipped a French fry into a pool of catsup. "Of course not. Zelma refuses to take responsibility. I'd say, don't let her anger upset you, but that advice wouldn't be realistic. Go ahead and get upset."

Glad for his understanding, she grinned. "What should I do? Throw things?"

"Why don't you direct your energy into discovering the real murderer? Or maybe now you think Zelma really is the killer?"

Nina sat back against the booth and heaved a deep sigh. "No, despite how badly she treats me, I still believe in her innocence."

"I'll keep digging. One of us will turn up something." He leaned forward. "In the meantime, I need an excuse to see you this weekend."

Nina laid down her fork and touched his arm. "You're good at drumming up excuses, but you don't really need one."

His eyes lighted. "Then we can spend the weekend

together?"

She thought a moment. "All except the nights."

"The nights…yeah, well, I figured that." He chuckled.

Relieved by his understanding, Nina laughed, too, then picked up her fork again and speared a piece of halibut. "What do you have in mind?"

"How about sailing tomorrow? The weatherman promises sunshine."

"Sailing?" She wrinkled her nose. "I don't know a jib from a jab."

"You're a quick study. Look how well you caught on to racquetball." He tilted his head. "Does sailing sound like fun?"

"Actually, it does." In truth, anything with Stephen promised to be enjoyable.

The following day, Stephen drove them to a boat rental on Lake Washington, and soon had them skimming across the rippling waters in a sleek, seventeen-foot sailboat.

Nina pushed Zelma's problems from her mind and concentrated on the tasks at hand. Back at the dock an hour later, they both agreed the outing was a success.

On Sunday, she went to his house for brunch. Nina watched him prepare their shrimp omelet. "I'm curious—are you hoping to impress me, or would you have this menu if you were by yourself?"

Stephen grinned. "Hmmm, I'll have to give your question some thought. But I hope you *are* impressed. I wouldn't want all my efforts to be in vain."

After breakfast, she sat beside him on the sofa while they read the Sunday newspaper. In the afternoon, they visited Jessica, enjoying tea and brownies in her apartment and then a game of pool. Nina found herself more relaxed than she thought she would be upon bringing the two together.

Later, at Nina's front door, Stephen took her in his arms and kissed her.

Nina returned the kiss, savoring the warmth of his body and the strength of his embrace.

At last, Stephen ended the kiss and pulled away. "I'd better leave before I get myself in trouble," he said with a teasing grin.

Nina knew that where he was concerned, she was already headed for trouble. What she didn't know was what to do about the problem.

****

On Monday, Nina had just settled in at the information desk when the phone rang. "Seaview Library. How may I help you?"

"I'd like to speak to Nina Foster, please."

The caller's voice sounded familiar. "This is Nina."

"Nina, this is Patti Hamilton."

Nina straightened and gripped the receiver. "How are you? I hope you're feeling better than the last time I saw you."

"I'm really not, which is why I called. You were so nice to me that day at the club, even though I'd been rude, and, well, I need someone to talk to."

Patti's unexpected announcement caught Nina off guard, but she managed a smooth reply. "Sure. I'm a good listener."

"I need to talk about Wildeen's murder…"

Nina glanced around but saw no one nearby who might overhear. "Go on, I'm listening."

"Not over the phone. Can we get together?"

"Of course." Her heart beat faster. Was Patti's request to meet the break she'd hoped for? "How about Wednesday? My day off."

"I can leave the club early and be at Josh's house at three."

Nina wondered if Josh's house was the best place to meet but decided to go along with Patti's choice. "I'll be there. Now, you take care of yourself."

"I will," Patti promised.

Later, during what had become a nightly phone call with Stephen, Nina told him about Patti's request.

"Good news. I hope you learn something to help Zelma."

"I do, too. I'll call you afterward and let you know."

Nina hung up, excitement surging through her veins. She could hardly wait until Wednesday and her meeting with Patti.

Chapter Sixteen

Wednesday came at last, and after housework and a light lunch, Nina prepared for her trip to Sapphire Hills. She wanted to be on time or even early, as was her habit. But before she left, Milt Forester, the condo manager, stopped by to discuss an incident of the previous night when the security gate floodlights were shattered.

"Some of the other residents want more security," he told Nina. "What do you think?"

The image of the mysterious car parked across the street from her unit popped into her mind, and a shiver rippled down her spine. "I agree, but do you know who knocked out the lights?"

Milt ran a hand through his gray hair. "Eva Miller saw a gang of teenagers on the street when she was comin' home from the movies, but we can't prove they were responsible."

Nina raised her eyebrows. "A teenaged gang? In Richmond?"

"I don't know if 'gang' is the right term." Milt shrugged. "But a bunch of kids was roaming around."

Nina gripped her car keys. "I'd like to think the town's parents have their children under control, but if not, then we need more security."

Milt nodded. "We'll meet soon to decide exactly what to do."

Finally, Nina was on her way to Sapphire Hills, but when she reached the subdivision's entrance, the time was already three o'clock. She rounded the marble boy and his dolphin, swung to the left, and drove up a winding road, only to find herself in the wrong cul-de-sac. Her stomach tensed. Now, she would be even later. Keeping one eye on her dashboard GPS—which she should have done in the first place—she backtracked to where she'd made the wrong turn and corrected her route. Finally, she found the street leading to Josh's rambler.

Not a soul was in sight, and the street had the silence of a ghost town. Nina parked at the curb in front of the house. As she stepped along the circular stones to the front door, she heard a motor running and smelled car exhaust. Wrinkling her nose, she stopped and turned toward the garage. The engine rumble definitely came from within, and smoke curled from beneath the doors. Nina gasped. She could think of only one reason why a car would run inside a closed garage, and it wasn't a happy one.

Pulse pounding, she ran across the grass to the garage. She tugged on all three door handles but none yielded. The doors must be locked from the inside. She hurried to the fence enclosing the back yard. She shoved open the gate and dashed across the grass to the garage's back door. The doorknob wouldn't give. Grabbing a rock from a flowerbed, she hurled it through the window. The sound of shattering glass pierced the air, and smoke billowed out the jagged hole.

Tossing her shoulder purse on the ground, she tore off her jacket and held it over her nose and mouth. Careful not to cut herself, she reached inside the broken window, located and turned the lock, and then withdrew her arm and turned the doorknob. The door popped open. More exhaust rolled out.

Keeping the jacket over her face, she ran into the garage. The outline of a white sports car appeared. Stumbling toward the car, she peered in the driver's side window, coughing and choking when the noxious air penetrated the jacket. Her eyes watered so badly she could barely make out the person slumped over the wheel. A woman with blonde hair. Patti.

Nina grabbed the door handle. For one horrible moment, she thought the car was locked, but then the handle gave, and the door swung open. Nina grabbed Patti's arm and pulled her from the car. She reached inside and turned the ignition key. The car's engine died. Good. At least, the poisonous exhaust would cease.

Although gasping from lack of breath, she succeeded in dragging Patti from the garage and onto the side yard's grass. Patti wore white shorts, a blue T-shirt, and tennis shoes. Under a tangle of hair, her eyes were closed, her mouth slightly open, and her skin a pale pink.

As Nina knelt beside Patti, she noticed a piece of paper floating along in the smoke. With Patti to attend to, she let the paper go. She pressed her fingers underneath the woman's chin, felt a pulse, and gave a silent cheer.

Nina grabbed her purse, pulled out her phone, and punched 9-1-1. The call completed, she kept an eye on the steady rise and fall of Patti's chest, to make sure she still breathed. While she waited, she sent up a silent prayer. *Please, God, let Patti live*. At last, the wail of sirens filled the air. Medics burst into the backyard and ran to her and Patti.

Scrambling to her feet, she jumped aside to let them take over. Although she insisted she was all right, one of the medics had her breathe into a small device he called a Breath CO Monitor. Thankfully, she passed the test and would not need treatment for carbon monoxide poisoning.

Another officer led her to the lawn chairs by the swimming pool where they sat while he questioned her. He wanted to know all sorts of details, such as when she arrived and whether she'd seen anyone else at the home or around the property.

Haltingly, she related how she found Patti unconscious in the garage. When she finished, she leaned back and gazed around. Several medics placed Patti on a gurney. A policeman guarded the gate where Nina entered. The gate opened, and another policeman stepped in. Behind him was Stephen. The sight of him brought a flood of relief. She half rose from her chair, wanting to go to him. She watched while Stephen spoke to the man he'd entered with, gesturing toward her as he talked.

Finally, the policeman nodded.

Stephen stepped to an area near the gate and beckoned to Nina.

"Okay if I join my friend?" she asked the officer who'd been questioning her.

He looked up from his clipboard. "Okay, we're through here. Just stay out of the way."

Glad to have someone to rely on in this crisis, Nina ran to Stephen and fell into his embrace. "They let you in."

Linda Hope Lee

"Mac's a buddy. I told him I needed to be with you and take you home when you're okay to go. Are you all right?"

"I am, but Patti—I—I found her in the garage." Nina choked back a sob.

"Is she still alive?" Stephen nodded to where the medics wheeled the gurney toward the gate.

"I hope so. She was breathing when I found her." Nina pressed a shaky hand to her forehead.

"How about you?" He drew back and studied her. "Are you sure you're okay? Maybe you should go to the hospital, too."

The concern in his voice touched Nina, but she shook her head. "One of the medics gave me a test for carbon monoxide. I passed just fine."

"Then I'll take you home." He shifted and grasped her shoulders.

"But Patti—" Nina swallowed against the lump in her throat.

"She's being taken care of. You've done all you can, Nina." Keeping an arm around her waist, he led her toward the gate.

Nina spotted a piece of paper half-hidden under a bush and put out a hand. "Wait, Stephen. See that paper? It looks like the one I saw drift from the garage when I rescued Patti. I let it go then because I was more concerned about her. But it might be important."

Stephen left her side long enough to retrieve the paper. "It's a typewritten note." He read the message aloud:

"'I killed Wildeen Bergman because she wouldn't give Josh a divorce. God forgive me for what I've done. Patti Hamilton.'"

208

Shock rippled through Nina, staggering her footsteps. "Patti killed Wildeen?" Could her confession be true? Had Wildeen's murderer been discovered at last?

"We need to give this message to the police." Stephen waved to one of the officers.

The tall man joined them.

Nina explained seeing the slip of paper float from the garage.

He took her statement and the paper, securing it in a plastic evidence bag, and then told them they could leave.

Outside the gate, Stephen led Nina to his SUV. "I'll have a couple of my employees drive your car to your condo later. Right now, you're coming with me."

Gratitude filled Nina. "Thank you, Stephen."

Once they were underway, she soon realized they were headed not for her home but for his. However, she was too tired and upset to argue. At his house, he took her upstairs to a bedroom overlooking the sound and tucked her into a king-size bed. Nina barely closed her eyes before she fell asleep. Sometime later, delicious aromas drifting up from downstairs nudged her awake.

Stephen stood, looking down at her. "I must say, this wasn't exactly the way I'd planned to get you in my bed."

At his sly grin, Nina sat up and mustered a smile. "Being in your bed under any circumstances wasn't in my plans, either." Then she sobered. "But what about Patti? Have you heard anything?"

"She's alive but in a coma. They sent her by helicopter to a hospital in Seattle for special treatment."

"A coma?" Nina's throat tightened. "Will she

survive?"

Stephen shrugged. "At this point, no one knows. Even if she does, she could be left with complications."

Tears sprang to her eyes, and Nina covered her face with her hands. "Oh, I'm so sorry. If only I'd arrived on time…" She told Stephen about her talk with the condo manager and taking the wrong turn in Sapphire Hills.

He sat on the bed and put an arm around her shoulders. "Don't blame yourself. You didn't know she planned to commit suicide." He gestured toward the doorway. "I've made dinner. You'll feel better after you eat. Can you come downstairs? Or should I bring the food here?"

Nina tossed back the covers. "I'll come down. Just let me freshen up."

"Sure. I put fresh towels for you in the bathroom."

A few minutes later, with her face washed and hair combed, Nina walked downstairs. Stephen had prepared a beef and vegetable stew, toasted cheese bread, and a tossed salad. He was right—she did feel better after eating. They carried their coffee into the living room.

He settled her on the sofa, put on a classical music CD, and then sat beside her. Slipping an arm around her shoulders, he drew her close.

With a soft sigh, she laid her head on his shoulder. Outside, the twilight faded into darkness. Boats passing by switched on their running lights, and overhead, stars popped out. "Being here is just what I needed," she said after a while. "But I should go home."

Stephen gave her shoulder a squeeze. "Why not stay here? The guest room isn't fixed up yet, but you can have my bed, and I'll bunk here on the sofa."

Nina tensed. Tempting as his offer was, even under the conditions he proposed, she wasn't ready for an overnighter. "Thanks, but I need to go home. When I get up tomorrow morning, I'll need to get ready for work."

Several moments passed. Wondering if he would press the issue, she held her breath. If he did, she might change her mind and accept. She wanted to. At least, a part of her did.

Finally, he withdrew his arm and edged away. "Okay, Nina, I'll take you home."

His sad tone made her feel guilty, and she laid a hand on his arm. "Please know I appreciate all you've done tonight."

He gave her a soft smile and covered her hand with his. "I know you do, but tonight isn't the time for heavy discussions. Best we get you home."

As Stephen had promised, at Viewmont Estates, Nina's car was parked outside the gate. He drove her car into the garage and then accompanied her to her front door. Taking the key from her hand, he slipped it into the lock.

"You're spoiling me," she said.

He brushed a thumb along her cheek. "I want to take care of you. Are you sure you'll be all right here alone?"

Despite her fatigue, she nodded. "I'll be fine."

He leaned close and kissed her cheek. "Goodnight, Nina. I'll talk to you tomorrow."

From her front window, she watched him drive away, so thankful he was at the Lorings to help her through the awful experience. Her thoughts turned to Patti. Would she recover? Had she really been responsible for Wildeen's death? So many questions yet to be answered.

****

A night's sleep restored Nina's strength but not her spirits. Over breakfast, self-reproach continued to plague her. What if she hadn't stopped to talk to the condo manager? What if she hadn't become lost on the way to Josh's? Would she have arrived in time to prevent what happened to Patti?

The biggest question, though, was why Patti chose to commit suicide before seeing Nina. She specifically asked Nina to visit. Why, then, had she attempted to kill herself before they were scheduled to meet?

Perhaps she changed her mind about wanting to confide. Then another thought occurred. What if Patti hadn't attempted suicide at all, and instead someone set the scene to appear she'd taken her own life? The idea that she might have been only moments away from confronting the person sent chills rippling down Nina's spine.

Nina called the hospital that Stephen named yesterday, but, as she had expected, was told only that, yes, Patti Hamilton was a patient. Well, at least she knew Patti was still alive.

At the library, her staff gathered around. They heard the news and wanted to know the details. She told them only that she and Patti became acquainted at the athletic club and Patti invited her to the Loring home for a visit.

Nina expected a summons to the police station to talk to Pete Russell. Instead, Russell came to the library. Appreciating his gesture, she counted on being more relaxed and in control on her own territory than at the station.

When he arrived, she led him to her office and motioned him to a seat.

Russell shook his head and remained standing. Propping his hands on his hips, he looked around. "Cozy office you have here."

"I like it." She sat behind her desk and followed his gaze to the bookshelves lining the walls. "Never enough room for all the books, though. Do you read much? I mean, besides for your work?"

"Don't have much time, but when I do, I usually choose a true crime story. No surprise there, huh?" He grinned and from his jacket pocket pulled out a small notebook and a pen. "But, to get down to business, I want to review what happened yesterday at Josh Loring's. Why were you there?" Narrowing his gaze, he raised a hand. "I know, you're about to tell me to read the statement you gave yesterday to the officers at the scene. I did. But I want to hear what happened straight from you. You might have thought of something else since then."

At the thought of reliving yesterday's horrible experience, Nina felt her stomach tense. Nevertheless, she took a deep breath and started with her recent encounter with Patti at the athletic club and moved on to Patti's subsequent phone call asking for a visit, and their arrangement to meet at Josh's.

Russell made a few notes and then looked up. "Did she say what she wanted to discuss?"

Nina hesitated, certain her answer would upset him but also knowing she must be truthful. "She, ah, wanted to talk about Wildeen's murder."

He stopped and stared. "Now, why would she want

to talk to *you* about the crime?"

Guilt over intruding into police business nudged her, but she pushed away the feeling and lifted her chin. "I'm looking into the murder. For Zelma."

He frowned and waved his pen. "Do you mean to tell me you've been running around town playing amateur detective?"

She met his glare with a steady look. "I'm surprised you didn't already know. Everyone else in town knows. But I haven't said anything about being a detective. I've merely made inquiries here and there."

"Look, take my advice and let us catch the bad guys." He thumbed his chest.

Nina smiled sweetly. "Of course, and if I hear anything I think you might find useful, I'll be sure to let you know."

Russell pointed to his notebook. "Let's get back to Patti."

Once again, while struggling to calm the rising tide of emotions, she explained the details about finding Patti in the garage and dragging her into the yard. "Is the suicide note authentic?"

"Do you know any reason why it shouldn't be?" He tilted his head and narrowed his eyes.

Nina looked away. "No, I don't," she finally said, her voice low. Without proof he was doing anything illegal, she wouldn't reveal her suspicions about Josh. Glancing at Russell, she wondered if he'd sensed her hesitation.

He paced a narrow path and then stopped at her desk. Picking up a blue glass paperweight, he turned it over in his hands. "We're still checking the note for authenticity. Hopefully, she'll come out of the coma, and we can find out exactly what happened."

"So, she's still in a coma. I was wondering. I called the hospital this morning but, of course, they couldn't tell me anything more than confirm she's a patient."

"I'm sure the doctors are doing everything they can for her recovery." He put down the paperweight and looked at his wristwatch. "Oh, oh, gotta go."

Exhaling a sigh of relief, Nina led Russell to the door. "Please let me know if I can do anything else." She opened the door and stood aside.

He stopped and regarded her with a stern look. "Yeah, you can let us do our job, and you stick to yours."

Right. She would do her job as she saw it, which meant continuing her investigation.

****

When Stephen texted Nina asking to come over that evening, she agreed without hesitation. She very much wanted to see him. However, they had barely settled on the living room sofa with their coffee when she answered a call from Josh.

"I didn't want to bother you at work, Nina, but I needed to thank you for rescuing Patti."

His forlorn voice brought a flood of sympathy. "I wish I had arrived earlier. Maybe I could've prevented what happened. I heard she's still in a coma."

"Unfortunately, she is. I was with her most of the day, along with her sister, Melanie, who flew in from L.A. Mel is her only family."

The mention of a sister reminded Nina how little she knew about Patti. "I'm glad Melanie could come. How are you doing?"

"Not so good. Bad enough what happened to

Wildeen. Now, Patti…"

Nina pressed a hand to her stomach. Knowing just what to say in this situation proved difficult. "I'm so sorry, Josh. Do you believe Patti's note and that she killed Wildeen?"

"She was awfully jealous of Wildeen, but to go to the extreme of murdering her? Hard to accept. Still, if she did commit the crime, then I suppose guilt could drive her to take her own life. I've been wondering why you were visiting."

His suspicious tone made Nina hesitate. What could she say without violating Patti's confidence? As always, she'd best stick to the truth. She settled closer to Stephen, hoping to draw strength from his presence. "She asked me to come. I think she wanted to be friends. We got acquainted at the club, you know."

"Yes, but you two are so different. I'd never expect a friendship to develop."

Neither had she, and Patti's request for a visit had been unexpected. "I regret we didn't get a chance to find out. Maybe, hopefully, we still will."

"Thanks, Nina. I'll keep you informed."

When the call ended, Nina set aside her phone and turned to Stephen. "Josh is having a difficult time accepting Patti murdered Wildeen. I still can't believe she would invite me to visit and then kill herself before I arrived."

Stephen rubbed his jaw. "Maybe she didn't attempt suicide and the garage set-up was a cover for murder. The killer didn't know you were scheduled to visit."

Nina leaned against the sofa cushions and folded her arms. "What if Josh murdered Wildeen, and then attempted to kill Patti because she, too, knew about his financial scams? He wants the cops to think Patti killed Wildeen and then herself. Then, both cases will be closed. Josh can keep cheating his clients with no one the wiser. What do you think of that solution?"

"A possible scenario, but who else might not want Josh's dealings to be discovered?"

She tilted her head and mentally reviewed her list of suspects. "Burgess Botts. If Josh is exposed, he will be, too. His share of the rip-offs would be discontinued."

Stephen picked up his coffee cup and took a sip. "Okay. Anyone else?"

"How about Elizabeth Botts? She wouldn't want her husband exposed or to lose the extra income."

"Now, we have three possible suspects." He held up three fingers.

"Yes, which makes discovering the murderer more difficult. Still, Josh seems the most likely person. Maybe his display of grief is just to hide guilt. I wonder if he has an alibi? We need to know if the suicide note was authenticated. Can you find out?"

"I'll do my best. My contact at the police station is usually willing to share information."

She straightened and beamed him a smile. "Oh, Stephen, what would I do without you on my side?"

He scooted close and put an arm around her. "I told you we make a good team. Now, if I could make myself indispensable in a few other ways…"

She laughed. "Let's not go there now. We have too much to deal with without *us* as a complication."

Chapter Seventeen

The following day, Nina sat in her library office writing her column for *The Richmond Review*—or attempting to. She'd planned a series on Art Techniques, chosen to coincide with Richmond's yearly art festival. The column's topic was watercolor. On her desk sat a stack of the library's best books on the subject, plus notes from interviews with several local artists.

However, so far, inspiration eluded her. Wildeen and Patti dominated her thoughts. Nina wanted to get her life back on track, to do her job at the library, and carry on with day-to-day living. But she couldn't put aside the tragedies. The memories lingered, festering like ugly sores, and popped up when she least expected.

Her grandmother lent a sympathetic ear, telling Nina she understood how she felt, but to not blame herself. "I'm worried about you," Jessica said during a recent phone call. "You're too involved. Why not let the police solve the crimes?"

"I know I should, Gran, but I just can't rest until I've done everything I can to help." Even though Zelma wasn't speaking to her, Nina still wanted to prove her innocence.

"Please be careful," Jessica admonished.

"I will," Nina had promised.

She certainly had enough work to keep busy. She

must finalize plans for the book sale, prepare stories for the weekly story hour, attend meetings of various professional groups, process new books, and manage the staff.

Plus, she must write the column for *The Review.* Focusing again on the screen, she read what she'd written and made her brain compose another sentence. Then another. She sighed and looked at her wristwatch. Maybe writing for the newspaper wasn't such a good idea, after all. She wondered if Zelma worked as hard on her novels. According to her, the words just rolled out of her mind and onto the page. Except for her most recent book, of course. The one she had plagiarized. Zelma's indiscretion had created a most puzzling situation.

Nina's phone chimed. A glance at the ID brought a smile to her lips, and she connected the call. "Hello, Stephen."

"Hey. How're you doing?"

"Not so good. I'm writing my column, but I can't stop thinking about Wildeen and Patti."

"You have a couple more days before I need your copy. What I have to tell you might put your mind to rest."

Nina gripped the phone. "Go ahead."

"Patti's note was printed on a printer found in the Loring home. The autopsy turned up traces of a sedative in her blood, consistent with her doctor's prescription for depression. So far, indications are Patti killed Wildeen and then guilt drove her to suicide."

Nina raised a hand. "Wait a minute. What about Josh's and Patti's claims they were together the night of the murder?"

"The police questioned Josh again, and he admitted he and Patti had an argument that night—over Wildeen, as a matter of fact—and they didn't stay together."

Nina shook her head and shifted in her chair. "I still can't believe Patti would kill herself knowing I was on my way to see her."

"Why don't we talk more later? The weekend's coming up, and I'd like to spend the time together."

"I want to be with you, too. My house Saturday, yours Sunday? I love your brunches, and in the afternoon, we can visit Gran, as usual."

"Sounds like a good plan. I'll think of something we can do on Saturday."

Nina hung up, filled with happy anticipation. However, soon her worries about Patti and what had happened returned to plague her. She still refused to believe the attempted suicide theory, but how could she ever prove she was right?

****

When Stephen arrived at her condo the following day, he suggested a ferry ride across the sound to the Olympic Peninsula.

"I'd enjoy a ferry ride," she said. "But rather than drive, let's be walk-ons. The across-sound traffic is heavy on summer weekends, and with a car, we'd wait in line a couple hours. Exploring Kingston on foot—the shops, the restaurants, and the beach—will be easy enough. We won't lack for activities."

Stephen folded the map he'd consulted and tucked it into his jacket pocket. "I made a good choice when I picked you for my tour guide."

Thirty minutes later, Nina stood beside Stephen on the deck of the *Hyak*, watching the dock and the town of Richmond recede into the distance. The sun beamed from a bright blue sky dotted with only a few clouds. Seagulls hovered about the ship's stern, hoping to be tossed a handout. They cawed and flapped their wings as they kept up with the rapidly moving vessel. Farther out, a variety of boats dotted the water, including a tug hauling a load of lumber to Seattle.

Nina leaned against the railing. "I never realized how much fun playing the tourist could be, until I had someone to play with."

He stepped closer and slipped an arm around her waist. "Are you saying you're glad I came into your life?"

She chuckled. "Yes, exactly that." Her gaze met his, and warmth that had nothing to do with the sun overhead filled her.

After debarking at Kingston, Nina and Stephen walked a short distance to the town's business district where they browsed art galleries, antique, and souvenir shops. Then, they chose a restaurant and sat on the deck enjoying glasses of Chablis and crab cake appetizers.

Nina sat back and took a deep breath of fresh air. How easy to forget her worries on a perfect day such as this one.

They made idle conversation for a while, and then Stephen put down his wine glass and leaned forward. "I hate to risk spoiling our relaxing day, but I need to tell you what I've found out since we last spoke."

At his serious tone, she sat straight, ready to listen. "About Wildeen's murder?"

"Right. I've finally finished checking the arrest and criminal records of all the names on your list of suspects. Everyone has a clean record, except one person." He raised his eyebrows.

"Who? Stephen, don't keep me in suspense."

"Wildeen's employee, Hamlet Green. He's been arrested for burglary and drug trafficking."

Nina frowned, unable to recall ever suspecting Hamlet was anything other than Wildeen's loyal employee at the bookstore. "Here in Richmond?"

"No, he's originally from California. He did time in a correctional institution near San Francisco. He goes by a different name now. His legal name is Hamlet Genovich."

"I wonder if Wildeen knew about his past."

Stephen helped himself to another crab cake. "If she didn't when she hired him, maybe she found out later and threatened to fire him, or expose him to the college, or to someone he cares about."

Nina folded her arms. "Would any of those actions be a motive for murder?"

He shrugged. "A guy with a history of violence might be easy to set off."

A memory surfaced, and Nina stiffened. "He was hostile at the bookstore when I questioned him about his whereabouts at the time of Wildeen's murder. But I wouldn't have guessed he was a drug addict and a criminal. What do you think I should do?"

Stephen finished a bite of his crab cake. "What can you do? The police are still responsible for solving the crime. So far, they seem to accept Patti's note and her suicide attempt. If only she'd wake up from her coma…"

Nina pressed her lips together and shook her head. "I keep hoping and praying she will. In the meantime, I have to do something to help bring the case to a conclusion. I just don't know yet what that something is."

He took her hand in his. "Don't forget about me. I'm here to help."

Warmth filled Nina. "You are wonderful, you know that?"

"Thanks. So are you." He leaned over the table and kissed her.

However, even though Stephcn's support comforted her, Nina still needed to decide on her next move. How could she discover the truth?

****

The following day, Nina and Stephen followed their usual routine. However, instead of taking her home after the visit with her grandmother, he suggested they drive to his house to watch the sunset. She agreed, and soon they sat on the sofa facing the window where they could enjoy the view. He put his arm around her, and she rested her head against his shoulder. The sun inched toward the horizon, filling the sky with bands of orange and gold. All too soon, the last rays faded into the darkening sky.

"I want your opinion on something," Stephen said after awhile.

"Okay," she murmured, sleepy now and barely aware of his words.

"Which do you think would be better—to take out the partition between the living and the dining room and make one big space, or to preserve the wall for a more cozy atmosphere?" Stephen gestured toward the partition.

She blinked her eyes to focus. "I've always preferred a separate dining room. The extra wall can be used to position furniture. A sideboard, for example, or a china cabinet."

"Good point. Speaking of furniture, do you prefer the pieces to match? Or different styles tied together with common colors? Never mind." He waved a hand. "Judging by how you've decorated your condo, I know you like furniture to match."

"I do. But, you can choose what you like. Your home should reflect your tastes and personality." Why were they having this conversation, anyway?

"But I don't plan to live here alone. I want to make sure my remodeling will, ah, meet with your approval." He slanted her a glance.

Her stomach knotted, bringing her to full awareness. "Stephen, please don't include me in your plans."

"Nina, you know I want to marry again and have a family…"

She stiffened and held up a hand. "Marriage and children aren't in my future."

Bracing his hand on the back of the sofa, he twisted to face her. "Are you serious?"

His eyes were wide with—what? Incredulity? Horror? "Don't look at me as though I'm some kind of alien." She folded her arms and turned away.

He slid his arm around her shoulder. "I'm sorry. But you can't mean what you just said."

"I certainly do." Nina kept her tone firm. Their relationship had been going well. Why did he have to pressure her for more?

"Which don't you want? Marriage? Or the children part?"

She shook her head and kept her back rigid. "I

don't want either." Her past relationships had all ended in disaster.

"But why, Nina?" He frowned. "You'd make a wonderful mother. I've seen how well you work with children at the library. You have so much to give a child."

His plaintive tone touched a chord, but she held fast to her convictions. "I wouldn't be a good mother."

"Why? At least give me a reason." He grasped her shoulders and gently turned her to face him again. Then he took her hand in both of his.

"I don't know exactly why." She took a deep breath "But my feeling has to do with my father leaving when I was young and my mother hating him for abandoning us. I never experienced being part of a family. I spent a lot of time by myself. Mother was always too preoccupied with her real estate work to pay me much attention."

Stephen knit his brow and studied her. "What about your grandmother? Didn't the three of you function as a family?"

"Not so much." Nina tensed. Talking about her unhappy upbringing was always difficult. "Jessica always blamed Mother for the break-up of her marriage, and sometimes, they were barely on speaking terms. After Mother died, Jessica and I became close."

"Since you never belonged to a family as a child, don't you want to have the experience as an adult?"

She bit her lip and looked away. "The idea of being part of a family scares me to death."

"Are you afraid history will repeat itself?" Stephen brushed back a lock of hair from her forehead.

At his touch, even though gentle, she flinched. "I

don't know, I tell you." Her voice rose. "Quit probing. Talking about my feelings is painful."

"Come here, Nina…" Stephen opened his arms and leaned close.

Avoiding his embrace, Nina scooted away. "Don't, Stephen, please. I see now I've let things between us go too far."

He shook his head. "Not true. Together, we can work out your problems."

"No." She stiffened.

He drew back and folded his arms. "You don't want to solve your problems. You want to keep experiencing the pain, like self-punishment, as though you're to blame."

His accusatory tone stung. Needing to put some distance between them, Nina scooted to the edge of the sofa and stood. "Don't be my psychotherapist. I've been to a few such doctors, and therapy hasn't done much good."

"Because you don't want it to." Stephen stuck out his chin.

"Will you stop challenging me?" She rubbed her throbbing forehead. "Please take me home now."

A few seconds of heavy silence elapsed. Then, without a word, Stephen stood, walked to the hall closet, and pulled out her jacket. He opened the jacket and held it out.

Avoiding his angry gaze, she slipped her arms into the sleeves. Then she snatched up her purse and followed him out of the house to his SUV. On the way to her condo, neither spoke. He focused on driving, and she gazed out the window.

At Viewmont Estates, he punched in the code to

open the gate and drove to her unit. At the front door, he pulled to a stop but left the car engine running. "I'll call you tomorrow."

His flat, distant tone sent a shiver up her arms. In preparation to escape, she gripped the strap of her purse. "Please don't phone, Stephen. Let's end this relationship before we hurt each other any more than we already have."

He turned, his eyes wide. "You can't be serious."

Her stomach churned and tears threatened, but she held his gaze. "I've never been more serious in my life. Good-bye, Stephen." She stepped from the car and headed up the walk to her front door. Sick at heart, she didn't look back.

****

At work the following day, as Nina sat in her office preparing a report for the home office, she couldn't keep her mind from wandering to her breakup with Stephen. Deep down, she'd known for some time he headed in a direction she did not want to go—could not go.

Her attitudes toward marriage and children should be dealt with and, hopefully, healed. But whenever she took a step in that direction, the emotional pain was so great she retreated. Once again, she stuffed the hurt deep inside where she hoped it would hide forever.

Yet, the thought of not seeing Stephen again left a terrible emptiness. No more phone calls and texts, no more adventurous Saturdays and relaxed Sundays. She straightened her shoulders and lifted her chin. She'd gotten along before she met him, and she would survive without him now.

Besides, she had other, more important matters to

consider. She still wasn't satisfied with the police's conclusion Patti attempted suicide. Something other than suicide was on her mind when she asked Nina to visit. What would happen to poor Patti? Would she wake up from the coma? If she did, would she be left with permanent damage?

What would Zelma do, now she was no longer a murder suspect? Would she and Sondra go on their book promotion tour? The police would have no reason to make public Zelma's plagiarism. Now, the only threat to Zelma's reputation was Nina. Would Zelma contact her and beg her to keep her secret?

Despite her preoccupation, Nina finished her report in time to keep her appointment with Sondra Wagner, who came to discuss more ideas for the book sale. After Nina settled on publicity and selected designs for bookmarks and flyers, she casually asked, "Are you and Zelma going on your book tour?"

Sondra smiled and clapped her hands. "We're leaving as soon as we can make all the arrangements. I'm so excited."

Zelma would continue her charade. Well, what she did was none of Nina's concern.

However, Wildeen's death and Patti's comatose condition *were* her concern. Nina must do something about both of those problems.

But what?

Chapter Eighteen

During the following week, Nina finished her column for *The Richmond Review* and emailed the file to Stephen. A few days later, the assistant editor replied the copy had been received and accepted. Nina did not hear from Stephen, nor did she see him around town. Not crossing paths was for the best, though, because meeting would surely be awkward and painful for them both. One day at the library, while Nina unpacked a box of new books, she received a phone call from Josh.

"I've decided to sell the bookstore," he said. "I have no reason to own it any longer. I'm much too busy with my own business to run Wildeen's."

Busy cheating your clients? She was tempted to ask, but bit back the words. "I suppose selling the store is best. Do you have potential buyers?"

"I haven't put the property on the market yet. First, I'll have the inventory assessed. Wildeen's financial records will help decide how much the business is worth, but I want a professional's opinion, too."

Nina set aside the box of books and concentrated on their conversation. "Determining the value sounds like a good idea."

"Would you like to look at the collection first? You might find books for the library or for your personal use."

His offer came as a surprise, and Nina took a

moment to compose her reply. "Why, how kind of you, Josh, but not necessary."

"I know, but you were a good friend to Wildeen. I'm sure she would approve."

At the memory of her friend, Nina smiled. "All right, I'll accept. May I look at the books during the evening? I have a busy schedule during the day."

"Fine by me. Hamlet can give you an extra key, and you can lock up when you finish. I'll let him know you're coming."

Nina hung up, excited about Josh's offer. In addition to selecting books for the library, she now had another chance to inspect Wildeen's office records. Hopefully, she'd find something she overlooked before, which would lead her to the truth.

Eager to begin the project, Nina decided to visit the store the following evening. On her way, she stopped at the Soup and Sandwich Deli and purchased a turkey sandwich and a bottle of lemon soda. She arrived at Bergman Books at five thirty. The store closed at six, which would give her half an hour with Hamlet. Considering what she now knew about his background, she wondered if she should be alone with him after closing. However, to fulfill her promise to Josh, she had no choice.

She found Hamlet shelving books in the fiction section. He wore his usual outfit of black turtleneck, jeans, and boots.

"Josh told me you were coming to pick out books for the library," he said.

Nina smiled and nodded. "I accepted his generous offer. Looks like you'll have a new boss before long."

"More likely, I'll be out of a job." He grumbled

and shoved a book onto a crowded shelf. "New owners usually bring in their own people."

"Sometimes, they do." She kept her tone cheerful. Hamlet was clearly out of sorts tonight.

"If I don't keep working, I won't finish school. Being a college grad will get me a job that pays a whole lot better than this one." He grabbed another book, looked at the title, and added it to the shelf.

"Well, I hope you reach your goal." She held up her deli bag. "Okay if I put my dinner in the fridge?"

"Sure. Do whatever you like around here, why don'tcha?" He scowled and waved a hand.

Nina headed down the hall to the office. Was Hamlet in a bad mood because he feared losing his job? Or for some other reason? Again, she had second thoughts about being alone with him. However, she was here and she might as well stay. She'd be on guard, though.

In the office, after placing her deli bag in the refrigerator, she couldn't help glancing at the floor near Wildeen's desk. The recently added rug didn't quite cover the bloodstain. She stared at the telltale brown spot for a long moment. Then, swallowing the lump in her throat, she grabbed an empty book cart and hurried to the main part of the store.

Surveying the subject areas, she began with the Psychology section. After perusing several volumes, she found an out-of-print biography of Sigmund Freud and set the book on the cart.

Hamlet passed, pushing his now-empty cart, the wheels rattling on the wooden floor. He didn't speak, but she sensed his stare.

A few minutes later, he walked by again with

another load of books.

The back of her neck prickled. She didn't see him again until six o'clock.

Then he appeared wearing a baseball cap and a jacket. A canvas pack was slung over one shoulder. "I'm shutting off all except the night lights, as usual. Otherwise, people might think we're still open. You can turn on the overheads again in whatever section you're working." He held out a key on a metal ring. "Front door's locked. Here's the key to the back."

"Thanks, Hamlet." Nina took the key and slipped it into her slacks pocket.

Hamlet gave a curt nod and disappeared down the hall.

A few minutes later, hearing the back door open and close, Nina took a deep breath. Now that he was gone, she could relax. However, her growling stomach signaled dinnertime. She took her sandwich and soda to the reading area and settled into an overstuffed chair underneath the dome. Soft light filtered through the glass, enveloping her in a warm glow. While she ate, she reflected on Hamlet's hostile attitude. Something bugged him.

Finished eating, she returned to her task. As Hamlet suggested, she switched on the light directly above the shelf where she worked, which provided enough illumination but wouldn't be noticed by passersby.

She worked her way through Psychology, Philosophy, and Religion. Her book cart held several dozen books. Checking her wristwatch, she saw the time was already nine-thirty. She'd stay until ten and use her remaining time searching Wildeen's office.

After boxing her books, she sat at Wildeen's desk and turned on the computer. Leaning forward, she studied the screen in anticipation. An examination of the inventory and correspondence files yielded nothing of interest. Disappointed but not discouraged, she shut down the computer and searched the desk drawers where she found Wildeen's manuscript, *Reflections of a Bibliophile*. She pulled out the folder, intending to take it. Surely if Josh were interested in the manuscript, he would have removed it by now.

Opening the folder and idly riffling through the pages, she came upon a sheet of notebook paper not part of the printed manuscript. The paper lay askew, as though hastily stuffed inside the file. Perusing the sheet, she recognized a list of the literary agents Wildeen contacted for representation. A dozen names were included, along with the dates of both submission and rejection. Poor Wildeen—she'd had no luck finding an agent.

All the names on the list were unfamiliar—except one. Nina stared. The name belonged to a person she wouldn't expect to appear on Wildeen's list.

A sound at the back door caught her attention. She turned to see the doorknob jiggling. Hamlet, returning for something he'd forgotten? Or, maybe Josh, checking on her? But why would either man have trouble opening the door? Nina tensed. Should she run to the front of the store? Or hide here in the office?

Before she made a decision, she saw the door pop open. The person who stepped inside was too large to be either Hamlet or Josh. His face came into view, and she gasped.

"Morry!"

Morry squinted at Nina. "What the hell are you doing here?"

His surly tone sent a chill down her spine. *Be calm. You can handle him.* Holding the notebook paper behind her back, she stood and faced Morry. "Josh said I could choose books for the library before he sells the store. Why are *you* here?"

Morry shut the door and stepped farther into the room. He was dressed in black and had a black briefcase slung over one shoulder. "Josh gave me a key to the place, too. He said I could look for a book one of my clients wrote."

His shifty eyes told her he lied. The pieces to the puzzle of Wildeen's murder suddenly fell into place. Nina sucked in a breath.

"Why're ya lookin' at me like that?" Morry stuck his hands on his hips.

"I—nothing." She took a step backward.

He leaned to peer behind her. "What're you hidin' behind your back?"

"Nothing." Heart pounding, needing to get away, Nina inched around the desk toward the back door.

He lurched to her side and grabbed her arm. "I wanta see whatcha got."

"Ouch. You're hurting me!" She pulled away.

He yanked the paper from her fingers and studied it. "What the—?" He looked up and twisted his lips. "You think you've got everything figured out, don'tcha? *Reflections of a Bibliophile.* What a buncha crap."

She rubbed her sore arm. "I have what figured out? Like I said, I'm here to get books for the library, before Josh sells the store." Nina eyed the paper. She had to

234

regain possession of the list.

"Don't lie to me, kid." Morry narrowed his eyes. You've been snooping. You're no dummy. You saw what's on this paper, and you put two and two together." He slapped the paper with his free hand.

"I don't know what you're talking about." She made a move toward the back door. "I have to leave now."

Morry stepped in front of her, blocking the way. "You're not goin' anywhere." He waved the paper.

Seeing her chance, she snatched the list from his outstretched hand and stuffed it into her slacks pocket. Wheeling around, she ran from the office and into the hallway. Her breath tight in her throat, she headed toward the front door, remembering too late she didn't have the key.

Morry followed close on her heels. His big feet slap-slapped against the carpet.

For so large a man, he moved surprisingly fast. As she flew by the counter, Nina grabbed a hardback book and with all her might threw it at the front window. With a thud, the book hit the glass, bounced off, and landed on the floor. *So much for that idea.*

She reached the front door only to find Morry blocking her exit. She spun and ran toward the office. As she neared the spiral staircase leading to the glass dome skylight, a thought flashed through her mind. Readers of mystery novels considered the heroine hopelessly stupid when she ran up stairs to escape the villain. But this situation was real life. As she moved, she formulated her plan.

She grabbed a handful of books from a nearby shelf and heaved all of them at Morry. Her aim was true, and the books hit his head, not hard enough to knock him out, but enough to delay him while she raced up the staircase. Taking the steps two at a time, she careened around each bend. Behind her, the stairs creaked and groaned under Morry's added weight.

She reached the top, grabbed more books from the shelves, and hurled them at Morry. Again, her book bombs found their mark. He teetered, but then clutched the wrought iron railing in time to stay his fall.

Spying a cart full of books, she pushed it toward the top of the stairs where the wheels hovered a moment before the cart rumbled down. Books flew everywhere, many hitting Morry. She hoped the cart would hit him, too, but he flattened himself to the railing and dodged it. She grabbed more books from a nearby shelf and threw them down the stairs.

Each barrage delayed Morry but only momentarily. Then he climbed over the mess and continued his pursuit.

Nina threw a stool, a straight chair, more books, and another chair. Finally, the staircase was blocked. No way could Morry reach her. Her veins pulsed with new energy.

Raucous laughter floated upward. Peeking over the railing, she saw him standing at the bottom of the staircase. A purple lump had blossomed on his forehead, and his cheeks were stained a bright red.

"You ain't so smart!" He shook his fist. "Now, you're trapped. Don't bother with the dome, because you can't escape there. I tried to get in after hours. The dome is padlocked."

Locked? A cold chill rolled down her arms. He had to be lying. She'd counted on the dome as her way to freedom. She ran to a tall ladder and dragged it under the dome. She was halfway up when she smelled gasoline. The odor of smoke and the crackle of flames followed. The fire already engulfed the reading area, and flames licked the bottom of the staircase. Soon, the entire lower level would be ablaze. Filled with dread, she looked up at the stars blinking through the glass. Freedom. So near and yet so far.

Chapter Nineteen

Determination drove Nina to climb the ladder with smoke curling around her feet. Smoke stung her eyes and clogged her throat, making her cough. At the top, she grasped the ledge circling the dome. She placed one knee and then the other on the ledge just as the ladder toppled and crashed to the floor.

Gingerly, she rose to her feet. Placing one foot heel to toe in front of the other, she made her way along the narrow ledge to the dome's latch. Would the window be locked, as Morry warned?

Finally, she found the padlock. Sure enough, the lock was secure. She had no way out. A sinking feeling invaded her stomach. What now?

In the distance, sirens wailed. Fire trucks. Rescue was on the way. Filled with new energy, she yanked on the padlock, again and again. Finally, something gave. Not the lock itself, but the hasp. She pressed against the area, and damp splinters stuck to her fingers. The wood was rotten. Years of good old Northwest rain had eaten away the frame. Was the wood rotted enough to release the hasp? Hope surged within her veins.

With the fervor of a trapped animal, she clawed at the crumbling wood. Discovering the hasp's buried screws, she dug at them. Her hands were cut and bleeding, but she didn't care. No price would be too great to pay for freedom.

Smoke wrapped around her like the tentacles of an octopus. The fumes stung her eyes and filled her nose and throat. Then, just when she was ready to give up and accept her fate, the hasp broke free. Yes! But did she have enough strength left to open the dome? Balanced precariously on the ledge, she reared up with all her might, shoving a shoulder against the curved glass. The dome remained closed.

Coughing and gasping for breath, she lunged at the glass. Again and again, and finally, just when she feared she must give up, like a suction cup wrenched from its surface, the dome popped open. Nina squeezed through the narrow space. Before she gained complete freedom, the dome fell, landing on her legs. Pain stabbed her calves, rippled upward through her thighs. Even though still a prisoner, she had fresh air. She took several deep breaths before smoke oozed from the crack in the dome and drifted over her.

The sirens sounded closer now. Help would arrive any minute. She must let the rescuers know she was stranded. Propping her elbows on the roof, she strained to pull her legs from the dome. If only she had something to grab, she might pull herself free, but the roof was flat. Using her elbows as leverage, she inched her way along, gritting her teeth to shut out the pain as her legs scraped against the frame.

At last, she freed all but her feet. Loud sirens indicated the rescue vehicles entered the street below. Then the sirens quit, replaced by the shouts of the firefighters battling the blaze. Nina yelled at the top of her voice, but with so much noise below, she doubted anyone heard her.

By twisting onto her side, she freed first one foot

and then the other. Her shoes came off, falling back into the store, but they were a small loss. Despite the pain in her legs, she dragged herself on her stomach to the edge of the roof.

With enormous effort, she raised up enough to hang her head over the elevated rim. Vaguely, she was aware of a crowd below, and firefighters in helmets and suits, and water spraying from hoses.

"Up here! Up here!" She raised an arm and waved.

One of the firefighters looked up. "Someone's on the roof! Hang on, we're coming!"

Gasping and panting, Nina rolled onto her side. Moments later, footsteps stomped across the roof. Two men lifted her, and then one carried her over his shoulder down a ladder. The pain in her legs made her wince with his every step. At the bottom, medics placed her on a gurney.

A man broke from the crowd of onlookers. "Nina!"

She looked up and saw Stephen. Her heart took an unexpected leap. "By g-golly, the news hound is still c-chasing after the police."

He grinned. "Yeah, I heard on my scanner about a fire at Bergman Books. I mighta known you'd be involved."

"Morry Snyder set the fire… Tell them to g-get Morry. Now."

Stephen widened his eyes. "Morry did this? Okay, sure, Nina, I'll tell 'em."

He disappeared, only to return as the medics loaded her into the ambulance. "I'm riding with her," he told the attendant.

"Yes." Surprised at how right having Stephen by her side felt, Nina clasped his outstretched hand. "I want him to come, too."

****

"Do you have enough pillows? Are you comfortable?" Stephen asked Nina.

Nina settled into the spot he'd made on his sofa. "I'm fine. You can quit spoiling me now."

He grinned and shook his head. "Nope. Spoiling you is one job I'll never give up."

The day was a bright, hot, Indian summer Sunday in September. After a superb brunch of crab omelet, hash browns, and toast, they carried their coffee into Stephen's living room to read the newspaper. Nina's left leg rested on a leather hassock, and her cane leaned against the sofa. She exchanged her crutches for the cane only last week, when the cast was removed from her broken leg. The break was painful but healed well.

"I still feel responsible for what happened." Stephen put aside the newspaper and moved closer to Nina. "I shouldn't have let my pride keep me away, especially when I knew you were still hunting a murderer."

Warmed by his concern, she patted his arm. "I would've gone alone to the bookstore, anyway."

He wrinkled his brow. "Yeah, but at least I'd have known where you were."

"You found me soon enough. Thanks to you, the police found Morry, too." Pete Russell told her Morry came to the door that night in his pajamas and claimed to have been asleep. But investigators found his briefcase in the bookstore wreckage, which placed him at the scene.

"The evidence against him piled up, didn't it?" Stephen sipped his coffee.

Nina nodded. "Besides his briefcase, the bookmark I found in the Bottses' rose garden had his fingerprints and handwriting. The list of literary agents in Wildeen's file proved she sent him her manuscript."

Stephen refilled Nina's coffee cup from the carafe he'd brought from the kitchen. "Keep talking. I like reviewing how you put together all the clues to prove Morry was the killer."

"Pete Russell and his men helped a bit, too," she said in a dry tone. "Morry's confession left no doubt."

"Right." Stephen put down the carafe and sat back. "According to what Morry told Pete Russell, the night of the Bottses' party Wildeen asked him to come to the bookstore at midnight. She showed him photocopies of pages from *Love's Eternal Triumph* that matched the writing in Zelma's *My Restless Heart*. Unless he reconsidered and represented her book, she would expose Zelma's plagiarism."

"He just laughed, which made her angry. He said she attacked him first. To defend himself, he grabbed the rearing horse bookend and struck her. He hadn't meant to kill her. Her death was…an accident." With a shudder, Nina put down her cup and hugged her arms.

Stephen frowned. "Remembering is hard on you, isn't it? Maybe we shouldn't discuss the case, after all."

She gave him a soft smile. "I'm okay. I expect I'll always have heartache when I think about what happened to Wildeen." She took a deep breath. "Anyway, Morry told Russell he didn't know Zelma had been to the bookstore prior to his visit, and when she became the prime suspect, he panicked. He framed Patti for Wildeen's murder and faked her suicide."

Stephen nodded. "According to what I read in the

police report, after finding the gate to the back yard open, he hid in the Loring garage and made a loud noise. When she came to investigate, he grabbed her and knocked her out. Then he dragged her into the car, found her car keys conveniently hanging on a nail nearby, and started the car's engine. He wrote the suicide note on her computer."

"He came to the bookstore to look for Wildeen's copy of *Love's Eternal Triumph*, which she'd refused to give him earlier. If he couldn't find it, he planned to burn down the entire store." Remembering that awful night, Nina took a deep breath and clutched her stomach.

"Desperate man." Stephen pressed his lips together. "He even admitted to stalking you on several occasions, too, hoping to find out if you'd discovered anything."

"I was really lucky to escape his intended harm."

Stephen took her hand. "I agree. His committing murder over Zelma's plagiarism seems extreme, though."

Nina met his gaze. "Not if you know his background. Pete Russell told me that all his life, Morry has been a loser. He's gone from one job to another, none profitable or successful. All the while, he piled up gambling debts, betting on the horses at Longacres and making frequent trips to Las Vegas. His creditors hounded him. He was desperate."

Stephen patted her arm. "I'm sure glad you escaped from the bookstore that night."

"So am I." Nina ran a hand over her forehead. "I hated to let him destroy all those books, but I had no alternative."

"You did just what you should have. I'm proud of the way you kept your head in a crisis." Smiling, Stephen gave her a hug.

She settled against his shoulder. "I'm glad Patti finally woke up from her coma. Even though she has no memory of what happened that day, at least, she's alive. Do you think she'll stand by Josh if cheating his clients is discovered?"

He nodded. "She loves him, and he loves her, too. He's hardly left her side since she was attacked. I'm betting they'll stay together."

"I hope so. They've both been through a lot." Nina's thoughts drifted to other events in the aftermath of her traumatic escape from Morry. With the help of Sondra's publicity ideas, the library's August book sale proved a huge success. Even Larry joined in the spirit of the occasion, distributing the flyers advertising their prizes. Nina's broken leg limited her participation, but she presented the awards to the winners.

The sale earned enough money for Larry to purchase his coveted reference materials, Arlette to have her book and video choices, Myo a new computer, and Holly new furniture for the children's room.

Nina received a letter from Wildeen's family expressing their concern and sympathy for what happened and thanking her for discovering the truth about their daughter's death. They extended an invitation to visit if she was ever in Sedona.

Stephen shifted in his seat. "All the loose ends are wrapped up, then? What about Zelma? Have you heard from her?"

The mention of her old friend brought a wave of sadness. "Not to speak to, but she sent me an email.

Hand me my phone, and I'll read it to you."

"Sure. I'd like to know what she had to say." He picked up her phone from the coffee table and held it out.

Nina accessed the email, cleared her throat, and read.

"'I want you to know, Nina, that I told my publisher the truth about My Restless Heart. *He was upset, of course, and withdrew the book from the marketplace.*

"'I returned my advance. Writing another book for Best Books Press is not an option, but I will continue writing and am confident another publisher will buy my stories.

"'I was shocked to hear about Morry. I would never suspect him to be a murderer. To me, he was always a lovable guy. I was sorry to hear how he almost added you to his list of victims.

"'But, in light of all that's happened, I'm not ready to resume our friendship. Maybe someday we can try again. In the meantime, I wish you the very best. In another year or two, look for my name on the bestseller list.

Zelma.'"

Nina put aside her phone. "I'm glad Zelma finally owned up to her deception, but I regret the loss of our friendship." She heaved a deep sigh. "I've lost both my best friends."

"Friends are important, and losing them is always sad. I understand how you feel." Stephen grasped her chin and gazed into her eyes. "But you've gained a new friend—me."

Nina smiled. "New friends are always welcome,

245

too." She was happy her relationship with Stephen was restored. His unexpected appearance the night of the fire made her realize how much she missed him and wanted him in her life. Then she sobered. "But I can't promise I'll change my feelings regarding marriage and children."

"Don't worry." He patted her arm. "We'll put aside those issues and enjoy our time together."

His words warmed her. "Thank you, Stephen, for your understanding." She cleared her throat. "I, ah, especially like our weekends…" She slanted him a glance.

"So do I. We'll continue to spend weekends together, then?"

"Of course."

"Even the nights?"

His light tone teased. Nina laughed. "Especially the nights."

"All right!" Stephen laughed, too, and drew her into his arms.

They exchanged a long, sweet kiss, and then Nina snuggled against him, feeling secure and happy. Although uncertain where the future would take them, she knew that right now, here with Stephen was where she belonged.

Enjoy the opening scene from *Secrets To Die For*, the next book in the Nina Foster Mystery series:

"Do you think the rain will ever stop?" Nina Foster gazed out the first floor window of the soon-to-be library at Marley Manor, the retirement community where her grandmother, Jessica Bingham, was a resident.

"We live in the Northwest, my dear." Jessica looked up from unpacking a box of donated books. "And it's January. You know what we always say around here—better rain than snow."

Nickel-size raindrops pelted the surface of Marley Lake, which provided much of the home's setting. Across the water lay an undeveloped area where tall pine and fir trees swayed back and forth like frenzied ballet dancers.

Nina was about to turn away and continue her unpacking when something caught her eye. Leaning closer to the window, she made out a person in a yellow hooded slicker trudging along the path bordering the lake. Alongside trotted a small white dog wearing a matching yellow raincoat. "Someone is out walking a dog in this storm."

Jessica came to stand beside her. "That's Ellie Larkin and her Pomeranian, Nigel. Ellie's from the Midwest. She was an accountant for a manufacturing firm. You've met her, Nina. She and I are good friends."

"Yes, I remember Ellie." The image of a tall, bony woman with iron gray hair popped into Nina's mind. "Why are she and Nigel walking in this miserable weather?" She hugged her arms. "Couldn't she put him outside for a couple minutes if he had to go?"

"Ellie walks her dog every day around this time, rain or shine." Jessica looked at her wristwatch. "Yep, four-thirty. You could set your watch by them." She frowned. "I've been worried about Ellie lately."

"Why?" She turned to Jessica, neatly dressed, as usual, in brown slacks and a rust-colored sweater that complemented her strawberry blonde hair.

"Because she's often confused and forgetful. A certain amount of memory loss is to be expected at our age. But yesterday, she couldn't remember which mailbox was hers, even though the boxes are marked with apartment numbers. Plus, she often mumbles about secrets."

"Secrets? Do you know what she's talking about?" Anything that suggested a mystery intrigued Nina.

Jessica shrugged. "I haven't a clue, but she becomes very agitated."

Nina folded her arms and leaned against the window frame. "Hmmm, do you think she has Alzheimer's? Or some other kind of dementia?"

"I hope not." Jessica wrinkled her brow. "If she does, she'll have to move into a memory care facility. I'd really miss her."

"Does she have relatives to look out for her?"

"Only her nephew, Roger Blanton, and he hangs around hoping to get some of her money."

Nina nodded. "Okay, now I'm remembering more about Ellie. She won the lottery a couple of years ago, didn't she?"

"Right. Sixteen million." Jessica waved a hand. "After taxes."

"Wow." Nina widened her eyes at the thought of winning so much money. "I think I've met Roger, too."

Jessica nodded. "Yes, I'm sure we've all been together at least once when you've come for Sunday dinner. I never cared much for Roger." Jessica pursed her lips. "He's a weaselly, whiny guy, always complaining he needs money."

"Doesn't he have a job?"

"He calls himself an 'entreprencur.'" Jessica harrumphed. "I call him a bum."

Nina turned again to the window, pushing aside the curtain. Ellie was bent into the wind, her yellow slicker billowing out behind her. Nigel's bushy tail drooped, displaying his lack of enthusiasm for the outing.

Nina propped her hands on her hips. "Someone should go and bring Ellie and Nigel inside."

Jessica shook her head. "She wouldn't come until she was ready. She can be stubborn, especially if she's having one of her spells." She leaned closer to the window and pointed a forefinger. "Oh, look, not to worry; they're turning and heading back."

Sure enough, as Jessica spoke, Ellie wheeled around to head in the opposite direction. Nigel, his tail wagging, scampered after her.

"She'll be okay now." Jessica smiled. "We'd better get back to work."

As she turned from the window, Nina caught her reflection. Strands of her shoulder-length, brown hair escaped the loosely-tied ponytail and hung like exaggerated commas around her face. On some women that might look chic, but on her the tendrils looked messy. But, then, who could keep a hairdo in this wild weather?

She caught her grandmother's reflection. Jessica could. Her curls were never out of place. The only variation with her hair was the shade, which changed from reddish blonde to red, depending on her whim.

But Jessica was right—they'd better get back to work. As the managing librarian of Richmond, Washington's Seaview Library, Nina used her expertise to establish a library at Marley Manor. Today, in the initial stages of the project, she and Jessica unpacked boxes of donated books and stacked them on several long tables in the center of the room.

Around the room's perimeter, newly constructed, floor-to-ceiling shelves stood ready and waiting to be filled. The smell of recently applied oak stain lingered in the air. Several groupings of comfortable chairs and reading lamps completed the furnishings. "This space will make a lovely library," Nina commented as she crossed to the table where they'd been working.

"You are so nice to organize it." Jessica made a sweeping gesture that included the entire room.

"You know books and libraries are my passion." Nina reached into a box and pulled out several hardcover books. "I hope we get enough donations to fill the shelves."

"Not to worry, dear." Jessica picked up a knife and slit open a box. "Director Marshall applied for a government grant. Plus, he's set up a Library Fund, and residents are already contributing. You'll have a budget to buy books to your heart's content."

Nina looked up and grinned. "Really? That's good news. Current titles will round out the collection."

"I put a sign-up sheet on our bulletin board downstairs asking for volunteers. The next time you come, we should have a crew to help us...Oh, look, here's an Agatha Christie I haven't read." She held up a book. "I'll be the first to check it out."

The muffled ring of her phone grabbed Nina's attention, and she hurried to the chair where she'd left her shoulder bag. Digging into its voluminous depths, she pulled out the phone. "Hey, Nina."

Stephen Kraslow's deep voice resonated pleasantly in her ear. Stephen was from New York City, having left his job as a journalist to assume ownership of Richmond's weekly newspaper, *The Richmond Review*. "Hello, Stephen. What's up?" She hoped he wasn't canceling their evening together. She looked forward to being with him.

"About dinner tonight—"

Oh oh, he was canceling. Her shoulders slumped. "You don't want to get together," she blurted. "You have something else to do—"

"Nina, stop jumping to conclusions. No, instead of eating at your place, I thought we could go out."

"Why? I know I'm not the best cook in the world, but—"

"Going out has nothing to do with your cooking. I have something I want to discuss with you."

Something to discuss that required neutral territory. What could that subject be? Nina's stomach tensed. "Do you have a restaurant in mind?"

"How about Henry's, at the harbor?"

Henry's was one of their favorite places. "Okay, but what do you want to talk about?"

"Uh uh, not until dinner. Can you meet me at seven? I can get away by then."

"All right. I'll be there." Nina hung up, biting her

lip. Noticing her grandmother's gaze, she forced a smile. "That was Stephen."

"So I gathered. You two still playing 'your place or mine'?"

Nina tucked her cell phone into her purse. "Come on, Gran, we've been seeing each other for only six months."

"I married Tyler after three months and—"

"I know; you lived happily ever after." Nina finished a sentence she had heard often enough to know by heart. "A short-term courtship worked for you and Granddad, but I'm too cautious to jump into a committed relationship after only a few months."

Jessica placed the box she'd emptied under the table and picked up another one. "I didn't think you would commit to a relationship, period."

Hearing her grandmother's dry tone, Nina shrugged. "Okay, so I admit to being a little scared of commitment. Stephen hasn't proposed marriage, anyway."

"Maybe tonight's the night." Jessica slit open the new box.

"I don't think so. He's not ready."

"How long since his wife passed away?" Jessica stacked books on the table.

"Two years." Dating a widower was a new experience.

Jessica pulled another handful of books from the box. "That length of time seems long enough to adjust. If I were you, I'd be prepared. Wear something romantic and fix your hair nice."

Her grandmother's suggestion lingered uneasily in Nina's mind. What if Stephen planned to propose tonight? What would her answer be? Did she love him? She certainly admired him and enjoyed his company.

But her mother's marriage ended in abandonment, and Nina's few relationships all failed, leaving her more than a little afraid of commitment. The truth was, the idea of marriage scared her to death.

A word about the author…

A resident of the Pacific Northwest, Linda Hope Lee writes contemporary romance, romantic suspense, and mystery novels. She also enjoys watercolor painting, photography, collecting children's books and anything to do with wire-haired fox terriers.

www.lindahopelee.com

~*~

Other Titles by this Author
Dark Memories
Finding Sara
Loving Rose
Marrying Molly
The Red Rock, Colorado Collection
Under Gemini

Thank you for purchasing
this publication of The Wild Rose Press, Inc.

For questions or more information
contact us at
info@thewildrosepress.com.

The Wild Rose Press, Inc.
www.thewildrosepress.com

To visit with authors of
The Wild Rose Press, Inc.
join our yahoo loop at
http://groups.yahoo.com/group/thewildrosepress/

www.ingramcontent.com/pod-product-compliance
Lightning Source LLC
Chambersburg PA
CBHW070338260626
47160CB00003B/1082